eye
to
eye

Also by
grace carol
and Red Dress Ink

FLYOVER STATES
(where Doris and Ronnie began...)

eye
to
eye

grace carol

**RED
DRESS
INK**
TM

EYE TO EYE

A Red Dress Ink novel

ISBN-13: 978-0-373-89582-3
ISBN-10:   0-373-89582-8

www.RedDressInk.com

Printed in U.S.A.

ACKNOWLEDGMENTS

The author would like to thank the following people for their humor, encouragement and enlightenment: Bob Bledsoe, Alex Cordero, Aelred Dean, Romayne Rubinas Dorsey, Jim Elledge, Elaine McSorley Gerard, Amanda Hong, Brian Ingram, Jane Ingram, Tom Ingram, Jane Hill, Mimi Lind, Lori Lipoma, Kathryn Lye, Neeti Madan, Mike Mattison, Margaret Mitchell, Tania Modleski, Bernadette Murphy, Carol Muske-Dukes, Elaheh Partovi and Zohreh Partovi, Meg Pearson, Michelle Ross, Rosalie Siegel, Maurya Simon, Linda Sims, Bruce Umminger, Judy Umminger, April Umminger and Sabrina Williams.

To students of the ordinary and profound.

ronnie

A few years ago, I did something crazy. Something that no rational, normal person would do. I didn't murder anybody—though there were times I felt like it—but it was drastic behavior nonetheless.

I went to graduate school. In Indiana.

I left a job paying forty thousand dollars a year, a man who loved me, and the City of Angels, for a twelve-thousand-dollar-a-year stipend, a mountain of student loans, men who sorta kinda liked me, in a town of college kids and corn.

That's where I started wanting to murder people.

Then something completely unexpected happened. Grad school ended up being worth going into debt for. I learned a ton of stuff that had nothing to do with making a ton of money (dumb and dumber?) and I met a man. A nice man. Not the man of my dreams, though. Thank God. Since the man of my dreams was actually the man of my delusions. His name was LaVarian Laborteux.

In grad school, LaVarian was the only black Ph.D. around for miles and miles, and I was a single black female in search of my Denzel Washington/Cliff Huxtable. I fell ass-over-common-sense. My true common sense was pointing me to a man named Earl, a big, burly bartender with long, sandy hair and a bushy beard. He says he fell for me the moment I walked into the bar. The first time I saw him, I thought he was a hick, a good old boy on a Harley, and I couldn't for the life of me see how he and I fit together.

I read sociology and literature books for fun. He hadn't read a book for pleasure since he was ten years old. I was constantly politicizing everything and complaining about how everything was politicized. Earl hadn't even known what politicizing meant and then, when I explained it to him, he said, "Oh, well, things ain't got to be as complicated as all that." He's white, and I'm black. To that Earl says, "Yep. That's a complicated thing sometimes, and sometimes it ain't." He has a knack for stating the obvious and the true.

Still, I was igoring my common sense and the fact that I had the hots for Earl and that he was smart in ways that were different than me, ways that academia would never appreciate. By then I'd found out LaVarian wasn't exactly available—even though we'd already slept together, *several* times—by reading a footnote in an essay he'd written. A footnote in which he thanked his *wife* for helping him write the essay. Jackass. And then, soon after that, Earl put it all on the line and basically told me he was tired of my nonsense: He was a man and I was a woman, and he was going to take me out. Very macho. And very Italian of Mr. Erardo Lo Vecchio. Earl's real name. I like Italians—it's my tendency toward the macho, and yes, I am a feminist.

After grad school, I did something else crazy. I moved back home to L.A.—with Earl. Without any money. We ended up living in the first shack, I mean, apartment, we could afford. We blew all of our money on first and last months' rent, plus the deposit. We spent our last four thousand dollars to move and get settled and now Earl, big fish out of water that he is, is bartending down the street from where we live, and I am a tutor. A tutor of Satan. I was hired by Ian's family, but he's really the one in charge.

My boss is sixteen years old. Now. I'm not one to complain, but if I may for a moment. It's a hard life and a cruel world when you're a thirty-one-year-old woman and your livelihood depends on whether or not the teenage boy you're tutoring thinks you're a "total bitch" or a "complete idiot."

I've had the pleasure of hearing my boss mumble both of those sweet nothings while I tried to help him toward his pretty-much-solidified future of privilege. My paycheck isn't in immediate danger, but if Ian stops mumbling or stops talking period, my fat checks—proof that rich people just throw money at problems—will be but a memory. For now, I've got time because I'm still new, Ian's still here and his parents—TV writers and guilty liberals—don't want to fire the black chick right away.

"They think they'd look like racist assholes," Ian informed me the second time we met and I ripped him a new one for not doing what was the one and only reading I'd assigned him. "*The Bluest Eye* sucks, and you suck, but I'm stuck with you until I fuck up so much they think I'm hopeless. Then, they'll get rid of you with a clear conscience. So," he'd said, "I see, in your future, you being nice to me." He tipped back in his chair and pulled at the gelled tips of his spiky black hair.

Good times, I tell you. Good times.

I knew right away I was in trouble from the moment I first laid eyes on the kid, laid eyes on where he lived. My own biases kicked in, I have to admit. I've never met a rich person I liked. I had never truly met a rich person until Ian—but that hasn't stopped me from disliking them. It's not what rich people have, it's what they have and take for granted. Two minutes with Ian and his surly indifference to all the stuff he had, and would likely always have, and I knew I would have to keep *my* bad attitude in check, let alone his. When I was a kid, my mom, dad, brother and I lived in a two-bedroom apartment in what used to be called South Central L.A. that was about the size of Ian's foyer. Now, my family is solidly middle class (though I've slid down the ladder a bit since grad school). We moved to the suburbs after a gang extended a verbal and knife-accessorized invitation to join. So now, years later, my brother and parents' homes are at least twice the size of Ian's foyer.

After I drove up and met Ian, he and I were alone. His parents had trusted my girlfriend Bita's husband when he'd recommended me, and they'd hired me, sight unseen. It was a lucky favor because I'd come back home without a job and needed one right away.

"Hi," I'd said. "Nice to meet you." I extended my hand.

"Whatever," Ian said, and stared at my hand with his arms crossed. Light from the heavy, castlelike front door shone in his face and highlighted the blue tint in his spiky hair.

"Whatever? That's how you talk to people you just met? Jesus." I made a face at him like I smelled something bad.

He shrugged.

"You're rude," I said. An asshole was what I was thinking.

"And you're a complete bitch and a total idiot."

If I had been a cartoon, steam would have sprayed out of my ears and my eyes would have popped out of my head. However, since I wasn't a cartoon, I counted to four so I could regain my composure. I wanted to ask him if he was out of his goddamn mind by speaking to me like that; instead, I decided not to sound like a teacher or a parent. Reverse psychology and all of that. I said, "Dude. Seriously." The corner of Ian's mouth turned up in what was possibly a grin. "Only spoiled white boys talk to people like that." His eyes narrowed into slits, and he coolly stared at me with that corner of his mouth still turned up. We stood in the hallway facing each other, invisible holsters strapped around our waists. Finally, Ian snorted.

"I guess we're supposed to work in here or whatever," he said.

I followed him into a room off the foyer. That day, I spent only an hour with him telling him that we were going to read books and simply discuss them, to sharpen his analytical skills, to enable him to articulate his thoughts. I gave him the Morrison as his first assignment. He grunted and gestured until I was done talking, and then I let myself out.

He was right. At least about the idiot part because I decided I would work with Ian despite his bad attitude. I told myself it was because Earl and I are broke, but I know myself. And if I'm honest, I know that it's about seventy percent because we're broke. I'm also stubborn as hell, and I was not going to get chased away that easily, not by a little punk like Ian. It was war, and I would win. That was the other thirty percent that kept me working with Ian.

That was last week, so here I am again just like Donna Summer said, working hard for the money. Ian and I sit in his backyard, though "yard" is a sadly, inadequate way of putting it. His "yard" is one of those vast museum gardens, like at the Getty. There's a long, rectangular pool and statues all around seem to mock me with demure grins or pitying stares. I imagine them placing bets with each other. "I give her two weeks," the knock-off *David* says, while Venus gives me a bit more credit. "Ha, David, a month. Easy."

Ian faces the pool, though it would be natural to face me at the table. We've still got Toni Morrison between us. "Ian," I say. "Give me a break, here."

He sips his lemonade.

"Why?" He puts his hands behind his head and stretches.

Because I'll strangle you and have to go to jail?

"This is a complete waste of time. If I'm not feeling it, I'm not feeling it. Everything will work out for me, even if I fuck up in school."

So true. The statues stare at us as if they agree with Ian. I'm losing. I sip my lemonade and decide to stop dealing with a kid.

"'Not feeling it?'" I ask, closing *The Bluest Eye*. I slouch in my chair. "What're you, *down* or something? Chillin' with the homies?"

"You're hardly a homie," Ian says, looking directly at me, finally.

"What's *that* supposed to mean?"

"It means that I know *way* more about music, about hip-hop, than you do, which is why I don't need any of this shit, which is how I'm going to be successful."

Dear God. Please, not another blacker-than-thou-white boy. Earlier, just to make conversation, I had asked Ian what was on the iPod that he always seemed to be playing in order to ignore me. He rattled off a list of folks, most of whom I'd never heard of. But so what? Now I'm not black? Prince Ian of Beverly Hills is, because of a playlist? Not a day went by in our apartment growing up that I didn't hear the blues, jazz, R & B. I hadn't even heard of the Beatles until I was thirteen. Weird, not something to be proud of, but still. It's time for someone to get schooled. I stand up, pack up books.

"Okay, Malcolm X. You know hip-hop?"

"Did I stutter?" Ian asks.

"Right. Smart-ass. Who is Gil Scott-Heron?"

Ian shrugs.

"Heard any spirituals or work songs before?"

"Work songs? What are you *talking* about?"

"Ever hear James Brown——"

"No shit——"

"James Brown, *Live and Lowdown at the Apollo, Volume One, 1962?*"

Silence.

I look at Ian, lounging by his pool, drinking lemonade his housekeeper brought out for us because his rude, lazy ass wouldn't get it for us himself. "You don't know shit about hip-hop," I tell him. Goodbye job. "See you next week," I add, for a touch of performative bravado and walk away. But I won't be surprised if I never see the kid again. My boss had gotten hopeless a lot sooner than I thought.

It's a nice Friday night in September, so after I flee Beverly Hills's rolling lawns in my used Honda and pace around our apartment, imagining homelessness, imagining how to tell Earl my big mouth may have landed us in the streets, I decide to leave and walk down to the Baseline. This was where Earl bartends. It's only a short ways away from Dodger Stadium. Our grand idea is that Earl will bartend to save money for law school—labor law—and I will keep writing on the side, and tutor full-time. The tutoring was a job opportunity I reluctantly accepted from Charlie, Bita's husband. Beggars with MFAs, which stands for Money: Forget About It, who still have no idea what they're doing with their lives, can't be choosers. At least we've got an apartment. Small, ever-so-slightly rickety, overpriced, but *ours*.

I walk slowly to the bar, listening to my flip-flops slap the pavement. I notice that the Echo Park Market has been tagged again: the words FROG TOWN stretch across the awning. Cars pass by blasting Mexican banda music, and the neighborhood terrorists, two brown Chihuahuas, yip and snarl at me as I pass their chain-linked fence. I also notice that the mattress that's been on the sidewalk the last four times I've walked to the bar has been picked up.

When I enter the Baseline, it's quiet, except for the Rolling Stones on the jukebox, singing "Angie." Seven on a Friday night is still too early for the hipsters. It's a big bar with three rooms, and I linger near the doorway so I can watch Earl without him knowing I'm there. I like to do that sometimes, and I get that fluttery feeling in my stomach, just like when I used to watch him at the Saloon in Indiana. Now that he's all cleaned up, sans long hair and Rumplestiltskin beard, something about the bar's lighting makes him look dramatic, dare I say: like a movie star. Not in a barely-out-of-his-teens sort of way, but in a badass, old-school, one hundred percent man sort of way. Tonight, he seems a different Earl than the one I met in Indiana. He's wearing a tight white T-shirt, and I watch his arm muscles flex as he wipes down the counter and nods when a tall guy appears asking for a drink. Tall Guy's body language tells me he likes what he sees when Earl's large hand nearly wraps around the Campari bottle as he pours. I wait until Earl turns his back to the bar before I park myself on a stool. As I fix my shoe, a blonde waitress who I've never seen comes up and hugs Earl from behind. He smiles, but takes his free hand and peels her arm off him, and then she goes down to the other end of the bar to

pour more drinks. Who in the hell is this, feeling up Earl?
When he turns around and sees me, his face lights up and the
dimples come out in full force.

"Well, well, well," he says, crossing his arms and leaning into
the bar. "Cat dragged in something right pretty."

"Hey, baby." I lean into the bar, too, and give Earl a long kiss.

Tall Guy looks surprised—and disappointed. After all, Earl
did take the blonde's hands off him.

"He's my boyfriend," I say, wanting to show off Earl. I eye him
up and down as if I want to eat him. Earl turns red and gives
me a look that says *behave*.

"Lucky girl," Tall Guy says, and stands up with his drink. "I'm
obviously wasting my time and money here." He winks at Earl
and walks off.

"Have a good night, buddy," Earl calls after him sincerely, and
that's why he's a hit with both sexes. Earl pours himself a glass
of water and drinks it in three gulps. He puts the glass under
the counter and then grins at me. "What're you drinking,
trouble?"

"Who, me?" I ask, and blink dramatically. Then I grab him
by the front of his T-shirt and kiss him long and hard again.

"Hey, dude," a lanky guy says. He's been standing at the bar
the whole time and we didn't even notice. He looks like
Timothy Hutton. Hell, he could be Timothy Hutton for all I
know—or care. I'm kissing Earl Lo Vecchio. "How about a
drink?" he asks. "I mean, since we *are* in a bar. And since you *are*
the bartender. Unless it's too much trouble, I mean."

Earl gives him a serious look. The guy has no idea how

deeply and swiftly Earl could imbed his foot in his ass if he felt moved to do so. But then he smiles at him. "You're right, buddy. I'm being rude. Not doin' my job. What'll it be?"

I narrow my eyes at Earl and tilt my head. In Langsdale, he would have had much more to say to this guy. He winks at me. "I'm taking it easy, being mellow here in California."

"Who's the blonde?" I ask, when Earl's done getting the guy's Greyhound. "Your new girlfriend?" I smile. I've never worried about Earl wanting someone else. We haven't been together long enough for me to worry about that, especially with Earl being the solid, straightforward man that he is. Still, I don't like the *liberties* Blondie's taking, like the bar's her world, the world is her oyster, and she could slurp Earl down.

"Oh," Earl says, sounding a bit weary. "That's Katie. Hey, Katie. Come on over here a minute."

Katie laughs loudly at something her customer has said, takes his money and puts it in her tip jar. "What is it, honey," she says to Earl. Up close I see that she looks barely legal. *Honey?*

"Katie, I'd like you to meet my woman, Ronnie."

Katie's eyes widen ever so slightly, but then she plays it off. She gives me a quick once over, pausing over my braids. "This is your girlfriend?" She blinks and extends a hand.

That's what the man said. In the words of my pain-in-the-ass tutee, Did he stutter? "Hi. Veronica. Nice to meet you."

Katie nods. "It's only my third night. My first time working with Earl. He's made it so easy for me!"

Doesn't mean you have to *be* easy. *Honey.* "Yeah, Earl's that way," I say, and then the small talk gets minuscule.

"Well, better go do my thing," Katie says in a bright, babyish voice.

"Nice to meet you," I reply, but she's already walking away. I smile at Earl. "She seems nice."

"She's all right." He takes my hands in his big warm ones. "I'm wondering about you, though. How you doing, sweetheart? How's that little boy treating you? Am I gone have to take him behind the toolshed?"

I laugh at the thought of a toolshed in Ian's palatial garden. "Oh, you know..." I don't want to complain to Earl, not right now. He's had to listen to me complain too much; me, the woman who says she's never one to complain. "Let's just say that I needed to come down the hill to see you, and that I can only drink Diet Coke tonight, in the interest of avoiding alcohol abuse."

Earl holds his hand up. "'Enough said, baby. Diet Coke, coming right up."

Seeing Earl makes me feel better, but while he gets my drink, I get sad again all of a sudden. Earl calling me trouble gets me thinking about Doris, my best friend, and my former partner in misery at grad school in Langsdale, Indiana. If she were here, I'd definitely be having more than Diet Coke. I'm so proud of her that she's Dr. Weatherall. *Professor* Weatherall. She didn't let the academic crazies chase her away like I did. I was considering a Ph.D., too. But like one of those challenges on *Survivor,* I ran out of stamina, and gave up after trying to balance myself on a narrow pole. But Georgia—Professor Doris Weatherall in Georgia—tickles me, as they say in the South.

"Doris," I'd said, tossing her shoes into a big box when we packed up her apartment a few weeks ago, "you're going to have to learn how to get the vapors."

"Don't," she'd said. "I'm going to kill myself."

"C'mon. You've got a *great* gig. Atlanta's a cool town. And didn't you say there's all this hiking and pretty nature and stuff?"

"Listen to you. *Nature.* You break out in a cold sweat at the thought of grass. Now I know you're really trying to make me feel better."

I shrugged.

"It's true, though. Atlanta's supposed to be a cool town." Doris sighed. She suddenly flopped down on her couch. "I just wish you were coming with me. It'll suck not knowing anybody."

"La-uh-dies don't say *suck,* Miss Weatherall. A true Southern lady does not, and I repeat, does *not,* use such coarse language."

"But they give their friends the middle finger," Doris said, demonstrating.

I covered my mouth daintily and fanned myself. "I do declare, I believe I might faint. Somebody give me a mint julep."

"What *is* a julep, anyway?" Doris stood again, absently surveying her Langsdale apartment.

"Fuck if I know," I said. "I barely know what mint looks like. It looks like green, right?"

"Oh, I see. La-uh-dies don't say *suck,* but they say *fuck.*" Doris shook her head. "Wow. You and Earl are a pair. The country boy and the city chick who's not even sure if mint is green. This just proves that there's someone for everyone."

I held up a pair of black platform heels. "You should totally give me these. Southern Belles don't wear these kinds of shoes. They wear, like, white pumps or something, don't they? These are L.A. shoes."

Doris clasped her hands together and pointed her index fingers at me like a gun. "Put the shoes in the box and step away from the collection," she said.

"Jeez." I held my hands up in surrender. "I'm a get Earl after you if you don't act right."

Doris slapped her hands together, trying to get the dust off them. "Earl? He's a teddy bear. He'll be on *my* side."

I smiled at that. Earl was crazy about Doris. He liked her mouth, that it was big, equally big as mine. Earl didn't get shrinking violets. One more reason to love him.

Earl and I were going to help Doris drive to Georgia the next day, but not before we tied one last one on that night. We all went to the Saloon, and for the first time Earl wasn't the bartender. He'd given notice two weeks before, and was a customer like everyone else.

"Until we meet again," we all repeated.

"To Boozy and Floozy," Earl said, raising his glass to me and Doris. Zach, Doris's guy, clinked Earl's glass enthusiastically. Doris and I glared at them both until they lowered their glasses. But then Earl clinked his glass with ours and flashed those dimples.

Driving on the interstate the next day, Doris seemed worried about Zach, didn't think it was going to last, especially since they were "taking a break" from each other.

"I don't know," she said, tuning the radio. "I don't know if he has enough ambition."

"But Earl's a bartender. You like *him,*" I tried to reason. Personally, I thought Doris and Zach had come too far to let ambition, or a lack thereof, get between them.

"A damn good bartender," Earl said from the back of Doris's Toyota. He was laid out lengthwise, but curled up because he was too much man for a Toyota.

"Yes, but Earl wants to go to law school——"

"But not to make money," I say.

Earl sang along to the Hank Williams tune coming from the radio. He sounded good. Real good. I hadn't ever heard him sing.

"It's *not* the money," Doris said, but couldn't elaborate as to what *it* was exactly.

So it was only the four of us that night before we hit the road. All the way to Atlanta, we split the driving, and got Doris to Georgia faster than you could say Rhett Butler.

It's dusky outside and every so often the door to the Baseline swings open, and a warm breeze comes in, along with somebody covered in tattoos or still wearing sunglasses—indoors, at night. And what about the women walking through the door? Maybe it was because I was in graduate school in the Midwest far too long, where style and any attempt at fashion was frowned upon, got you labeled as a dum-dum, but looking around at the women, looking at Katie in her perfect, taut body, I feel dowdy. I thought I was looking effortlessly chic. Instead, my sundress feels too thrift store, a little too tight. My flip-flops are a little worn, I have to admit. Or maybe it's seeing how Ian lives, how a lot of people live or try to look like they're living in L.A. I knew all of this, saw all of this before I left, but because it wasn't *my* life, I didn't think about it so much, either way. Now I feel like a visitor, a tourist, being wowed and amazed by so many ordinary things. Coming back to a place that has changed so much, or being the person who went away, who has changed so much, has made me nutty, made Earl look at me with worry more than once since being here in L.A. I can get past this.

I've been through worse: the two most scarring experiences of my life were working at McDonald's in high school, and living five years in Langsdale, Indiana. I only lasted for one year at McDonald's and finally quit when I realized I couldn't take one more day of asking folks if they wanted an apple pie with that, only to hear them yell through the drive-through speaker exactly what I could do with that apple pie.

Sure, my hard time at Langsdale lasted much longer—you have no idea how much longer. Five years in small-town Midwest as a black woman in graduate school should be calculated more like dog years. I was only there five real-time years, yet my psyche aged ten years. I have souvenirs from both McDonald's and Langsdale. The not-faded-enough imprint of a kamikaze fry that somehow *jumped* out of boiling lard and landed on my forearm. I once nearly got into fisticuffs with some Shakespearean at a party, who blah, blah, blahed about an article he'd read about our "litigious" society, and how that one woman who sued McDonald's over spilled coffee on her thighs was "frivolous" and "greedy." I *saw* the photos of that woman's thighs, which didn't look none too pretty after a cup full of hot-ass coffee settled on them, and they didn't look frivolous—they looked fucked up. And I showed the Shakespearean my fry tattoo. That shut him up.

It was the beginning of a long epiphany, really. I was trying to figure out what to do with my life: continue on with a Ph.D., or leave and do something that was a better fit for me? I took the MFA and ran with my second souvenir: Earl.

When I first met Earl, he looked like the lost member of ZZ Top—or Grizzly Adams—and I saw myself as a kind of Clair Huxtable—if she were more broke, showed *a lot* more skin, kept her hair in braids, never went to the gym and cussed like a sailor. If you try to think of these two kinds of people dating, and you feel your mind refusing to wrap itself around that image, think about how I must have felt about it. But God bless Earl. He only thought about what he wanted and how to go about getting it. He never worried about what anything *looked* like, this man who would never use the phrase "politic-ize." He never even worried about what our life would be like in L.A. Before leaving Langsdale, Earl was already thinking about quitting bartending and studying labor law because he was tired of his family and friends—a long line of factory workers just like mine—getting screwed over. "I cain't bartend for all the rest of my days, Ronnie," he'd said. But he decided to do it just a little bit longer in L.A. to save for school and get settled.

And so, in an anything-for-love gesture, my boyfriend, a man who cares nothing about the looks of things, moved with me to my hometown, a city that is obsessed with the looks of things. All the time packing up my life in Langsdale, Indiana, I thought about how Earl would adjust, fit in. Turns out that I'm the one having to readjust. I'm a native Los Angelino who has had it up to here with loud, self-important cell-phone conversations about "project meetings" while I'm trying to eat my lunch. I'm one flip out away from the next Hummer I see taking up two parking spaces outside Starbucks. And don't get me started on the hipster uniform for the up-and-coming Hollywood set. For the guys, a hundred-dollar haircut so that one's hair looks effortlessly "I'm-too-cool-to-comb-my-hair messy," faux Elvis sunglasses, ironic T-shirts of '70s and '80s icons. In general, it's the look of a fifteen-year-old skateboarder, even if you happen to be closer to thirty. The women have three looks: anything that makes one look like a thirteen-year-old, anything that makes one like a hooker *and* a thirteen year-old, and anything that looks like what Doris refers to as *the mask*—that is, at least four layers of makeup. I wanted to live in Echo Park because it used to have none of the things, none of the people, that made me nutty. Turns out they've migrated, crawling away from the west side, leaving a trail of dumb, money-making Hollywood scripts behind them. So, Earl and I are living in a neighborhood we can hardly afford to stay in and given first, last and deposit on any new place, we can't afford to leave.

Who in the *world* would have thought that I'd find myself sometimes longing for the relatively simpler life of Indiana? Sitting out on Earl's porch, listening to him tell stories about growing up in a small town, or watching a free movie in the park

at night while fireflies drifted past, or—and this is really scary—
longing for the days when I sat in a graduate seminar of self-
important academics in training, throwing around Foucault and
bell hooks with shaky authority. But I'm confronting my longing.
I admit my longing: I've complained to Earl since moving back.
Okay. I've ranted, monologued, delivered hour-long dissertations. In typical Earl fashion, he's not phased one bit. He's on easy
street, relaxed and loving his adventure in L.A., the traffic, the
smog, all of it. Earl responds to it with a shrug, a shake of his
head and a grin. Meanwhile, this Ian kid has nearly sent me to
my first visit to a therapist in all my thirty years of living.

Hearing that Toni Morrison's *The Bluest Eye* is "lame" and
school is "retarded" and he is "going to be a music producer, so
who needed this shit anyway?" makes me panic about the
purpose of trying to teach anyone anything. He hadn't even tried
to read the book. After that first meeting with Ian, I went home
to Earl, and I was still stunned. He pulled me up from the couch
and gave me one of his bear hugs. "It is what it is, darlin'. You're
home. You're an L.A. woman."

"It's not the same," I said mournfully into Earl's T-shirt. "And
if it's not rich Hollywood kids driving me to drink, it's all these
other fools running around who are not even *from* here. People
pose so hard, it's a wonder they don't break a goddamn bone."

Earl grinned at me. "I ain't from here. You like me all right.
And anyhow, it ain't who's from where, it's who sees eye to eye,"
he said. "You can't blame folks for trying to get somewhere.
They're just trying too hard, is all. Getting above their raising
is what Daddy used to say."

"Being a pain in the ass is what my daddy calls it."

"Actually," Earl said, giving me another squeeze, "my daddy calls it that, too." Then he winked, let me go and ran his hands through his newly short hair with the neat, sandy waves that looked slightly retro, and I made up my mind to stop whining, to count my blessings. I was living in the place I was born, raised, and wanted to be with a good person, a smart person, a handsome man. Someone who understood me. Cain't beat that with a stick, Earl would say.

I kissed his freshly shaved right cheek, right on his dimple, and said, "Thanks, Erardo, baby. Thanks for being so sane."

Earl tugged on one of my braids. "Erardo. I still ain't used to you calling me that."

"Viva Italia!" I shouted.

He shook his head. "I wish you never knew I was Italian. Hell, I don't even think of myself thataway."

The only reason I knew that Earl's real name was Erardo Lo Vecchio was because it showed up on my caller ID the first time he called me. I've continued to get a kick out of his name since then, and for a long time I was obsessed with Italy and Italians, anything that was a combination thereof. I've calmed my Italian lust, although Doris would say that's arguable. She would also say that my lust for Earl had nothing to do with his Italian pheromones wafting toward me. She would say that in spite of my hard head, I was seeing him for the true man he was, the true man he is—a reluctant Italian who's much more Billy Ray than Bruno, who's crazy about me and gets what I'm saying, even though we were raised on two different planets. Planet Indiana and Planet California.

* * *

Earl keeps giving me Diet Cokes and now that it's later in the evening, nine o'clock, things are picking up. I watch him banter and carry on with Katie, who I try to like, but she's way too flirty with Earl for me to give her a break. I didn't think I was the jealous kind. But now, I watch her closely. If you looked up the antonyms for *willowy* and *blond,* in both cases the thesaurus would say my name. Veronica Williams. Curvy and dark. All night, Katie's been chatting it up with Earl, laughing and lightly touching him to guide him out of her way as she moves fast around the tight space, taking orders and pouring drinks. She and her cleavage are working hard to charm the customers. But maybe I should see that she's working hard. She makes her job seem easy and breezy, but she's a bit too hyper about it.

Earl told me she wants to be (surprise!) an actor. "An *actor,*" I said. "Figures."

"I thought ladies was called 'actresses'?" Earl questioned at the time.

"Do you go to doctresses?" I asked him. "Or get tickets by police officeresses?" That whole diminutive tag for jobs that happened to be done by women always killed me.

"Got it," Earl said.

The busier it gets, the more I think it's time for me to walk back up the hill because I never want to be out on the street too late at night. I've not been gone from L.A. so long that I forget the dark streets can be full of creepy motherfuckers who think it's cute to chop up women. Besides, Earl's getting too busy to keep me company while Katie's working overtime to keep him company. For a moment, the images of them together get to me and I have a fleeting thought that the two of them *look* like they should be together, but I shake it off. I try to get his attention while The Beastie Boys fade out on the jukebox. When Ray Charles kicks in, Earl perks up. He's nodding his head to the music and I can see him whistling, even if I can't hear him over the orchestration.

"Earl!" Katie hollers. "Sing it. You know you can sing. Don't be shy!"

Earl puts a drink on the counter and looks around the bar, searching for me. I'm down at one end, so cup my hands around my mouth and shout, "Sing, baby!" I love to hear him sing. It's just busy enough, but not too busy that folks can't hear Earl sing if he really belts it out. He shrugs, holds his towel out, as if to say, *should I?* I nod, blow him a kiss, point to my wrist watch, and thumb toward the bar exit.

Earl grins, mouths *I love you,* and waits for the next verse before he joins Ray.

His voice is strong and deep over the din of the bar. He waves goodbye, but sings at me, so I can't leave. All the folks whistle at Earl and egg him on. I'm mesmerized, and I'm thinking if Katie sees what I see, if everybody sees what I see, Earl's going to fit right in, in the land of looking good.

When I turn to leave, I catch something out the corner of my eye. It's Katie. This time, when she touches Earl to move around him at the bar, she stands behind him, gives him a squeeze from behind and rests her face against his back. I get a feeling, a sick feeling. It surprises me, this feeling, and it takes me a little while to recognize that it's fear. But I don't even know what I'm afraid of, exactly.

doris

Question: What do Ezra Pound (brilliant imagist poet, grand-
daddy of literary modernism, borderline fascist) and
Doris Weatherall (struggling feminist poet, practicing postmodernist, and dater of borderline fascists*)
have in common?

Answer: a) Unrequited love for T. S. Eliot. (including much
hotter movie version of Eliot, craggy-faced
Willem Dafoe in his early days.)
b) Belief in the power of language to convey image,
and image to convey experience.
c) Mantralike devotion to the phrase "Make it New."
(Not to be confused with the now-Dr. Weatherall's

other favorite reality show catchphrase, "Make it
Work.")

d) All of the above.

(* For those unfamiliar with academic lingo, "practicing post-
modernist and dater of borderline fascists" means that although
I have a liberal job in a liberal profession, I subscribe to *Us
Weekly* and date the occasional republican, à la Maria Shriver.)

Okay, before everyone runs screaming at the somewhat pretentious comparison of my life to Ezra Pound's, let me tell you
why I think an old-school poet like Pound is an appropriate model
for a woman like me, why "d," dear readers, is the correct answer
to today's multiple-choice pop quiz. As poetic mandates go, what
could be more appropriate than "Make it New," especially when
being a professor-professional poet requires that you uproot your
life, choose between your job and your boyfriend and start brand-
new in a brand-new city at the less-than-tender age of thirty-two?

Pound believed in the power of image, so let me start by
giving a few from the past three weeks of my life. First, August
10, me, packing up the shards of sanity that still remain from
seven years of graduate school in Langsdale, Indiana, where I
recently completed my Ph.D. in poetry writing. It's almost as
useful in real-world terms as devoting one's life to the study of
foam patterns at the top of cappuccinos versus lattes. I use this
metaphor largely because failed Ph.D.s in poetry often find
themselves intimately reacquainted with the making of coffee—
although I must say that my sisters at Starbucks might have a

benefits package to rival that of my new employer, Atlanta State
University. Into my trunk went the spoils of years spent shopping
cleverly at flea markets for the perfect blend of kitsch and acceptable adult decoration. My signed Marilyn Monroe framed
picture from a yard sale in Terre Haute, although it may have
only been signed by the three-year-old running around in a
saggy pair of underwear and "Got Milk" T-shirt; a formica coffee
table set with red chairs and slightly rusted aluminum legs (and
fifties styling to rival June Cleaver's, might I add), and more, all
loaded up in Indiana, and unloaded in Atlanta, Georgia, into my
swanky midtown loft where I stare at them and wonder if I am
actually a nouveau Beverly-hillbilly. Can I make this work? Can
the old me become new again?

Image number two, this from only a couple of days ago: August
27, on the cusp of the first day of class and me, lost and frustrated
on the streets of Atlanta. I had been trying to find the newly
opened Ikea, and wound up somehow driving twenty miles past
it to Marietta, where I encountered a giant mechanical chicken
the size of a three-story building—the "big chicken" of "you are
officially outside the Atlanta city limits" fame. Knowing I was lost,
I pulled into the parking lot of the Army-Navy surplus store, only
to be greeted by a row of "Yankee, go home" bumper stickers,
which I couldn't help but take personally—and at the same time,
I felt like gesturing at them and saying I WISH I COULD EVEN
FIND MY STUPID HOME. A perfectly nice gentleman behind
a counter of death stars gave me polite directions back into the
city, and I tried hard not to sound like the displaced New Yorker
that I am.

The euphoria of the initial move had worn thin, and all of my excitement at having found a job was slowly being replaced by the thought that making new friends in one's thirties was not as easy as doing so in one's twenties. My next-door neighbor, a funky singleton of about my age, had mentioned drinks, but hadn't followed through yet. I had gone to three coffee shops before I realized that one couldn't simply sit at a coffee shop and expect to make friends—that smiling at strangers merely made one look deranged, not friendly. Ditto for the same behavior at power-yoga, my other attempt to be social. Although there were some nice-looking men, particularly one bald, black man who could have been Michael Jordan's twin, whose downward dog was a thing to behold—but I digress. That, plus I am separated by the entire contiguous United States from my best friend of the past half-decade, and I am not one of those writers who enjoys ongoing solitude. Solitude makes me cut weird bangs, overpluck my eyebrows and eat too many Nutter Butters.

Driving back from the outer edges of the city, the only thing that kept me from weeping in frustration at the glacial pace of traffic was the knowledge that Zach, my boyfriend of three years, was arriving in seventy-two hours to help transition me into my new life. So when I finally re-entered my apartment, the one spot of familiarity and comfort in Atlanta, I had moved past relief to gratefulness at the sight of Zach's number on my caller ID. Zach, calling to tell me that "things had come up," and he wasn't going to be able to drive from Langsdale, Indiana, to Atlanta, Georgia. "We'll talk later in the week," he said. "I can tell you're tired, and I don't want to upset you more."

Image number three: this, today, August 29, the day before my debut at Atlanta state as Dr. Doris Weatherall. The "money shot" of the entire move was my entering the building that houses the English department to start a job where I am no longer grad-school-wastrel and Oprah-watcher Doris Weatherall, but fully bona fide assistant professor, Dr. Doris Weatherall, with attendant adult salary and health plan. In honor of my confirmed adulthood, I am wearing a Katherine Hepburn—worthy ensemble of grey tailored pants, white shirt and Pradalike naughty-conservative lace-up shoes with decidedly nonsensible heel. I moved up from Miss Clairol to the Aveda salon, and my hair is dyed a rich red-brown and cut in long layers that reach about an inch below my shoulder.

I feel glamorous and professional.

For about five minutes.

The glamour wears off after I drop my books in my office and go back down the hall to my mailbox. On top of the various catalogs and beginning-of-school calendars sits a letter, with DORIS W. scrawled in serial-killer-like spidery writing across the front of the envelope. I open the envelope to see what looks like a hand-stamped logo of CLASSROOM in gigantic capital letters, with the middle of the letters slightly hollowed out to fit the word *politics* in small letters. Circled around the writing is a thick, red line with a slash through it, similar to the implied "no" in "no smoking" signs. Even creepier, below it, in the same handwriting are the words, "We are watching you. Watch yourself!"

From behind me, I hear, "That's what they didn't tell you

about during your campus visit." A thin blonde whom I vaguely remember from my interview last winter as Dr. Asa Davies takes the sheet of paper from my hand and traces her finger around the red circle. "No politics in the classroom—get it? And be warned, they have moles in all the classrooms. They actually tried to sue me last year, but it got thrown out of the kangaroo campus court. I teach postcolonial lit. Try keeping politics out of that. I suppose I should change my reading of *Robinson Crusoe* to explain how Friday found his true calling and learned his place in the brave, new, Eurocentric world. Welcome to Atlanta State University, where the inmates have a hand in running the asylum. Like I said, things they never tell you about on your campus visits."

She shrugs her shoulders, and then, like some academic oracle, she turns and disappears down the hall.

I fold the paper in half and put it in my new tote bag, a gift from Zach when I first secured this job. Before taking any job, candidates go on "campus visits," where they are put through a rigorous round of interviews, job talks, and given a chance to see what the campus is like for themselves. And while helpful, campus visits are sort of like first dates. Unless the school is beyond help, they put on their best face and pitch as much woo as an underfunded state university can. I knew that the student body was conservative as a whole, and I knew that there had been some stirrings in the Georgia legislature as to what should be taught in the classrooms. This is a state, after all, where they put stickers on high school science books, saying "evolution is a theory"—which, I assume is also *inside* the textbooks, as "theory" is scientific for "all but written in stone truth." I figured that as a poet I could fly under the radar, but it would appear that I had figured wrong.

I return to my office, a concrete block with cell-like rectangular windows ringing the top—enough windows to let light in, but not enough to see the goings-on of the world outside. Atlanta State University is located on the northwest side of Atlanta in a block of buildings that could only be converted housing projects. I was shocked when I first saw my "office," a cubicle that might just as easily have been used to interrogate prisoners in some *Escape from Atlanta*–style Kurt Russell TNT late-night urban guerilla warfare movie. It's no ivory tower—it's not even any Langsdale University, for that matter, which, while rural and threatening to unleash the children of the corn, was truly beautiful.

The address for the university is deceptive. When I was mailing out applications, twenty-eight in all, to every job for which I was qualified within a thirty-mile radius of a large metropolitan area, Atlanta State University on Peachtree Grove Avenue sounded idyllic. I had images of a hip-but-lush campus, cordoned off from the city, with actual peach trees from which I might nab a late-afternoon snack. Never mind that I'd never seen a peach tree. Never mind that I now know that calling anything "Peachtree" in Atlanta is somewhat akin to naming a baby boy Mohammed in the Muslim world, or calling helpless newborns "Apple" or "Roman." No peach trees bloom on Atlanta State University's campus. In fact, only a smattering of sad, straggly saplings all but grope for light between evenly-spaced gaps of pavement lining the streets nearby. But in the academic job market, a job is a job, and by the time they offered me a position, teaching poetry no less, it was yes-I-said-yes-I-will-yes. Yes.

My office is newly painted, a periwinkle-blue that I hope will make me creative and productive. Half-unpacked boxes of books have all been shoved against the walls, cramping me into the middle of the room. I've been provided with a computer and a phone, three chairs and a minirefrigerator that looks as if it was thrown away from a dorm in the midsixties. I lean back in one of the chairs and prop my feet on the refrigerator, looking again at the "We are watching you. Watch yourself." Not exactly words to warm one's heart.

What the neo-Nazis are about to find out, however, is that I, Doris Weatherall—*Dr.* Doris Weatherall—am nothing if not a contrarian. When all the world is wearing platform heels, I schlep around in ballet flats. When the "natural look" demands a clear and overglossed lip, I slather on the 1950s movie-star reds, vamping my pout to the absolute max. And when some bossy campus fascists tell me not to talk about politics in my classroom, I redesign my opening speech to address the topic directly.

This semester I am teaching "Introduction to American Literature," "Beginning Poetry Writing," and the upper-level seminar on "World Literature." But the first class of the day tomorrow is American lit—perfect venue for discussing the nature of politics in the classroom. I lock my door and open a copy of Ben Franklin's autobiography, looking for a way to tie the week's first reading with my rant about free speech and a liberal arts education. My computer chimes gently in the background, letting me know that Ronnie is awake and online. I open my IM screen.

ME: Are you awake? The McCarthyists are alive and well and living in Atlanta. I got a letter in campus mail telling me not so nicely to keep my big liberal trap shut. I guess it's back to poems about trees and birdies.

RONNIE: There have got to be better ways to make a living. Are we too old to learn pole dancing?

ME: I am pretty sure that I am. I'm not even sure I'm capable of learning basic yoga. How's Earl?

RONNIE: Asleep. We see each other two waking hours a day. How are you settling in? Meet any new neighbors?

ME: I have an exotic bohemian living next door. I am going to try to make her be my friend and teach me to dress for the city. Hard to meet new people here. I think I'm going to get a dog. Both for a friend and protection from potential campus Nazis.

RONNIE: You mean some rat dog?

ME: I mean a *small* but fiercely protective dog. By the way. I strongly suspect that I am about to get dumped.

RONNIE: Whaaaaattt?

ME: Well, I got "let's take some time off-ed," which is the

last stop before dumpsville. I am trying to repress this
information completely, as it will only give me a mini-
nervous breakdown for which I truly have no time.

RONNIE: Why? What's going on with Zach? Did
anything lead up to it?

ME: (now feeling sad) Everything led up to it. I'll call you
later. Must prep Ben Franklin for tomorrow.

RONNIE: Sounds like a party.

ME: Ha-ha.

After signing off from IM, I put the Ben Franklin aside and
unpack one of the boxes marked "OFFICE." A mug swaddled
in newswrap sits atop two piles of books. I unwrap it to find the
gag gift that Zach bought me as a joke on our first-year anni-
versary. The words on the mug read, "OPPOSITES ATTRACT,
THEN THEY DRIVE EACH OTHER CRAZY." Funny, and unfortunately, prophetic. Zach and I "met cute" almost six years
ago, if by cute you mean that I got really sloshed on pink wine
and kissed him because he looked like Harvey Keitel, and he
kissed me back because he and his girlfriend were "on a break."
Then we avoided each other for two years, followed by an
intense month of summer teaching where we were thrown
together by the forces that be, and our Hepburn/Tracy antics
eventually gave way to love. Zach and I knew each other for a
while before we started dating, and like any adults in a relationship, we learned to overlook each other's faults. I learned to love
a man who groomed his toenails in public, and he learned the

subtle difference between a pencil skirt from Old Navy and a pencil skirt mailed to me from my sister in New York, post-Barney's sample sale. I went to my first jam band concert, and he got his first haircut that cost more than twenty dollars. Though by the end of our third year together, the differences were starting to wear—not so much the superficial differences, but my anality versus his total lack of motivation. The straw before the final straw probably came my last evening in Indiana.

"It's only going to be Langsdale with accents," Zach told me at the Saloon. We were at the local watering hole with Ronnie and Earl, my best friend and her ersatz-hillbilly boyfriend, a Langsdale local who had actually agreed to follow Ronnie to the West Coast for love. It was all I could do to get Zach to follow me back to my apartment at night.

"Nothing wrong with accents," Ronnie said, squeezing Earl playfully beneath the chin.

"You better make sure to eat up when you get there," Earl said. "Looks to me like you're wastin' away, Doris."

Earl was right. Between arguing with Zach about his latest career change—opening an old movie theater to show classic films in Langsdale, *instead* of finishing his dissertation—and thinking about a new job, the move, everything, I'd been forgetting to eat. And not to go off on Zach, but do the words NO MARKET mean anything to anyone? Selling vintage movies to the locals seemed to me a uniquely vexed venture akin to opening a designer boutique next to the Wet Seal and expecting the tweens to come running. You can't just walk in and sell tofu burgers to a meat-and-potato populous. Don't even get me started.

"There's no danger of Doris starving," Zach said. "Believe me."

Hmm. Zach stood up and stretched, then headed for the men's room.

"Sooooo," Ronnie asked, "A little trouble in paradise? What are you going to do about the move?" Earl's brows knit together with concern. Ronnie and Earl were wearing matching black T-shirts from a Tom Waits concert they'd attended in Chicago, a fashion accident, but proof that they were on the same wavelength. A reminder of how far off Zach and I had gone—his hippie sine running counter to my urban cosine. That night, Zach was wearing Birkenstocks to my Charles David, a Target T-shirt to my Betsey Johnson baby-doll dress, and patchouli to my Hypnotic Poison. No, things were not going well.

Things hadn't, in fact, been going well for the past few months. They had been made worse by a trip in late July to Atlanta where we both sweated for about three days straight and looked for a place for me to live. A brief snapshot from the visit:

"I like this place," Zach had said, when we were shown the ever-so-chi-chi loft, with exposed brick walls and tin roofing in which I now live. The building seemed quiet and well maintained.

"It's a studio," I said. "I'm not sure I'm a studio-loft kinda gal. And where are you going to put your stuff?"

Zach sighed. He'd grown his hair out long, a little longer than I like it, and had it knotted in a lazy ponytail. When he went to run his hand through it, it got stuck.

"Didn't we already talk about this? I thought we talked about this."

"No," I say. "I started to talk about it, and you started drinking, and you said things would all work out, and I said that I was getting older and might want a kid and marriage, and even if I didn't, that you still can't just drift and job jump forever. Is this ringing any bells?"

"That?" he said. "I've almost forgiven you for that conversation. Just let things be, Doris."

"I can't just let things be, Zach. And don't give me some faux-Buddhist crap about not pushing the river or letting flow rule one's life. I'm totally hippied out."

"And what's that supposed to mean?"

There are certain phrases that are never part of a healthy relationship, such as *"We need to talk. I'd like you if…"*, *"You remind me of my mother,"* and of course, *"What's that supposed to mean?"* (Frankly, I'd add *"You'd do it if you loved me"* when related to any and all less-than-kosher sexual experimentation, but that's a totally different story. I broke up with a boyfriend once during a stunning argument that ended with me yelling *"I intend to take my ass-virginity to my grave."* I suppose in this day and age that makes me a bit of a prude. So be it.)

Anyway, the issue at hand is bickering. Zach and I were bickering. And once you become a bickersome couple, it's a short ride to bitter and trapped.

"Forget it," I replied, the fear of a potential break-up beginning to feel very, very real. "I was kidding about the hippie thing. Stop being so sensitive."

And *"stop being so sensitive."* Another definite no-no. We'd gone from a fun, opposites-attract academic thrill ride of a couple, to a *Lifetime* movie-of-the-week, complete with recycled dialogue and the occasional semipublic tantrum. There were moments when I actually thought that all our story needed was a B-list actress to banish us forever to made-for-TV movie hell.

What he thought I meant was the fight we'd had the week before. It started out innocently enough. I'd bought a fabulous vintage piece of lingerie off of eBay, in which I felt very Marilyn. It was a baby-doll slip-type piece in sheer pink. Nothing kiddie-porn, but still naughty enough to be nice. And did Zach, the überhippie of my dreams, even *notice?* The answer, unfortunately, is yes. He took one look at me and said, *"Jesus, you trying to look like Mrs. Roper?"* Then he tried to recover with: *"You know I just like you naked, baby."* To which I responded, *"Of course you do, it requires the least amount of effort."*

So much for a sexy evening. I then proceeded to turn into someone's mother, yelling things like "YOU HAVE TO FINISH YOUR DISSERTATION." In a pink nightgown. In false eyelashes. I was going for a look. "YOU CAN'T QUIT AND OPEN SOME STUPID MOVIE THEATER." Just plain mean of me—stomping on the however ludicrous dreams of another.

Our final weeks together in Langsdale didn't do much to repair any of the damage. And my last night in town felt more like the last night before an execution. Painful and full of dread.

"He's still staying here in Indiana," I said to Ronnie, sloshing around my watered-down Jack and Coke and lone cube of ice. "I think we might have technically broken up last night. But it was such a horrific conversation that I refuse to go back in and clarify. I think that when I get to Atlanta, I'm trading in the whole men thing for a dog. Something I can properly accessorize that leaves me alone when I'm trying to write poetry and shuts up as long as it's fed."

"You think that a dog'll do that?" Earl asked, laughing. "Poor dog!"

Zach returned from the bathroom and sat next to me with his legs splayed apart at a ninety-degree angle, rubbing the fine hair on his knees and putting as much emotional distance between the two of us as possible.

"Don't know," I replied, thinking that I still wanted to cross that distance between us, that even his knobby, hairy knees were making me sad tonight. "The way things are going, it's worth a shot."

And then Zach and I did clarify things. We broke up, at least temporarily. Six weeks and then he says he'll visit, that we'll re-evaluate, blah, blah, blah. Two days later he called to say that it was all a mistake, that he would come to Atlanta before the semester started and we'd talk about things then. Now, he's canceled. Sometimes being in a relationship feels like having eternal detention, where you just keep getting re-evaluated and hoping that someone will either promote you or let you off the hook once and for all.

This afternoon, though, in my Atlanta office with a ninety-five-degree heat, and ninety-five percent humidity, it feels more like Doris + boxes piled all over office of fabulous new job +

only Doris to unpack them = maybe Zach and I should have tried a little harder. Still, I can't turn this into Sadlanta, or I won't be putting my best foot forward at the new job, and I'll have that horrible stink of needy and alone, which potentially healthy-minded new friends *and* boyfriends can smell from miles away. I do not want to become the emotional equivalent of deershit, in which only animals with no home training are permitted to roll.

I take the opposites attract mug, wrap it back in newspaper, and return it to the box.

After finishing class prep for my first day, I load my exhausted self into the Toyota and head back to my apartment. Frankly, I have decided that I would be doing well if all I did at the end of the day for the next six months is go home and tune in to find out just who *will* be America's next top model. If item one on my to-do list is "do new job well," then item two is the recycled-from-kindergarten "make new friends!"

The only thing more challenging than finding a new boyfriend in a strange city, which I honestly can't even begin to think about right now, is finding a new girlfriend. And no, I don't mean that I am taking "Make it New" to mean my sexuality. Aside from having no real inclination to lesbianism, I feel that having dedicated the past fifteen or so odd years to understanding men, I couldn't even *begin* to take on another gender and the attendant issues. No, I mean the sort of girlfriend/wingwoman you need for cruising the local hot spots, gossiping about your bad dates, and talking each other into unnecessary purchases at the Lenox mall. I don't mean a *best* friend, as I couldn't begin to replace Ronnie, but someone who is not backstabbing, overly obsessed with finding a husband, borderline in the single-white-female sense of appropriating one's hair/fashion sense or is just plain boring as sin.

I do have a candidate for girl-friendship, who is qualified in virtually every respect mentioned above, aside from the husband-hunting, which I now believe she has taken to such extremes that it almost wraps back around to not caring at the end of the day. The candidate in question is my next-door neighbor, Antonia, or "Toni" as she likes to be called.

I met Toni not long after I moved into my apartment. My first few nights in midtown, I started to wonder if I'd made the right choice about neighborhoods. When Zach and I visited Atlanta, midtown seemed like the perfect place—liberal, centrally located, dog friendly and relatively safe. At the time, Zach was happy that most of the hot boys were gay, but now it was starting to feel like one of those cruel "water, water everywhere" jokes that God occasionally plays on single women. Anyhow, my first week in the apartment, it seemed as if police sirens were going off every night: faint and intermittent, but frighteningly regular. I'd look outside my window or peek outside the doorway, but nothing ever seemed to materialize. Then I started to hear them during the day, and then, although I was beginning to question my own rational powers, it sounded as if they were coming from the apartment next door. I suppose it's possible that there was someone TiVo-ing *COPS* and playing it loud all night long, but then that raised an even more challenging question. Why would *anyone* in their right mind do such a thing? Besides, it didn't sound like television, it just sounded like a siren.

So I took it upon myself both to make new friends and find out what the hell was going on. I'd seen my neighbor once or twice disappearing in and out of her apartment. What I could tell about her was that she had a large blond afro and impeccably high-end bohemian fashion sense. Aside from that, I assumed that she was biracial, as she had toffee-colored skin and blue-green eyes. However, she could also have been an extremely funky white girl with a mystic tan obsession. Aesthetically, regardless of race, women in Atlanta tend to skew toward looking like Barbie. I pegged her at anywhere between twenty-six and thirty-five. When the sirens weren't going, I could hear her music, old-school R & B played late and loud, but not so loud that I couldn't get work done or sleep. I prayed to God that she wasn't a teetotaler and knocked on her door with a bottle of wine.

She opened the door wearing a pair of blue sweatpants, brushing her teeth and looking slightly bothered. "I'm sorry," she mumbled through the toothpaste, "I wasn't expecting anyone." Without waiting for me to respond, she made a "stay there" gesture and went to rinse out her mouth.

"Don't say it," she said. "You're the new neighbor come to kill me over that freakin' parrot."

"Excuse me?"

"That." She gestured to the corner of her apartment, where a parrot the size of my right forearm was suspended upside down from a cage that took up half the wall. The bird flapped its wings, nonplussed, and let out a sound that was part police siren, part car alarm. "My ex-boyfriend's idea of a gift to me. He found it in the classifieds and said that he wanted to give me something to last as long as our love. We dated two more months. But that freakin' parrot is for-freakin'-ever."

"A parrot is making that noise?"

"Nice gift, right? He gets it from this guy who bought it with his lotto winnings. It can mimic police sirens, ambulances and," she looked at the parrot and asked, "What's your favorite thing to say to the ladies?"

The parrot perked its head up and said, "Nice ass, beeatch."

Toni shook her head, and I couldn't keep myself from laughing.

"That's the funniest thing I've ever seen," I said. "What's its name?"

"Lotto," she said. "They probably had a dog named 'Bingo' and a goat named 'Craps.' But I guess the winning streak finally ended because they couldn't afford to keep him. So now the traumatic beginnings of his life have become the soundtrack to my own. I kept hoping that you couldn't hear it through the walls. I'm really sorry if it's disturbing you. I haven't quite figured out yet how to make him stop."

I walked over to the parrot's cage and tried to rub its beak through the metal grid.

"Fatties rule," the parrot said. "Fatties rule."

Toni shook her head. "I choose to believe that he means people."

"Can you get him to learn new things?"

"Only obscenities seem to take," she said. "We've been working on 'foxy lady' for the past week, but all I get back is 'nice ass, bitch.'"

"Nice ass, beeeeatch," the parrot corrected her, and started dancing from foot to foot, craning its head from side to side with spastic glee.

"I think he might have a personality disorder," Toni muttered. "So let me take the wine. You want a glass?"

"I'd love one."

I sat down on the overstuffed cranberry couch and Toni took the matching overstuffed chair to its right. She handed me an oversized wineglass, filled about an inch and a half with chilled white wine. I felt a bit like Alice in Wonderland, with giant furniture and giant utensils and a mad parrot bobbing in the background.

"So what do you do?" she asked.

"I'm a writer," I replied. "I write poetry, and I'm just starting a job teaching at Atlanta State."

Toni pulled a bottle of nail polish from a basket underneath the coffee table.

"Very cool," she said. "You mind? I need to do my toenails. I had an ex-boyfriend who couldn't stand to look at feet."

"I have nothing against feet." I immediately thought of Zach, who was prone to cutting his toenails in public. "So what do you do?"

"Long version or short version?"

"Doesn't matter."

Toni fanned the toes of her right foot as wide as possible and deliberately painted a thin coat of metallic champagne across the toenails. "So I did my undergrad at Vassar, in sociology, and thought I wanted to go abroad and study different people, all that. Did it for a year and hated it. So I thought maybe first-world social work was the thing for me. Didn't hate that, but it didn't pay the bills, either. So now I work at that part-time, consult for private industry part-time, and in my downtime, I'm writing a book, but it's a book with a sociological bent."

"Really," I said. "That's very cool. What's it about?"

"Dating. It's sort of half–Susan Faludi, about how the world is out to make single women in their thirties feel like they should be taken out and stoned and just put out of their misery, but I'm also interested in age, race, class and education and how they play out in Internet dating. So it's sort of a performance art piece, as well. I have about twenty profiles up on dating sites in the area. In some I'm young, in some I'm older. You know, twenty-eight, thirty-two, thirty-six, thirty-eight. In some I list myself as white, in some as "other," in some as African-American. And I change my education level, too, just to see if people spin themselves differently. Then I go on the dates to see how people act, what they say. What the white boys have to say when white Toni asks them why they only date white women, things like that."

"Any broad and sweeping conclusions?" I ask, sincerely curious.

"With race, whether they want a Nubian queen or a princess to pamper, the words may change, but the melody remains the same. The age thing is for real, though, and I'm trying to figure out whether or not the media generates ageism on the Internet, and whether or not men even really recognize when they're being ageist."

I find myself nodding along, Lotto style.

Toni reaches into the drawer of the mahogany end table next to the couch and pulls out a stack of magazine and newspaper articles. "If you don't mind me asking," she asks, "how old are you?"

"Thirty-two. Birthday's in a few months."

She considers this for a moment. "You've got plenty of time. But hear me on this, when you turn thirty-six, thirty-eight, the prospects get drier than the desert in August. And look at this, none of this is made up." She passes me an article that I skim quickly, making the case that men are happier marrying women who make less than they do and have no careers. Then she passes me a magazine clipping making the case for women under the age of twenty-five having the smartest and healthiest babies, then she hands over one about the chances of a woman over the age of forty getting married, and her waning fertility. By the end of the stack, I feel slightly dizzy.

"And people still argue against feminism," she scoffs. "You tell me the world doesn't still have a chip on its shoulder against a strong, successful woman."

"How recent are these?" I ask, looking for the dates.

"All within the last year," she answers. "I'm trying to compare societal attitudes against the real world. But the man online who is well over thirty-five, but won't date a woman over thirty-two, is alive, well and multiplying at a rapid rate. So you might as well get in the pond while you're still one of the sought-after fish."

For the first time since yesterday, I feel actual fear at the thought of Zach disappearing back into the alpha-male ocean.

"So what's your real age?" I ask.

"Thirty-four," she says. "Cusp of undesirability."

"That is sooo depressing. And you're still totally gorgeous."

"Age may be nothing but a number, but it's another of those real fictions. In Atlanta, today, you live the number." She finished applying a second coat of polish and gingerly placed her feet on the brown shag rug—very '70s retro-chic. "And because you're probably too polite to ask, I'll tell you my real race shakedown. My dad was Japanese and Swedish, and my mom was African-American and Irish, so I'm just about anything anyone thinks I am."

When I look at her face, I suppose that I can see all of it.

"What are you?" she asks.

"Irish, German, French, Native-American, and a little bit of Swedish for good measure."

"McMutt," she says. "American white girl." Then she yawns. I take this as my cue to make a polite exit.

Making new friends is never easy. Back in my apartment, I feel guardedly optimistic about Toni, but there's nothing like the ease of an old friend. I pour the dregs of a three-day-old bottle of chardonnay into a juice tumbler and dial Ronnie.

"Hello," she whispers.

"Ronnie," I say. "Why are you whispering?"

"Earl's asleep. He's working nights at the bar. Hold on, I'll take this outside."

There's a long pause, and I hear the faint drone of Lotto in the background doing his best will-the-ambulance-make-it-on-time screech.

"Okay," she says. "I'm outside. I have to drive over to Beverly-fucking-Hills in an hour to spar with Ian, so I'm gonna have to go in about ten. Teenagers with BMWs and personal trainers. Kid probably gets more in allowance money than they're paying me. So. Atlanta. You all moved in?"

"Unpacked the last box yesterday and even talked to the neighbor."

"So?"

"She was nice enough, I'm going to start a slow campaign to make her be my friend." I take a sip of my chardonnay, which has turned overnight from "oak-y" to "ass-y." "So tell me more about what you two are doing? Is that kid as bad as you say? Remember that girl I had at Langsdale, the one who was later picked to be on *The Real World, New Orleans?* I was teaching that class on autobiography and identity, I had them all reading *The Autobiography of Malcolm X,* and she looked at me with her terrible blond perm and god-awful Texas accent and said, 'Miss Weatherall, I think Malcolm X was a whiner!'"

Ronnie laughs. "I remember that. Ian's the other kind. Down-with-the-people from his mansion on the hill. I'm not sure which is worse."

"One-on-one is probably always worse. How about Earl? Is he going over as bartender to the stars?"

I conjure an image of Earl, in his mail-order Camel Lights T-shirt and tight jeans, trying to make an organic apple martini for a gaggle of starlets with surgically attached cell phones and

Ugg boots, wearing those bizarre ruffled miniskirts that look like ass-doilies.

"Everyone loves Earl. Maybe even more than they did at the Saloon. He's got the other bartender ready to buy cowboy boots and ride off with him into the sunset."

"Does that mean you're going to have to play sheriff? Knock some heads in the nouveau Old West?"

Ronnie gives a confident half-chuckle, which I remember well.

"So what's going on at school? Sounds crazier than Langsdale. And you have to fill me in on Zach. I can't believe you two would actually call it off."

"It's more like we called a time-out, but you know what that means."

"Maybe with someone else," Ronnie says. "But Zach may just need some time."

"Why do you say that? Did Earl talk to him?"

"No. But remember, as hard as it is to leave someone, sometimes it's even harder to be left behind. Try to remember how he might see things."

All I can see is the accusatory black typeface from Toni's headlines of horror—MEN DON'T WANT A MORE SUC-CESSFUL WOMAN. "I am," I say. "But it's not making me feel any better."

ronnie

With all my worrying about not having a job, I hadn't even thought about the fact that Charlie, who'd gotten me my job in the first place, would be after my ass, as well. He hadn't wanted to suggest me to the Bernsteins at all until I'd convinced him that I did know how to teach, that all my time in grad school hadn't been spent drinking and writing stories that nobody wanted to read. He'd never really understood the whole MFA thing in the first place. "What was that, exactly?" he asked. "So you, like, study writing, and that's it? They give *degrees* for that? And what are you supposed to do with that degree anyway? What kind of job? You couldn't possibly make any money with that sort of thing, could you?" I had sat next to Earl at their long dinner table that had been battered and sandpapered and then stained so that it would look as if they'd just found it in a barn somewhere and had not paid, Bita told me, three grand for it.

Bita, my best friend in L.A. who had known me longer than anyone, took one look at my face, said, "Charlie," and Charlie said, "What?" and held his fork and knife up, like what do you want *me* to do about the fact that she wasted three years of her life? Earl was still on good behavior—we'd only been in L.A. for a few weeks when we'd had that dinner—so he just squeezed my thigh under the table and didn't tell Charlie to "Hold on there, now, buddy," which is Earl's way of saying shut the hell up. Instead, he said, "Nice table. My mamaw had a table like this in her kitchen. Made it herself from wood out in the yard."

Charlie took a sip of wine and grinned at Earl. "Well, this is a four-thousand-dollar table, Earl." He stroked the table. "I doubt your, what'd you say, 'Mamaw'? I doubt your *grandmother* would have had anything like this."

Bita gave Charlie a look with her green, darkly lined eyes, which said, *Stop being an asshole,* but I didn't say anything. Though I was wanting to point out the fact that the table's price had somehow gotten inflated. Or had she been embarrassed and low-balled the price? That was possible, too. Charlie chewed his salmon, satisfied that he'd put Earl in his place. It's been the good old boy versus the Hollywood exec ever since the two met. But Earl knew how to fight his own battles. I was waiting for his comeback.

"Well…" Earl said, and took a sip of *his* drink, a Miller that Bita had bought a whole six pack of because she knew it was Earl's beer of choice. He let that "well" linger a little bit, as if the discussion was over. He crossed his arms and leaned into the table with them and I couldn't help it. I ran my hand up and down his arm and he covered my hand with his and squeezed. He gave me one of those sly grins where only one of his dimples was showing. "Well," he said again, finally. "You're right about that, Charlie. Mamaw would've never spent that kind of money on a table. Always told me, she said, 'Earl, nothing but fools throw away good money behind stuff that only fools don't know how to make their own selves.'"

"Charlie," Bita said, standing up and putting her napkin on the table. A cloth napkin with little cherries scattered everywhere that complimented the soft white stain of the table perfectly: a crisp, ironed cotton. "Honey, help me with the salad." And Charlie gave Earl one last glance before leaving the table with Bita.

When they left, Earl turned to me. "Darlin', you don't have to work for folks that know Charlie. I'm bartending. We can figure it out until you find something else." But I wanted to be working right away. One thing Earl didn't understand was that scraping by in Indiana ain't the same as scraping by in L.A. And this is why, in spite of my love for Earl and the kind of person he is—the no-bullshit kind—we are a strange match, partially because I was *slightly* more high maintenance than he'd ever be. Earl could really rough it, if he had to. Me, me no like-y. Earl could get by on a fire, a tent and a can of beans. Doris used to call him Mountain Man when we first used to see him at the Saloon. Little did we know.

I, however, *needed* to be able to get a coffee whenever I wanted one. I needed to grab a sandwich in the neighborhood whenever I wanted one. Nothing fancy, maybe a wrap at The Coffee Table or a breakfast burrito at Eat Well. I needed to buy something halfway cute at Gap or Old Navy on a whim, even if I didn't actually *need* those things. I needed a job. Period. I had an MFA, but I hadn't gone on the job market like Doris had, and it was too late—for now. I had to take what I could get. And I wanted to teach.

"Nope, Earl. I gotta have this job."

"Well, did I mess it up for you then? Giving Charlie that little talking to?" Earl frowned and looked toward the swinging door to the kitchen.

I shook my head. One thing I was certain of. Bita would damn near castrate Charlie if he didn't help me out. He was the money maker, the guy with all the pulls and connections and the TV shows in the works, but Bita was the boss. I even thought I could hear her raise her voice in the kitchen, though it was hard to tell over Coltrane's frantic "My Favorite Things," in the background. I hated having to rely on Charlie Flannigan for anything, but beggars—and caffeine addicts—can't be choosers.

The door swung open and Charlie came out holding an enormous ceramic bowl that they got during their last trip to Italy. Behind him came Bita with plates carefully stacked. "This is good salad. Everything organic," she explained, winking at Earl who thought the whole organic thing was a little silly.

"I'll call the Bernsteins about that job," Charlie said dutifully. And then he asked Earl with fake camaraderie, "Hey, Mr. Lo Vecchio. Get you another beer?"

"I'd be *de*lighted," Earl said. "Thank you," and then he turned to me to make sure I appreciated his gesture.

Now it has been exactly two weeks since Charlie has gotten me that job, and exactly five days since I've fucked it up. Earl has taken his bike out and is exploring L.A. even though I only allow him to do this after he promises that he won't get killed by an idiot driver. I'm lounging on the couch, flipping channels and hoping that the phone will ring and hoping that it won't. I'm waiting for Charlie to call and yell at me, or waiting for the Bernsteins to tell me that I will be getting my last check in the mail. On television, a couple is having to eat scorpions for the final fifty-thousand-dollar prize. That's good money. *Really* good money. Earl and I can try out for something like that. A little deadly, venomous creature, in comparison to Ian, ain't shit. Both are the same, actually, but one pays more money. And one, come to think of it, was less humiliating. At least with the scorpion, I wouldn't have to be working, literally, for Mr. Charlie and Mr. Ian.

When the phone rings, I have to follow the sound before I answer it. Where did Earl put it last? Our apartment is so small, every room you can see from the front door. The kitchen. I had it in the kitchen when I was boiling eggs for lunch. I'm budgeting now, two boiled eggs is lunch. I may even eventually be one of these skinny women running around town without an ass before too long. I grab the phone before the third and last ring and look to see who it is before I press the talk button. Bita Flannigan.

"You're calling to do Charlie's dirty work. I'm fired."

"Now what? Who said what to who? Who's going to have to shake hands and say sorry, now?" Bita takes a drink from something. I can hear ice cubes clinking against a glass.

"I'm fired. At least I think I'm fired. Me and that Ian had a, uh, exhange."

"He's a little shit, anyway," Bita lisps.

"Hey, chew that already." Bita loves to eat ice. It's a really bad habit she's had since college—it's in lieu of eating food, that she eats ice. The chewing made me want another egg. I had exactly two more eggs in the fridge, and two hundred dollars in my checking account. I'd save the egg for later. How sad. I was rationing.

Bita crunched in my ear. "You'll either get that job back or something else'll come up. It always does."

I say nothing. Bita is always flip about stuff like this. She has the attitude of someone who has never known what it's like to worry about money, and in spite of the fact that I would have NO respect for anyone else with the same attitude (Ian), I love this girl. I blame it on Charlie and his four-thousand-dollar table.

"Can you come over?" Bita asks. " I mean, since you're unemployed and all on account of being a smart-ass." She laughs again. I look at my watch and see that it's 4:45 p.m., the beginning of rush hour, and I imagine the slow crawl of Sunset Boulevard all the way up to Kings Road, the street where Bita lives. I'll be stuck in all that west-side scenery, like the giant billboards advertising some new starlet's crotch, and then I'll have to pass that idiotic House of Blues with its fake rust and Disneyland colors.

I wouldn't even be able to pop into Tower Records, the only reason for driving down to that end of Sunset, because it's closed now, making it really and truly not the same L.A. I calculate how long it will take from Echo Park and estimate my arrival time to be 6:30 p.m. Not even for Bita, can I do it. Not today.

"I can't. I just can't face the traffic. Just thinking about getting in my car exhausts me."

"Jeez," Bita says. "Indiana has made you soft. A traffic wuss." I hear the clink of ice as she takes a drink of something. "No, wait. What are you, scared to leave Earl alone or something? Is he lonely without you?"

"Are you kidding? Earl's the goddamn life of the party these days. It's like L.A. would shut *down* if he wasn't around to oversee the place on that bike of his."

"He gets around," Bita says. And he did, too. When he isn't working at the Baseline, he is one with the city. He has really taken to the place. But Bita says it with a *tone*.

"Around?" I know what Bita's thinking. It isn't my imagination that Earl is being chased by Katie. I made the mistake of mentioning something about it, and now Bita is putting my man in the same category as Charlie, which makes me mad. He's fine, Earl. Out with a couple new buddies at the bar. He's no Charlie.

"You let me worry about Earl," I say. "You worry about Charlie." It's a snarky thing to blurt out and I'm already sorry about it. Bita is silent on the other end. "Listen. I'll come by later this week," I say softly. "Okay?" She's still silent. "Hello?"

"I'm nodding," Bita says.

"Well, I can't see that." I laugh.

"I don't know what's wrong with me," she says, and I hear her crunching ice again.

"Next week. For sure," I promise.

When I get off the phone, I decide to take a walk down to Echo Park to try to get at this Katie and Earl stuff that keeps bothering me. I find a piece of paper and a pen, and I write Earl a note:

Dear Earl,
You've been neglecting your duties at home, not earning your keep.
So I'm off to the lake. The dudes down there know how to treat a gal.
:)
Love,
Veronica

I sign off "Veronica," because Earl always says that it's my sexy name, and that "Ronnie" is my everyday, "gettin' around town" name. I'm almost out the door when the phone rings. Maybe it's Bita again. Or Earl.

"Yep?" I don't here anything on the other end. "Yep, yep, aww *yeah*," I say again. That always made Bita laugh. It was my Vanilla Ice impersonation. He was always saying that as filler. I think it was code for "I'm being very black right now."

"You sound insane. Drinking already? It's barely happy hour your time."

"D. Oh my God, I miss you. If you were here, we would already be hammered by now."

"Exactly," Doris says. "I'm beating you, though. Two hours ahead of you and already on my first glass of wine."

I sigh.

"What?" Doris asks. "No wine in the house?"

"No. I mean, yes, there is…it's not that."

"Uh, oh," Doris says. "What?"

I pause and consider not telling Doris. I'm always putting on a brave front whenever something's getting to me. And things with Earl are good. It's jerky to complain given he's come all the way to L.A., and when I know that Doris is having a hard time with Zach and finding somebody to run around with in Atlanta. "I think I'm jealous of that chick down at the bar."

"You've got to be kidding me."

"I wish I were."

"Okay. Is this, like, some reverse-psychology tactic or something? Because I was all set to pour and rant for two hours."

"I'm sure it's nothing." I dangle one of my flip-flops off my big toe and jiggle my leg. "What kind of wine are you drinking?"

"The kind that works. Talk."

"Nothing to say, really. I'm just feeling this weird, I don't know, dread or something. I saw Katie hug Earl at the bar the other night, and I got scared."

"*Really?*" Doris asks, and I can see her wrinkled nose and squinting eyes that say, "*You've really gone round the bend now.*" "You don't get scared, not of skinny blondes, anyway."

"I know. I know. Maybe it's just the stress of moving back home, and money, dealing with that horrifying child, being worried that Earl's okay—"

"Huh," Doris says. I hear her take another sip of wine, and then she let's me have it. "YOU HAVE GOT TO SNAP THE HELL OUT OF IT."

"But—"

"HELL TO THE NO," Doris yells, mimicking Whitney Houston's now-infamous catchphrase during her reality TV meltdown. That shit was hilarious—in hindsight—now that Whitney's drug free and clear of Bobby Brown.

I'm laughing, but still trying to make my point. "Doris, seriously—"

"You cannot, and I repeat *cannot* start any of this horse shite," she insists. "All that time when you were playing hard to get in Langsdale, I was seeing how hard Earl was working to get you. He's not going to toss you aside after moving *across the country*, for some halfwit, barely legal, dime-a-dozen L.A. floozy. Do you hear me?"

"Yeah. Really damn loud *and* clear."

"Okay, then," Doris says, and then I hear the tinny sound of her call-waiting beeping. "It's Zach, speaking of people who are hard to get."

"Get it!" I holler. "Don't be mean, either."

"Don't worry. I will." She hangs up on me.

Doris's phone call was perfect timing and I think it's a sign that it happened when I was about to go on a walk. We used to always walk around the trail at the Y in Langsdale, and one of us was usually knocking some sense into the head of the other while we walked and complained about stuff. Doris was the one who gave Earl my number. I gave her shit for that, but she knew I would never call Earl. I would have kept running and running.

In Langsdale, I worked in a car parts factory to make money during the summer. The whole time, I was working with Earl's cousin and didn't even know it. Unfortunately, the cousin, Ray, thought I was a snotty university student slumming it, which I was, I realized by the time I was done. Ray gave Earl an earful about me, Earl told me later, but he still wanted to be with me. He saw something of me, in him, Earl said, which sounded crazy at the time. But then soon after we started dating, something happened, all because of James Baldwin.

It was my fourth time on Earl's hog, and he'd take me all over town. He'd picked me up from the library, where I was doing some research, and when we got to Griffey Lake, Langsdale's most beautiful spot—turning leaves in the fall, woodpeckers and ducks and every other creature I usually want to avoid—we hiked up to a clearing to talk. We lay on our backs and looked up at the sky. One of my books was poking out of my backpack so Earl asked me what I was reading. I pulled out *The Fire Next Time* and passed it over to him.

"Read something," he said, passing it back to me.

"Seriously?"

"Yeah. I don't know James Baldwin." Seriously? I felt that passing notion of our difference. *He doesn't know James Baldwin.* But I started reading anyway. Written in 1963, during the times when the racial shit was truly hitting the fan in America, any reader could see that Mr. Baldwin was pissed off—as were most black folks in America. In essence, Baldwin argues that all of us, black, white, *whatever,* really had best get it together or we were all going to go down in flames together. Sure, he was talking about the times in 1963, but for my money, it's still very relevant today. As I read, Earl's brows were scrunched together. "What?" I asked.

Earl sat up. "I don't know." He ran his fingers through his hair. He looked of in the distance. A woodpecker concentrated on a tree nearby. "I feel mad or something." He wouldn't look at me.

"Mad at what Baldwin is saying?" Good. I got mad every time, too.

"Yeah," Earl went on, "I don't think… He's not… Well, hell, Ronnie, I feel like he's blaming me personally or something, whenever he says white people this and white people that. I ain't like what he's saying."

Oh *no*. Here we go, I thought. I sat up, too, and stared at Earl hard. All of a sudden I wasn't sure what I was looking at. "Not you, personally, maybe, but white people of that time, and white people of this time still have a lot of privilege. Black people or other people of color keep struggling to be treated as equals."

Earl nodded slowly. "But I ain't privileged," he said.

He had a point, but I was becoming disappointed. I couldn't do this. If he was saying that racism didn't exist, that Baldwin was insignificant, Earl and I could never, ever, see eye to eye. "I want to go," I said. I stood up, shoved Baldwin in my backpack, and started walking away from Earl.

"Hey," he called out. "Wait a minute!" He caught up to me and grabbed my arm. I jerked away from him. "Don't do that," he said. "Don't just cut me off, Ronnie." He stood with his fingers in his belt loops and looked down at his boots. "Tell me something. Talk to me. I want to understand what you mean."

"You want to quit bartending and go to law school. You want to help people who get treated badly. When Jimmy D. got fired at the factory, you were pissed off about that."

"Well, yeah," Earl said. His voice was getting loud. He was frustrated and trying to calm me down at the same time.

Jimmy D. wanted to see about a union at the car parts factory. He was out of there faster than you could say Norma Rae. Not even Ray, Earl's cousin who was the foreman, could do anything about it. I could tell he wanted to toss me out on my ass before he'd see Jimmy D. go, but I was only a temp. I let my backpack fall to the ground and crossed my arms. "So why is this so hard for you to understand? People don't like to get treated like crap. That's all." I stared at Earl whose face was a deep red. He looked miserable.

"Ronnie," he said. "Veronica." He took my hand in his and his voice got soft. "I didn't mean to upset you the way I did. I just thought I could tell you what was on my mind. I want to be able to tell folks who I care about what's on my mind. Talk to me. Let's talk about all of this. Make me see what you're saying." He put his hand on my cheek and stared at me. I was looking into blue eyes that were trying to get me to see him and give him credit for trying, and for being the person that he was.

"I don't want to explain. I want you to already know." The wind was picking up then, and something flew in my eye. "Dammit," I said.

"Let me see." Earl held my face in his hands and blew in my

eye softly until it watered. I blinked a few times, and then whatever it was, was gone. He wiped my cheek and then tugged on a braid. "Some things I cain't know until you tell me," he said. "I'm going to do whatever it takes to understand what you need me to understand." He was still holding my face, and so I leaned into him and felt his big arms wrap around me. We stayed at the lake and talked until it got almost too dark for us to get out of there, and Earl and I came to an understanding. We didn't know how all of this would end up, but we would always talk to each other, talk things through. Doris is right, I have to snap out of whatever this is I'm feeling. Earl is the real deal, Katie or no Katie. When the phone rings, I think it's Doris and I'm happy to tell her I've come to my senses. But when I look at the caller ID, I don't recognize the number or name. My hello is met with a Southern accent. Hmm.

"Hi. May I please speak with Ms. Veronica Williams?"

This voice sounds *exceptionally* Southern. Could be a bill collector—I am one of their favorite people—but they usually didn't sound this nice. I *could* say, "She's not home right now, may I take a message?" Classic. That's old-school bill avoidance right there. Not for amateurs. But I gamble, take a Vegas chance. "This is she."

"How wonderful!" The accent thickens. "My name is Arianna Covington and I'm calling from Burning Spear Press."

Burning Spear Press…Burning Spear Press…I'm hoping to remind myself, and then I realize that I don't care. I got traffic to look forward to. "I'm sorry, I can't afford any subscriptions or anything. Thanks for calling."

The woman on the other end clears her throat. "Oh no, honey. You misunderstand. I'm calling about your manuscript, your novel, *F: The Academy?* You sent it to a friend of mine at Smith Alloy, who passed, but she sent it to me. I liked it a whole lot and would like to publish it."

All at once I'm trying to figure out everything she's telling me. The manuscript I sent out after graduating Langsdale, sent out on a whim because Professor Lind, my Shakespeare professor, told me to, the manuscript that had exactly sixty polite, two-line rejection letters to show for itself, the manuscript that I had just thrown in a drawer and accepted as every writer's first novel that never gets published—until you're dead—was wanted by some publisher called Burning Spear Press. "Are you *serious?* This better not be somebody screwing around with me."

"No," Arianna Covington says, coughing slightly, "I'm not, uh, *screwing* with you. We'd very much like to publish *F: The Academy.* We think it's exactly the thing for our press. We're a new house, but we're big, and we're looking to publish promising up-and-coming writers."

And then I flip out on old Arianna. I scream. I carry on. *Thank you, thank you, thank you!* I barely hear what else she tells me, only that my book which, by sixty other editors has been called many things, from a boring meditation on class, to a humorless meditation on class, to a pointless meditation on class further marred by a tedious discussion about race, is something that Burning Spear Press is very happy to be publishing. Other boring stuff about contracts and money—surprise, not very much—is also mentioned. Then Arianna, in her charming accent, congratulates me once again and I can't wait to tell everybody: Bita, Doris, Earl, my family. Yet there's a lingering silence on the other end of the line that makes me uneasy. Damn. There's a catch. There's always a catch.

Arianna starts out nice and sweet. "If you are familiar with our books…though, I've forgotten, you're not…" She stammers all over the place.

"Yes?" Uh. Oh.

"Well, Burning Spear has a very particular demographic. It's a press that publishes exclusively African-American books by African-American women for African-American women."

"Uh-huh." It was starting to sound awfully claustrophobic, but I stayed quiet so she could keep talking.

"So, let me just be as frank as I can be, Veronica. We're wondering if you'd be willing to make Dottie's character black."

Dottie was based on Doris, but I was confused about the rest. "You mean dark? Like a villain?"

Arianna pauses. "No. I mean black, like African-American."

I like old Arianna. She's a crack up. "That's funny," I say. "I'm going to like working with you. You're hilarious."

Silence.

"You're joking, right?"

"No, Veronica. We talked about the book in meetings—we love it—but think it would read more smoothly, be more attractive to our readers, if Dottie was African-American."

Hmm. Was I getting punk'd or something?

"Are you there, Veronica?"

"Kind of," I reply.

"What are you thinking?" Arianna asks, after a moment.

"I'm thinking it's the craziest thing I ever heard."

"Listen," Arianna says, in a gently urging voice. "Dottie can stay the same person—more or less. You just identify her as black and keep the book basically the same."

"I don't know. It's a weird change. I mean, part of the point was that Dottie's white."

"Imagine that she's exactly the same, but just a different color. That's all."

That's *all?* It's a lot to think about. Honestly, I don't believe that Doris would be the *exact* same if she were black. Environment and culture, etc.

"So will you take the book if I don't make the change?"

Arianna sighs. "I'm not trying to make this sound like an ultimatum, but there are other books that better fit what Burning Spear does."

Oh, well, at least I got to feel good about being a published author for about five minutes. On the other hand, the more I think about it, *parts* of Dottie would be the same except a different color, right?

"Can I think about this for a day or two?"

"Of course," Arianna says. "Please call as soon as you decide."

After I hang up, I think about what an asshole ingrate I must have sounded like on the phone. *Let me think about it.* What a jerk. But there's something still exciting about this and I'm amped, amped with a caveat.

I grab my keys, ready to rush out the door to see Bita, when

I hear Earl's bike pulling up, deafening everyone in the neighborhood. It's strange he's home so early, but then I'm happy that he is. When I hear the key turning in the lock, I stand near the door so I can jump on him and tell him my news. When Earl comes through the door though, he doesn't quite seem himself. He's clearly tired and in a bad mood—which for Earl is never mean. More like distracted and worried.

"Hey, baby." I hug his thick torso before peering up at him. "What's the matter? You're home early."

"Yeah." Earl squeezes me before he walks to the fridge to get a drink. "There's nothing but half a can of Diet Coke in here." He sighs.

"And an egg," I say, waiting for Earl to pop his head up from the fridge and grin at me. But he doesn't.

"I sure could use a beer. Something cold." He straightens up and comes to me on the couch.

"What kind of bartender are you, anyway?" I say, pulling him down next to me. "Living in a house with no booze, just a pitiful can of Diet Coke." I pat his firm belly and settle in close to him. Earl only gives me a weak smile. He pulls away from me so he can take off his boots and then he sinks into the couch with a sigh.

"You sure are sighing a lot and saying a little. What's the story?"

"Just got tired out is all. Didn't feel much like going for a ride after all."

"What? You're not getting along with Jake and them anymore?"

Jake's a guy Earl works with from time to time. He doesn't bartend so much because he's just okay, not a pro like Earl. But he's a homeboy—of sorts—because Jake's from Illinois and claims the Midwest, like Earl does. He's younger than Earl, a kid mostly, only twenty-one, with dreams of "making it," and so on and so forth. Still, Earl likes him because he likes to ride, too, and isn't prone to "get carried away with himself," as Earl calls it.

"Naw," Earl stretches his arms behind our heads and pulls me close with one of them. The way Earl says "naw" seems to have an ellipsis at the end of it, but he doesn't volunteer much more. He's closing that whole strong-silent-type business, but I'm not having it.

"Cut the shit, Erardo Lo Vecchio. What the hell happened?"

Earl sits up and straighter, then turns to me so we're not side by side anymore. He's finally grinning, he likes it when I get my version of badass on him. I do sugar and spice and everything nice as often as I can, but I can go from sweetie pie to mother-fucker, like going from zero to ninety.

"Wellll," Earl says, dragging his proverbial foot right away. "It ain't nothin, not really, but at least part of this story, you ain't going to like it."

What Earl is saying is code for "You're going to want to snatch that skinny Katie bitch baldheaded." But since I'm trying not to be jealous, I don't say a word. I just tell Earl to go on and give me his story. "So?"

Earl scratches at his wavy, sandy hair and then folds his big arms across each other. "I was all set to go out with Jake…" Earl pauses and looks at me for what seems like longer than he needed to, as if he were considering something.

I nod. Jake was hot, though I didn't say much about that to Earl. He was a tall, lanky brother with a shaved head and dimples not dissimilar to Earl's. He's always greeted me with a smooth, "Whas happenin', sistah?" whenever I came through the door. His smooth, flawless, dark skin puts me in mind of Lavarian Laborteux, who I knew was for sure by now *Dr.* Laborteux and never letting anyone forget it.

"So me and Jake and them had made plans, but they had to cancel, except I hadn't heard all about them needing to cancel before I said yes, when Katie asked if she could come along, ride with me on the back of my bike."

What a pro, that one.

"And so I said yeah. I didn't see no harm in it, and then when we was all set to head out the door after work, Jake says hadn't Katie told me they wasn't going to go."

I raise my I-told-you-so eyebrows at Earl, because I'm always teasing him about his *very* well-fitting, *tight*-fitting Wranglers that show off *everything* Earl doesn't mean to advertise about himself. Earl wears them like the good old boys wear them, and shakes his heads at the hipsters with their jeans sliding damn near down to their ankles.

"I know it," Earl says. It's a phase he always uses when he gives me credit for being dead-on right. Earl strokes his face and stares at nothing in particular for a bit. He used to stroke his beard but now it's his face out of habit. "Anyway," he goes on, after a while, "Katie was standing right there and was put on the spot, said she thought they were talking about something else, not *tonight*."

"So you blew her off then?"

"Yep." Earl held my face by my chin and kissed me on the nose. "Told her I wasn't going out with only us two and then she said, 'What's the matter, Mr. Earl? Scared of your *girlfriend?*' And I knew she was making a joke, but I didn't like the way she said that. Something about it made me mad so I just had to get on away from the bar and come on home." He levels his eyes at me and then closes them. He sinks down into the couch. "I'm beat," he says. "Need to rest my eyes some."

I stare at Earl's face, then kick off my flip-flops so that I can lie down lengthwise on the couch and stretch my legs across his lap. He runs his fingers up and down my thighs, but keeps his eyes closed. "This is all I want to do for the night. Sit here like this with you. Beer or no beer."

I think about everything that he has just told me and he was half-right. I hadn't liked what he told me, but it really isn't Katie trying to pull her crap that bothers me, it is more the fact that something about it really bothers Earl. He was a good sport, quitting the Midwest and coming to crazy L.A. for some broad (me) that he'd met bartending. But it isn't that alone. I knew from the moment I took my first ride on Earl's Harley that we weren't going to ride off into the sunset, that we would have to work at this. And now, it's happening, the work. Something is up because Earl is confused over some puny little girl who's chasing after him.

"Erardo."

"Mmm-hmm?" Earl murmurs. His eyes are still closed and he is still touching my legs. He smiles. "Am I in trouble about something? You calling me Erardo. I cut the shit like you asked me to." Has he?

"Something else is bugging you, I know it. Start talking, bud." I sit up and poke him in the side.

"Ain't no getting around you, is there?"

"Nope." I swing my legs off of Earl and then I straddle him. I take both of his arms and hold them back behind his head. "You're my prisoner until you tell me the truth." I kiss him on the lips and then on his neck. His favorite place. And then I put my hand on his belt buckle and lift the buckle. "There's more where that came from, but you gotta be good. You gotta be a good boy and tell the truth."

I know I'm not being quite fair: a man can't have a serious conversation about his *feelings* with a woman grinding up against him on his lap. But Earl tries. He looks down at my hands on his belt buckle and I kiss a tiny bead of sweat that has formed on his temples. He tries to put an arm around my waist, but I put it back and keep his arms pinned behind him. Of course he could break my hold with a sneeze—if he wanted to. "Uh-uh," I say. "That's only for good boys. Now tell me the truth."

Earl's breathing hard and he locks his gaze with mine. I know that look. He's just about done playing. I put my face close to his so that our noses are almost touching and he tries to kiss me. I pull away. "Uh-uh."

"All right," Earl says, slow and steady. "You listening?"

"Yes."

"What's bothering me is this—I don't like people trying to come between us. I don't like people looking at us like we're strange when I grab a hold of you out on the street. I don't like people treating me like I'm some ass-backward, ignorant hick the minute I open my mouth. I don't like people talking at me slow, like I cain't hear, just 'cause I talk the way I do, I don't like people carrying on about me like I'm some cute dog they just found on the street, so goddamn amusing. I don't like you thinking and worrying about all of this because I see that you do. And I don't like the way folks try so damn hard to be seen around here. Don't like the Vietnamese food place you're always taking me, too, neither," Earl adds. "I know it's cheap, but a person cain't get full."

I don't know what to say. Earl's really not laid it all out like this since moving to L.A. I'm usually the complainer, the one's who's telling him what I don't like. He's been *my* rock, the guy who goes along. The guy who says everything is fine. "You should have said all of this before."

"I know it."

"We have to do a better job of talking."

"I know it."

I finally let his arms go, lie down on his chest and slip my arms around him. He smells like soap and sweat and feels nice and solid on our soft couch.

I notice that one of the sleeves of Earl's white T-shirt has a smudge of what looks like peach-colored make-up. There's a smudge of lipstick, too, which is too light to be mine. I wonder where it came from, wonder if I should ask Earl about it. I feel strange though, because these smudges had to come from *some-where*. Somewhere I wasn't going to like. Still, he'd already told me about his night, and that had to be good enough for now.

"Hey." Earl smiles. "I've been a fine prisoner." He's rubbing my neck and lifts the back of my tank top to run his fingers up and down my spine.

"But we're not through talking," I say, thinking about the smudge. Earl puts his finger to my lips. He tugs one of my arms out from behind him and puts my hand on his belt buckle, keeps his hand on top of mine and holds it there firmly. He levels those blue eyes at me again. We've sat and talked so that it's gotten very dark and there are no lights on in the house. Only the moonlight coming through the windows.

"We're through talking," Earl says.

doris

The Existentialists: A group of writers and philosophers who valued subjective over objective experience, and believed in the basic need for a woman, alone in her apartment, to grapple with the meaning of her life (with or without a nice bottle of chardonnay). Think of Kafka's hero waking up to find himself a cockroach, or Camus's Frenchman shooting an arbitrary Arab on the beach. Or maybe, most famously, Bergman's Antonius Block (medieval knight portayed with decidedly nonmedieval craggy hotness by Max Van Sydow) playing chess with death on a plague-ridden beach. (One never thinks of the existentialists as beachy, but a theme does seem to emerge.) As one might imagine, the existentialists tend toward deathi-

ness and despair, and are slightly over-represented among
the French. But as with fashion, cheese and chocolate, the
French got this movement right on the money.

August 31—Day one in the classroom.

There is nothing quite like teaching to make one question the path
one's life has taken. My first class at Atlanta State University is
American Literature, and having been only mildly shaken by the
stalker-y note in my box, I am prepared to meet the issue of politics
in the classroom head-on. What I realize upon entering the fluorescent glow of the bleakest and most dingy classroom I've seen
since the two-dollar showing of *Dangerous Minds,* is that my students
could almost assuredly not give two cents for what will come out
of my mouth in the next hour. I'd say that twenty-eight of the thirty
seats are filled, and unlike Langsdale's farmboys, these students
represent a far more polished demographic. Two women are
texting furiously, three gentlemen in the back are actually sleeping,
in the second row sits a woman who could be Paris Hilton's more
attractive twin, looking long, blond and expensive. Although she's
the genetic standout, they're a good-looking crowd to a one.

To steel my nerves I go to the chalkboard and write something that still feels alien, yet somehow empowering: DR.
DORIS WEATHERALL, and underneath it, AMERICAN LIT-
ERATURE SURVEY. And then, to the right, I try to draw the
"no politics in the classroom" symbol. I hear a weighted sigh
from behind me like the air slowly leaking from an overfilled
balloon, but turn to meet stone-faced silence.

After a brief round of introductions, I gesture to the chalk-board and ask:

"Does anyone know what this means?"

"No P.C.," says one of the former nappers, a tall, jockish young man with triple pierced ears and a barbed-wire tattoo on his arm below. Clearly this is an acronym with which these students are familiar, as I hadn't even thought of shortening "politics in classroom" to "PC."

"Right. It's Tommy, correct? Tommy Evans?"

"Just T," he responds. "The letter, *T*."

"Okay," I say. "T. So I received a rather ominous and anony-mous letter in my mailbox the other day."

Paris Hilton's hand goes up.

"Name first, please, I'm trying to get these down."

"Paige Prentiss," she tells us. "And it's not anonymous. Every new teacher received a greeting from the Concerned Conser-vatives for Constancy in the Classroom. It's not meant to be threatening, it's just a little tap on the shoulder."

All of this said in a Scarlett O'Hara, buttery-sweet as I twist the knife in your back, Southern accent. And, might I add, de-livered in a tone so condescending that you'd have thought I was some hysterical nut-job ranting about creatures living in the yellow wallpaper.

"You don't think that an unsigned letter that reads 'We are watching you,' is hostile?" I ask.

Ms. Prentiss shrugs and gives her best "what an idiot" look to the girl sitting next to her.

"Then riddle me this, girl and boy wonders," I say. "How

does one create an apolitical English classroom? What's the value of a liberal arts education if you can't question and challenge what you've been taught and believe? For instance this American lit survey, I'm mandated to teach four texts and authors Ben Franklin, Herman Melville, F. Scott Fitzgerald and Mark Twain. You can see Gatsby, Huck Finn and Moby Dick on the syllabus. Now, don't get me wrong, I love all three books, but why might a person consider this choice of books political?"

(Chirping of crickets faintly heard in the distance.)

"Okay. What do all of these books have in common?"

Ms. Prentiss raises the lone hand. Curses!

"They're all classics of American literature."

"Yes," I agree. "But so is Frederick Douglass's autobiography, and so is Toni Morrison's *Beloved*."

"All dead white men," T. interrupts.

"Correct. And when the only four required texts are dead white men, that sends a message. Every choice we make is political, the very act of what we bring into the classroom is political, so while I will never judge you or grade you on what you think or believe, there is simply no way to make this an apolitical space. If that's what you're looking for, I suggest you find another teacher and classroom."

Although I'm quite pleased with my rendition of today's homily from the church of liberal humanism, with two minutes left, the notebooks are being closed and backbacks being nondiscreetly zipped. "Okay, go on, we didn't get to my Franklin intro, but next class, it's all Franklin and the American dream. So get cracking."

* * *

On the way back to my office I pass the closed office door of Dr. Antonius Block, professor emeritus. He's retired but for the occasional poetry workshop he teaches once every two years. Professor Block is one of the reasons I was most excited to get this job at Atlanta State. He's the sort of prima-superstar that every department likes to have on their rosters regardless of how often they teach or how difficult they are with daily departmental duties. Antonius Block, who was born in the southernmost extremity of Mississippi, has claimed that not only did he pre-date Bergman's knight, but that his parents wouldn't have known enough to name him after the iconic figure if they tried. Block's name fits his poetry: sparse, existential and merciless. Okay, to be fair, at times it's most merciless to *women,* especially the not three but four women he's been married to in his sixty-three years, but he's the sort of artist that I forgive every bit of misogyny for, for the sake of his art.

I'm reading the various articles posted on the front of Block's office door. There's critical praise for his National Book Award-winning collection of poems, the cover of his first book, which won the Yale younger poets prize, and a sarcastic cartoon about two cows reading poetry. Asa Davies comes out of her office, coffee cup in hand, and gestures dismissively at the brag sheets.

"It's as if Hitler were actually an artist with talent," she says. "You know he hasn't taught an actual class in three years, yet he's managed to sleep with two undergraduates in that time."

"Really?" I say, pretending to be scandalized when I know this sort of behavior is far too routine to be scandalous. "But the man can write. His book of sonnets is the best since Hopkins."

Asa's lips are pinched together. "Tell me how you like his sonnets when you've had the pleasure of a department meeting with him where he argues against every form of literary analysis since close readings. How was the first class?"

"Okay," I say, heading toward my office. "They're an interesting crew."

"By interesting you mean slightly above root vegetables, right?"

I smile, and try to remain positive. "I'd say they're turnips at the very least."

After spending the next hour prepping for my evening class, I hear a faint knock on my half-opened door. Silhouetted in the door frame like some film noir movie star is Paige Prentiss, looking far less surly than she did in American lit. Let me stop for a moment to paint a better picture of Ms. Prentiss. Long blond hair curled Farrah-style, a Tiffany heart necklace around her neck that looks both authentic and platinum, white wife-beater tank-top, flowing aqua peasant skirt. I know from my lust-tour of the Nieman-Marcus shoe department that she'd managed to afford gold Chanel sandals which crisscrossed thinly up her calves, revealing perfectly manicured toes and a perfectly even mystic tan. She opens a large Coach bag (the straw tote trimmed in lime-green leather after which I salivated, but could also not afford) and faces me with a nose so straight, teeth so white, and eyes so blue that the *Village of the Damned* comes to mind. Paige Prentiss, whom, might I add, as one of my advisees, I had been looking *forward* to meeting because of her outstanding test scores and Phi Beta Kappa—level grades.

"Take a seat," I offer, gesturing at the empty chair across from my desk.

"I just wanted to apologize," she begins, smoothing her dress against her thighs and crossing her legs demurely at the ankles. "I'd so been looking forward to meeting you, and I know that you're my advisor, as well, but so many of the professors here are disrespectful about the beliefs of others, and I assumed from the way you started the class that you were one of them. But I really like the books you've picked, and I can't wait to get started reading them. Dead white men and *all*." And then she whispers conspiratorially, "And it's nice to have at least one woman around here who knows how to dress like a lady and not some angry feminist."

"I may not be angry," I tell her, trying not to lose my cool. "But I am most definitely a feminist."

Paige shrugs, looks at my trim pencil skirt with the slightest flare at the bottom, and says, "Well, at least you don't look like one."

Arrrghhhhhhhhhhhhhhhhhhhhhhhhhhhhhhhh.

"I came to see you because I do so want to graduate with honors, Ms. Weatherall, and I want to make sure that I do whatever it takes in your class to make an A."

"Dr. Weatherall," I correct her. "And you'll get an A in my class if you show up for all the classes, do the homework, write brilliantly and participate actively." First day of class and the grade-grubbing has already begun.

"Yes," she acknoweldges, as though the title were somehow unseemly. "Dr. Weatherall. It's just that you *look* so much like a Ms."

And then she gives me a smile as if I'd been knighted. No wonder she has such glowing letters on file from the male faculty. She was playing me like I was judging Miss Georgia Peach.

"Well, I worked very hard to become a doctor."

"Yes, I saw your book of poems. I thought that one about shoes was sweet. I think that women *ought* to be allowed to write books about shoes if they like. You'd never know it goin' to school here."

Who did this child think she was?

"Well, Miss Prentiss. If you read the poem carefully, I think you'd have noticed that it was about more than shoes. There's careful attention to class and class markers in that poem. Manolo slides versus department-store copies..." I was starting to sound defensive. "And the rest of the poems are hardly about shoes."

"Oh, *that*," she says. "That whole tired class thing. Lord, you try escaping this place without a whole wagon-load of that hooey. That's why I felt I had to say something in class today, I get so *tired* of it all. Dr. Block says it's only the words on the page that matter, not what your professors try to slop on it. Some mornings I wake up and wonder if this is America or communist Russia."

She smiles at me, and for the first time I see the intelligence behind the act—the Paige Prentiss who could score 1460 on her SATs and still play Scarlet for anyone willing to watch. It wasn't a pretty sight. And then it vanished.

"I guess I'll be seein' you in class," she concludes, extending her hand. "French sandals and all."

I honestly don't know whether she means her sandals or my own, so after she leaves my office I untuck my right shoe and check for the brand. *LaParda.* My latest designer shoe warehouse purchase. I assumed the shoes were the dollar-store equivalent of deodorants marked "Seekret" or "Shure," but evidently these shoes are not your everyday knockoffs, but superdeluxe knockoffs. Faux French Prada. So either Ms. Prentiss was speaking narcissistically, or she was making fun of me. Looked to me like the two of us would be gearing up for a real brand war at the O.K. Corral. An age-old showdown between money and irony, "the real world" and academia. *Chanel,* one; *LaParda,* zero.

"Doing research?" I hear from the doorway.

I look up to see Asa, who has clearly had some Sibyl-like personality change since the last two times that I've seen her. She's smiling, and I realize that she's one of those women whose face totally transforms when she's in a good mood. She was an effortlessly pretty, cherub-faced platinum blonde—hair cut in a chic but functional short bob. She had on salmon-colored Capri pants and a pale beige shirt and a pair of Birkenstocks that I knew were part of the Heidi Klum line, designed to bring a bit of glam to the hippie-set.

"I'm sorry that I sounded so curt in the hallway," she states. "It's been a crazy month for reasons I don't want to bore you with, and I've been overtaxing myself trying to make my postcolonial literature class perfect, the syllabus at any rate. I had a rough time of it last year. You'd think that the complaints coming from the students would be beneath notice, but I spend more time in meetings defending my teaching last spring than I did teaching. It creates a mean environment. I don't want you to feel like the department is poison your first weeks here. We should have a drink once things calm down and talk about Atlanta. I'm doing a nonfiction essay class this semester, as well, so I can pick your brain about that."

"Great. I understand. It was a little creepy getting that letter in the mail my first day. But I have only good memories of how encouraging your were last year during my campus visit. You had longer hair then, no?"

"Impossible to keep long hair in the Atlanta summer, but my partner likes it."

"Partner" is academic speak for any and all of the following: husband, wife, lover, boyfriend, girlfriend, live-in help, fellow writer. So, while in the real world "partner" signals "alternative lifestyle," in academia, it simply means that said person is fluent in the über-PC parlance of the day. Now I have to play the pronoun game.

"My ex-boyfriend," I say, calling Zach an "ex" out loud for the very first time, "wouldn't have noticed if I'd shaved my head. Or he would have been really utilitarian about it—less money on shampoo and no hairballs in the shower."

Asa groaned.

"David, my partner, he's finishing his sociology dissertation at Emory. We try to keep fighting to a minimum, since he now meditates an hour every day before approaching the keyboard.

It's probably good. It keeps me from complaining about the Paige Prentisses of my day."

"Omigod," I say. "Is she, like, the well-dressed spawn of Satan?"

"Worse." Asa moves from the doorway and sits where Paige had sat only moments before. "She heads the Concerned Conservatives, and even once suggested they not allow anyone in who wasn't Christian, but they didn't want to not appeal to the Hitler youth of all faiths. Don't let her fool you with that accent and posturing. The double-C's are a hundred percent behind that bill of rights for students. They even had an article about Atlanta State in the *Chronicle*. It's like they want to go back to the days when you couldn't even read *Huck Finn* or *Catcher in the Rye*. Don't even think of assigning Carol Churchill. I had parents coming into my office over that one. Parents. Is this high school or a liberal arts education? It's Big Brother all over again. Or in Paige's particular instance, little sister."

I put my hands to my ears in genuine disgust.

"I thought this would be better than Indiana. Politically speaking. And when did Christian become synonymous with conservative? As an occasionally practicing Catholic, I resent that."

Asa tucks her right leg underneath her left thigh in a yogalike posture.

"Don't worry about getting lumped in," Asa says. "I talked to Paige about it once and she's quite sure that the Catholics are Mary-worshippers headed straight for hell. She just doesn't think it's polite to say so. This was when I tried talking to Paige.

She loved that I was a lapsed Episcopalian. She seemed to think that she'd get brownie points in heaven for talking to me about Jesus. Of course, since I received my official letter of complaint, we don't talk about much of anything anymore. Believe you me, there's nothing terrifically spiritual about the double-C's. And nothing Christian about Paige Prentiss."

"I have her in two of my classes. Just had her in American lit, and I saw that she's in my advanced poetry workshop tomorrow."

Asa makes as though a cold shiver is running through her body. "I can loan you cyanide."

"The worst thing," I say, "is that her poetry does *not,* in fact, suck. I got a few poems in advance for the first day, and hers were among the best. They're not *about* anything, but they don't suck."

Spoken by a woman who writes about her shoes, I think, hoping Asa isn't thinking the same.

"In my opinion," Asa mimics, her speech decidedly more clipped, "if it's not *about* anything, then it sucks. Period."

The words of a true post-colonialist. Asa pronounces *sucks* as if she found it in the dictionary for uneducated Neanderthals, right after *booby* and *neato.* I make a mental note: tone down the casual lingo while at work. I'm no longer going to be forgiven the fact that I can discuss Freud and Lacan in late-eighties Valley-speak. Ronnie and I used to discuss literary theory Romy and Michelle style. "Like, how totally demented is Freud with his clearly misogynist, totally un-self-reflexive hysteria horseshit? Tony Soprano has more self-awareness.

And before I go off on his repressed blow-job mania, did you check out those shoes on Zappos?" No, that will no longer fly in my professorial incarnation. Asa has ever so gently, every so placidly, let me know that use of the word *sucks,* on the job, is clearly not cute, not postmodern, and definitely not "academic."

The next two weeks of school are lonely but uneventful. Asa does little more than say "howdy" in the hall, and Toni has twice promised an evening out trolling for single men, but has had deadlines come up each time. Her parrot, though, has branched out in his imitations to add to his repertoire an emphysema-like cough that he evidently picked up "in the crack house." I have looked longingly at a number of ads for dogs, but haven't been able to commit. Besides, none of the classifieds have yet to seduce me with, "rarely barks, housetrained, has a taste for birds." And like a total idiot, while I have committed good amounts of my time to watching television, I always have an ear out for the phone, half hoping that Zach will call and tell me that he made a mistake, that he's moving to Atlanta, and that my fears of dying alone have all been as silly as grown women in miniskirts and leggings.

The sad truth: yesterday I saw a thirty-five-year-old in black leggings and a jeans skirt cut just below the ass, and my phone has not been dancing off the hook.

Instead, I have worked on my relationship with Southern food, probably the one thing about the South that couldn't possibly be overrated. On my drive home from the campus, I've taken to detouring from my usual route to make a pit stop at the OK Café, home of the best macaroni and cheese I have yet to find in Atlanta. So far as I can tell, the standout thing about Atlanta is the food. Midwesterners, I have now decided, are fat for no good reason whatsoever. Southerners, however, have a point. Between the ten kinds of greens around town, the fried chicken, the red velvet cake, the banana bread pudding, the shrimp and grits, the turkey meat loaf with mushroom gravy, all washed down with the omnipresent calorie bomb, sweet tea, you could pack on ten pounds without batting an eye. And with no one to witness my demise, I'm on my own mini-mission to reach size twelve by the end of fall term.

At the loft, alone, again, I sit down to watch an exciting evening of reality television, bowl of macaroni in hand, *Us Weekly* in lap, nice glass of chardonnay at my side. If this is how one slides into defeated middle-age, then let the games begin. Here is the problem with my brain: in terms of word association, middle-age begets old, which begets barren and hagged out, which begets why didn't Zach love me, which begets no one will ever love me, which begets time to eat a little crap for the team, which begets me reaching for the telephone, telling myself that I don't *really* care, that I'm just really bored and dialing Zach's number in that half-conscious-but-determined state of I-know-I-shouldn't-do-this crossed with what-the-hell-here-goes-nothing. I've successfully ignored his silence, trying to make him believe that I'm out having a grand old time in Atlanta, rather than Hoovering macaroni and developing a semi-intimate relationship with my television and conversational skills with the ghost-parrot through the wall.

"Doris?" he says, picking up the phone on the seventh ring. Only Zach would resist owning an answering machine well into the twenty-first century. "Lemme turn the music down." I hear the latest Elvis Costello blaring, then fading, in the background. And then, to my horror, the dull murmur of a woman's voice growing from faint to audible. "Zach, you want to put these away?" Not a voice that I recognize.

"Who's that?" I ask. Drunk and defensive.

"You remember Samantha? I think I told you about her."

No bells are ringing.

"From my composition class?"

"You mean your *student* Samantha?" I ask, properly disdainful.

"I mean my *ex*-student Samantha. She gave me a lift to the grocery store."

"And now she's inside helping you unpack your groceries? Cute." This is definitely the day for hating how I sound, but I can't stop myself. "What is she? Twelve?"

"C'mon Doris, she's only doing me a favor." Then he remembers something. "It's not like we're still dating. I assume you're not sitting at home pining for me in Atlanta. I took that for granted from the deafening ring of my phone."

He's got to be kidding. Not calling one's ex is standard operating procedure for those possibly getting back together—dating nymphets barely past Humbert Humbertdom is not.

"So you *are* dating her. Pervert. Remember what we said about students? Like shooting fish in a barrel."

Zach exhales like he's smoking a cigarette.

Then he inhales like he's smoking a cigarette.

"Are you smoking?"

"Maybe."

"Zach!" He quit two years ago. Secretly though I'm pleased that he must be depressed, doing the male equivalent of macaroni binges and Lifetime movie marathons. Or, I correct myself, trying to look cool for his no-doubt nicotine-addled waif of an ex-student.

"So is this just some late-night fault-finding mission?"

My phone beeps. I'm putting together a biting rejoinder, but first I click over to hear Ronnie's voice. Ronnie, who, after listening to a call-waiting-shortened summary, tells me, "GET OFF THE PHONE WITH HIM NOW BEFORE YOU MAKE A COMPLETE ASS OF YOURSELF."

Zach is none too happy to rid himself of my carb-fueled hysteria.

"Ronnie," I exclaim, "My friend! My real, nonacquaintance, nonacademic friend. Come to save me from myself."

"Don't drink and dial, Doris. That's the oldest one in the book."

"You think they can teach that to the parrot? So that I can knock on the wall and he can yell back 'put it down, beeatch.' You know, train him to fly out of the cage like Batman and knock the phone out of my hand when he catches booze on my breath?"

Ronnie laughs. "You'd have one knocked up telephone."

"Not funny!" I swing my legs over the arm of my chair. "What's shaking in Hellay? Can I expect to see Earl on the big screen anytime soon?"

"Nooooo. But you can expect to see me in print."

I almost drop my chardonnay.

"Are you saying what I think you're saying?"

"I hope so," she says. "I'm still hoping it wasn't a prank call. Not sure I'll even believe it until I have a signed contract in front of me, but it looks like my novel is going to come out sometime next spring from Burning Spear Press. I spoke to the editor yesterday, called me out of the blue, and after a whole stack of rejections, there you have it. Out of nowhere."

"Next spring! That's like turbo-publishing! Are you going to be rich? Okay, and forgive me my poet's ignorance, but what exactly is Burning Spear Press? One of those lefty presses out of Cambridge or San Fran?"

Ronnie sounds excited, if disbelieving.

"I don't know. I've been meaning to look it up, just haven't had the chance."

"Don't remind me about your neo-Ludditism. I know from the weekly posts I receive. It's like being friends with a missionary."

"So I haven't really been able to check them out properly because my laptop is acting up again, I only know that they're a black press."

Chardonnay glass in one hand, I move to my kitchen counter and sign on to the Internet.

"Luckily, my friend. I now have wireless. I've gone from the Flintstones to the Jetsons in two short months. All the computer techies at Langsdale would be very impressed. And have I said congratulations? CONGRATULATIONS!"

I know how hard Ronnie has worked for this, how we used to sit around at Langsdale and fantasize about how our first books would look. Probably the same way I imagined other women sat around and fantasized about future children or husbands. I wanted something kitschy but literate, appropriate for the title of my collection, *Man Trouble in the Nuclear Age*. The cover I got was close, a woman next to an oven, pulling out a tray of cookies, smiling, but in the window behind her you could see a mushroom cloud bellowing. Very literal, my publishers. And Ronnie had always wanted something closer to the old *Catcher in the Rye* covers, plain with white or black letters, allowing the fiction to speak for itself. And here she was, only months away from seeing that dream come true.

"Sorry," I say. "It's slow connecting."

"Admit it," says Ronnie. "You poured yourself another glass of wine."

"You'll never know and I'll never tell."

I Google Burning Spear Press and click on the first entry.

"So?" Ronnie asks.

I take a big sip and try to break the news gently.

There's nothing neo-Garvey about Burning Spear, nothing "fight the power." The only thing vaguely African about the Web site is a red, green and gold cocktail napkin, on which sits a gigantic martini glass with a "spear" of olives resting inside, and "burning" flames around two figures, male and female, framed in the background. At the top of the page the words "Burning Spear Press" appear in scripted lettering, with "Fire for the Rest of Us," beneath it. To the side of the main image are bullets on recent releases, authors, press, etc. The usual. And when I look more closely at the page, I see that Burning Spear Press, is "the new, hip, ethnic imprint." Their covers are mainly cartoon figures with hands angled jauntily on hips and purses dangling from the crooks of their silhouetted arms. If male writers were subjected to marketing like this, then their books would all have Amstel light bottles and Rogaine in shadow on the covers.

"Doris?"

"Good news first?"

Ronnie groans. "I don't like the sound of that."

"The circulation is huge. It looks like most of the books are done in print runs of the tens of thousands. Which, might I add, having had a print run of five hundred on my poetry collection, is no small feat."

"Quit beating around the bush, Doris."

"Wellllllllllll. It's an African-American imprint."

Silence.

"An African-American imprint? Tell me, I beg you, that they're branching out into literary fiction."

I scroll down the "About Us" page.

"Kind of. It looks like they're going to do one literary, or as they're saying 'adventurous' novel every other month. Seems they did one last month. *Murder on the South African Express.* I think I saw that book. It looked like a real book."

I don't tell Ronnie that by "real book" I simply mean hardback book, that the cover showed a woman in what could only be described as a dashiki mini-dress boarding a train, leopard-print luggage case in hand.

"I have to get to the library."

"The good news is they're publishing your book. Don't lose sight of that."

I peruse the other recent offerings. *Brown Sugar and Maple Syrup, Grooving with Mr. Thang,* and *Catcher of the Fly* (with a decidedly non-Salinger cover). I have to concede that some of the covers are quite clever, and it looks like *Catcher of the Fly* was reviewed favorably in both *People* and *Time* magazines, and a Barnes & Noble notable book. So regardless of the covers, what's going on between the pages is evidently interesting. The most important part.

"Some good reviews on one of these. And don't forget the zillions of copies. Oh, and look, believe it or not, even though the publisher is in New York, looks like Burning Spear has an office in my fair city. And for the record, presses can mean anything these days. Pam Anderson gets published by the same folks who put out Gish Jen. Burning Spear could be radical chic. Maybe you can get them to fly you out here, make sure your cover is normal and everything."

"Do publishers do that?"

"Big publishers might. For all I know, my poems were published by the Keebler elves, but you know how poetry goes. We practically pay them to put us into the world, and as much money as I've spent on contests to get that stupid collection out there, ready for ridicule by Georgia teens, I might as well have self-published. Would have been cheaper. No matter what happens, no matter how you feel when you do find Burning Spear Press, repeat after me: published is better than not published. Big press is better than obscure."

"You'll have to add one more chant to the chain—black Doris is better than white Doris."

"Whaddayamean?" I ask. "I already feel my next-door neighbor would prefer a black Doris to a white Doris, so don't toy with my emotions."

Ronnie explains that, demographically speaking, white Doris doesn't make much sense to potential readers. That editors aren't even sure that they believe in white Doris.

"So I'm like the Easter Bunny? Or Santa Claus? Why doesn't white Doris make any sense? You know that I'm going to have a full-out existential crisis when I get off the phone."

"Yeah, well, I think I'm going to have a full-out literary identity crisis when I find the Web page for Burning Spear Press."

"Published is better than not published," I repeat. "Published is better than not published. Black *and* white Doris agree."

I hang up the phone and decide, after closing down my computer, that it's best that I didn't get to discuss my Zach interaction with Ronnie. She tends to side with Zach anytime I'm being irrational and prideful. But the mental image of some tattooed, pierced, twenty-two-year-old swooping in on my ambition-free ex-boyfriend? Me no like. I can just imagine them, smoking cigarettes, and her twenty-two-year-old take on his situation: *that's really cool, man, I think it's cool you want to open your own theater. Why be part of the system? Let's make love and eat shitty twenty-nine-cent ramen on your decade-old futon. Coooooool.* The image is enough to convince me that I'm going to have to venture to the one place I never thought I'd be looking for men: the Internet.

By the sound of Stevie Wonder through the walls, I know that Toni is home, so I decide to seek out her expert advice on the subject and attempt to further forge a friendship. I take my half-opened bottle of wine, since it's the only one I have left, and knock on the door like some sad charity case.

"Doris," she says excitedly, a half-opened bottle of wine on her own coffee table. "Fellow single woman fighting the good fight. Have I found an activity for the two of us."

"Is it low cal?" I ask. "I think I'm taking up obesity as a hobby."

Toni has her computer open, and is clearly online and drunk typing.

"I'm losing it, Doris. I know I've been AWOL, but something terrible has happened." She falls back into the couch cushions and lets out a sigh that lets me know "terrible" is code for "wonderful, but problematic."

"First off, no judging," she says. I like this rule, since it excuses me from all behavior with Zach, so I nod in mock-solemn approval. "Okay, so I went out with this horrible fascist who liked white, thirty-two-year-old Toni. His profile says the only ethnicities that he'll date are white and Asian, and he's looking only at women who are at least two years younger and two inches shorter than he is. I mean, his profile is loathsome. I was all fired up to make out with him and then tell him he had biracial cooties and go home and write three paragraphs about it."

I know exactly where this is going. "But you liked him," I interrupt.

"More than like. I still half hate him, but aside from the profile, he has yet to say anything really fucked up, and I can't see that he's racist in daily life, but I know that he is crazy with the race thing because I read his profile and we even talked about it. He said that he 'just knows what he finds attractive,' which was clearly me."

"So he just doesn't know what he finds attractive. He needs your help."

"I'm the one who needs help. I need an intervention."

"What's his name?"

"Tino," she replied. "Can you even believe that? Big hairy Italian. He's not my type at all. But when we talk, it's like we were pods on the same spaceship. We like the same books, same movies, we crack each other up. We even went to the same stupid church camp in New Jersey when we were teenagers, but two years apart. I think my body is against me."

I pour the dregs of my wine bottle into the glass.

"Or it knows more than you do."

Toni shakes her head defiantly. "Never. We've been on five dates in the past two weeks, so I must take immediate action. You and me, we're going speed dating. Copelands. Tomorrow. He must be replaced."

Like living in Los Angeles and having passionate affairs with pool boys, speed dating is something that I knew about only from my favorite source of trashy information—the television. On television, speed dating looked like a fast, acceptable way to meet a veritable bounty of professional men. The news magazine special that I'd seen on speed dating showed a large room, dimly lit, with white tablecloths checkerboarded in half-empty wineglasses. The clientele were all thirty- and forty-something, laughing urbanely over no-doubt literate conversation.

Speed dating in Atlanta—the nontelevised version—I was soon to learn, was something altogether different.

The next night, Toni stopped by my apartment looking equal parts glamorous and jittery. She was nicely put together in the official Atlanta spring/fall uniform of sweater twinset in a bright yellow pastel, dark denim jeans, low sandals with an open toe, übercoiffed hair and manicured nails. Fashion wise, Atlanta is like if you crossed L.A. with a Lily Pulitzer warehouse. Coiffed, conservative and colorful. Very done and very *matching*. "I know, I know," she says, gesturing at the outfit. "But I don't like to scare the lawyers. Sometimes the loud prints make them skittish, and I wasn't kidding, I need to find a replacement, fast."

I, however, am dressed in my very own version of "Langsdale chic," a carefully honed homage to years of shopping in the rural Midwest, meaning a mismatch of Target, thrift stores and the occasional online Bluefly purchase. Today it's an Isaac Mizrahi button-down white shirt, cuffed jeans from the Salvation Army, and my all-time-favorite shoes, Marc Jacobs's take on ruby slippers, a delicate Mary Jane with an agony-inducing heel, but well worth the punishment. Funky, yet feminine. Furthermore, I worked to get my general appearance city-ready—tweezed my eyebrows; polished and filed my chipped, uneven nails; spent thirty-five minutes with Miss Clairol changing my roots from dull silver to nutmeg; and the evening before I even used whitening strips on my coffee-dyed teeth. If I didn't feel unstoppably gorgeous, at the very least I felt presentable. In Langsdale this would have been "supermodel"; in Atlanta, it was "average."

Toni drove, and I tried hard to pretend that I wasn't fearful for my life. Unlike Langsdale, where the speed limit rarely tops forty-five, or New York, where public transportation is the de facto mode of travel, residents of Atlanta are *drivers*. The first time I rode in a car with Antonia, truly, I feared for my life. In Atlanta, a speed limit of fifty-five means seventy for all but the far right lane, and seventy was about as fast as my Toyota could handle. I stayed out of the far left lane unless passing one of those confused and/or passive-aggressive souls who drive the speed limit. Toni's BMW, however, was made to go eighty, ninety, even ninety-five. These are all speeds at which my Toyota would no doubt begin to shake uncontrollably, lose bolts and hubcaps along the way. But Toni was also a true Atlantan in that driving the actual car was secondary to all the other activities she engaged in behind the wheel. She rarely signaled, fiddled with the CD player, answered the phone, and then cursed the poor souls driving around her for not being able to read her mind when she crossed three lanes in three seconds to make her exit. From what I've seen of Atlanta drivers, it's as though the turn signal were simply a decorative touch or design flaw. Psychic driving, I told Ronnie.

As we're moving, Toni flips down the visor and applies a final round of lip gloss and mascara. I try to ignore that the speedometer reads seventy-eight and concentrate on the evening ahead. "Okay, don't kill me, but I had sex with Tino."

"When?" I ask. "Since yesterday?"

"Since two hours ago. And it was great. I can't date him, Doris. Tino and Toni? Think about it, we sound like pizza-bites. It would never work. If you hear me saying I'm going to do it again, you must say no. And it's undermining my project. Now I have to write an entire chapter on 'sleeping with the enemy.'"

"But what if he's not the enemy?" I say. "What if he really likes you?"

Finally, finally, she puts the visor back up and looks at the road. Speed: eighty-six.

"Change the subject," she insists. "I need you to change the subject. Have you ever dated online?"

"No, but I worked on my profile today. I'm trying to do what you said, sound witty and light, not bitter and desperate."

"Good," she replies. "And dumb. Believe me, the more I misspell, the more I hear back. Did I tell you how many misspellings were in my first e-mail to Tino?"

"No," I say, "I'm just excited to meet professional men. My ex, Zach, God bless him, I was the only one with a car, the only one with a job, the only one who seemed anxious to get out of Langsdale, Indiana. He's still there, dating some tadpole of a female."

"That's a man for you," she says. And while normally my rejoinder would be, *no, there are crazy women, too,* I decided to be un-PC and let it slide. Let Zach, the man who knits in coffee shops, who has tried to reform non-lipstick lesbians and who prides himself on being a 'feminist' get lumped in with the other Y chromosome Cro-Magnons. That's what happens when one dates kinderwhores instead of charming, employed women of a certain age....say, oneself. My brain is clearly corkscrewing down some obsessive spiral, which is the last place I need to be before walking in to meet more men.

The venue is crowded with women dressed like Antonia and men in business casual, all nervously sipping on drinks in plastic cups and making small talk. The online sign up said the age range was from twenty-five to thirty-five, but the demographic looks skewed toward the twentysomething end of the range, although I do spot a man who is forty if he's a day. It's not as if you have to send in paperwork with a certified birth date for these events, so clearly the online truth stretching isn't just confined to online. About half of the men are white, and the other half appear to be African-American, Indian or Middle Eastern. There's slightly less ethnic diversity among the women.

"Slim pickin's," Toni points out.

"This will give you a window into my old life, but I was just thinking, *wow, look at all the single men.* I'll have to tell Ronnie that I'm not in Kansas anymore."

"You're definitely wearing the shoes for it," she says, and I can't tell if she's approving of or merely amused by my choice in footwear.

A slight, chipper woman with tightly permed strawberry-blond hair directs us to choose a number and for the ladies to take a seat at one of the tables. "The men will be rotating," she explains, drawing large imaginary circles in the air, "and the women will stay seated. There will be one break for drinks and, ladies and gentlemen, remember to take notes. You think you'll remember all twenty of the lovely bachelors and bachelorettes, but survey says you won't." Big fake smile and dramatic pause. "Anytime after midnight tonight, you can post a yes, no, or friends for each of the singles you meet, and if and *only* if your choices match, you'll be given the e-mail of your desired date-ee. Any questions?"

A woman who is probably close to my age and clearly trying to approximate a living image of a blow-up doll whispers, "Yeah, can we weed out the shorties?" I don't quite laugh, but give a half-smile that I hope acknowledges her, rather than the comment, and remember that there are plenty of ways that men don't have it so easy, either. Especially in Atlanta, where having a hippie-dippie good heart clearly just won't cut it for some. And looking at porno-judgmental lady, and looking at the shorties looking at her, I know that every response for her on the shorties' score-cards is gonna be a "yes." There's something vaguely tragic about the whole superficial, dysfunctional mess. I'll be damned if it doesn't make me miss Zach.

Two hours later, my mouth is dry, my head is ringing and Shirley Temple was right; I need every note that I've made to keep one John straight from the next Paul. For the most part, a nice but undistinguished group of gentlemen. In typical Doris fashion, the only man I'm actually attracted to is a semi-professional gentleman working at Emory on a post-doc—the slightly newer, more professional model of Zach. His name is Andrew, and in the thirty-second pause between when he asks what I do and when I answer, the conversation that will inevitably follow flashes before my eyes. A discussion about the hideousness of dissertating life, the perils of academic publishing, and the generally tragic snobbery of your average department—be it mine in English or his in Psychology.

So I lie, deciding instead to say that I do something totally porno.

"I'm a stewardess," I say. And then I think *flight attendant, idiot. Flight attendant!* "I just like saying that. It's sexier than flight attendant."

Andrew nods appreciatively. His hair is sandy blond and cut in a shaggy, long bob, the hot-hippie look. He has a large silver band with Celtic lettering on his middle finger, but otherwise, no jewelry. His hands are smaller and more feminine than I normally like, but I decide that sexy-stewardess Doris will forgive such physical shortcomings. Especially since this new Doris also has the sneaking suspicion that there is lipstick on her teeth—something the airlines would no doubt *never* tolerate.

"Stewardess, flight attendant," he says. "That's the thing about academia. You have to check everything you say. That's why I like meeting women who won't dissect *Dumb and Dumber* for whether it's sexist or not. Can't a movie just be funny?"

Stewardess Doris most *definitely* thinks a movie can just be funny.

"I love *Dumb and Dumber,*" I say. "And *View from the Top?* Some of the other flight attendants," and I make quote marks for emphasis when I say "flight attendants," because I am *really* into being Stewardess Doris, "they thought it was really bad for our image, but to be honest, I like those outfits. I'm so not into the whole pantsuit thing."

Andrew smiles approvingly as they "ding" for the men to rotate tables. So I've lied in an all but pathological way, but it did cut through the monotony. Andrew smiles warmly when he leaves, and even though I know no good comes of lying about one's life, I check the "yes" box on my scorecard without a moment's deliberation. Three computer engineers follow, then a tax accountant, then a young Republican so straight from 1984 that his upturned polo shirt nearly sends me back in time. As does his assertion that "he'd like a woman who wants to raise children and live a traditional life." That one sent me all the way back to 1884. The final man to approach my table is a late arrival and the last thing I expected as a newcomer to the city: a familiar face. I've seen this gentleman three times at my local Starbucks, ordering a grande coffee with soy milk and Sweet 'n Low. I'd pegged him for gay, but that shows how much I know.

"Maxwell," he says, shaking my hand warmly. He looks as if he's wandered in from some Mediterranean resort, in a fitted yet flowing rust-colored linen top, beautifully tailored pants, and leather sandals in a deep, rich brown. His head is shaved, and he's one of only two African-American men in the room, but seems completely comfortable.

"Doris, and I think I've actually seen you around."

Maxwell smiles and sips his vodka tonic like he hears this line all the time.

"I noticed you right when I walked in."

A line if I've ever heard one. Hooray! A line!

"Really," I say, crossing my legs seductively and giving a tight-lipped smile (in case of lipstick on teeth).

"Have you seen this morning's paper? Front page of the lifestyle section? Celebutante wedding of the decade? Maggie Mae Mischner?"

I give Maxwell a genuinely suspicious grimace. Maggie Mae Mischner is locally famous, and I quote, for wanting to throw "the wedding Scarlett O'Hara would have had if there hadn't been a war." Interviews with Maggie Mae, who is heir to a diet soda fortune, would lead one to believe that she hadn't really read *Gone With the Wind* carefully, or necessarily made it through the movie. They would, however, lead one to believe that her family hopes the bottom never falls out of the carbonated-beverage market, as the nuptials are rumored to be costing well over half a million dollars. The dress alone, featured prominently on Page One of *Life and Style* is all hand-beaded and hand-laced—a gigantic antebellum monstrosity that should command an extremely wide aisle, and supposedly cost well over fifteen grand. And she and I look nothing alike. I don't know where the fair Maxwell is going with this one.

"Have you seen her mother?"

I might actually have to kill him.

"Unless she had Maggie Mae when she was twelve and a half, I don't like the direction this is going," I say.

Maxwell laughs. "You're a ringer. And she's a fox."

Now I laugh. "Fox," I repeat. "Do people still say 'fox'? I

think I had stickers that said 'fox' and 'groovy' on my lunchbox when I was in first grade."

"Which was when?" he continues. "Nineteen ninety-two?"

I have to respect the attempt to salvage himself.

"Flattery will get you everywhere."

"You're cuter," Maxwell says, either flirting or just trying to make me less nervous. "She's a little on the thin side for my taste. I like my women thick."

"Yuck," I say. "It sounds like you're describing a steak."

Maxwell laughs. Why can't I stop offending this man?

"Well, that wouldn't be me. I haven't had a steak in six years. Or even a piece of fish."

"Really?" I ask, disbelieving. "Next you're going to tell me those shoes aren't even leather."

"They most certainly are not. Cruelty-free footwear, the only way to walk."

I officially have no idea what to make of this man, but I discreetly mark "yes" by the name Maxwell when he leaves the table, hoping even more than I did with Andrew that he does the same.

After commenting on the generally uninspiring crop of men in the room, Toni drives most of the way home in silence. I imagine that she's thinking about her life, about the ways in which you plan your attractions and how rarely such plans match reality. I don't think it's quite possible to be a single woman and not engage in a little existential angst. The moon is three-quarters full and reddish-yellow above the city, not the clear beacon it seemed to be in the skies above Langsdale. More like its sullied cousin. The high of the evening wears off, and I miss how easy it was with Zach when it was good. The way he really knew and understood who I was. And how I'm a blank slate again when it comes to dating. What I really just had was a fun evening with a bunch of strangers, all projection and optimism. Nothing I can count yet as real.

ronnie

I knew Doris would be happy for me. I knew she'd say, "You're getting published. Yipee!" She did that. She's a good, dear friend like that. But she also tends to tell me stuff I want to hear, not what I need to hear. So I'm not going to believe the hype. Not yet. But the more I researched Burning Spear Press at the library, the more I got excited. As Doris had mentioned, there were some wacky titles, sure. *Catcher of the Fly* was the winner. It unfortunately seemed to take itself seriously. A giant zipper, à la the Rolling Stones's *Sticky Fingers* album cover, with a giant, red-fingernailed hand grabbing at the crotch. But *How Stella Got Her Divorce Papers Back* seemed to be obvious satire even though I didn't read any text, so I believe the press is up for my book, *F: the Academy,* a satiric look at university life with Doris and

myself serving as the basis for characters. We'd gone to Langsdale University, but I'd changed the university's name to
Farmdale, a play on being in the Midwest and all that. So I'm
starting to feel okay about it now. Coming around. There seems
to be something for everyone at Burning Spear. I could be a hot-
shit writer by next year.

In the meantime, though, while waiting on that Pulitzer
Prize, I have to work like regular people. My work, as it turns
out, is more like a sentence, since I still have to tutor that pain
in the ass Ian. As I drive to Ian's house, I think about Bita and
Charlie, and how perfect their lives seem to anyone who doesn't
know them well. I think about how so many people think
Charlie is the cat's meow, but then, when you really get to know
him, you find out he's the doggie's doo-doo. Still, he did me a
solid, as they used to say in the seventies. I was so worried that
I was going to get fired, and it turned out that Charlie saved my
ass. I found out I still had the job after I went over to Bita's later
in the week, like I had promised. Bita and I relaxed and cooked
together. She's got one of those beautiful kitchens straight out
of a magazine: warm lighting, everything's shiny and brand-new.
The stove's one of those old *looking* stoves that's actually state-
of-the-art. Marble counter tops. I was happy, drinking wine,
basking in the beauty of her home. Bita had me chopping fennel
or some strange thing. For a salad. She's forever making some
elaborate meal out of some fancy cookbook. Whenever I'm
going to Bita's house to eat, I know I better grab a cheesebur-
ger or something before I get there, because first of all, it'll be
hours before you actually get food in your mouth, and second

of all, it's always some outrageously healthy thing that has you damn near starving *while* you're eating it. Bita, I always say, you're *Indian,* for God's sake. Can't you do better than this? Charlie doesn't like it, she always says. He likes light foods, not spicy foods.

The fennel looked like weeds. I put a bit in my mouth and made a face. "You know what you ought to be cooking tonight? We ought to be barbecuing one of those big-ass Fred Flintstone rack of lambs that's, like, tipping over his car in the opening. Do you remember that? And a big casserole dish of macaroni and cheese with a pound of milk, cream and cheese." Etta James was wailing in agreement from the CD player that Bita keeps in the kitchen.

"Charlie's the one who knows how to barbecue," she said, furiously stirring some cream in a gigantic silver bowl. "Asshole."

I wiped the fennel off my shiny knife and put it down on the cutting board. "What now?" But I already knew. Charlie was cheating on Bita. I didn't say it out loud, but as Earl says, *A person gets a feeling.*

She put her finger in the cream and licked it. "Good. This is good."

"You don't want to talk about it?"

"This soufflé, Charlie and I had in Lyon last year. It was the cutest little rustic place. Really simple food and French people who weren't pains in the ass. I've made this soufflé three times since then. Reminds me of the trip."

Bita was standing next to me, and so I gently tucked behind her ear some of her long, dark strands that were hanging in her face. She was avoiding my eyes, keeping busy. "Charlie's working late. I don't think he's going to join us for dinner." She pointed her spoon at the bowl in front of her. "Put the fennel in the cream."

The fennel went in the cream? Scary. The things I did for love. I sprinkled in the fennel while Bita stirred.

On television, old-school television, anyway, when the husband comes home and says, "Honey, I'm home," it's usually occasion for happiness. The wife runs up in her apron, gives the husband a kiss, gets him his slippers and a cocktail. Even Lucy, the original Rosanne, did that occasionally. So when Charlie came home in the middle of our dessert—something normal, thank God, cheesecake and Ben and Jerry's—and said, "Hey, honey, I'm home," and had the nerve to kiss Bita on the top of her pretty little head and ask, "what's for dinner?" It was all kinds of ironic and wrong. Bita looked at me, and I shoveled more ice cream into my mouth. Though Charlie, he's a slick one. He's not making all that dough in Hollywood for nothing.

"Meeting got canceled," he said, pulling up a heavy, expensive "rustic" chair. He took a sip of Bita's water, then he twirled the half-empty wine bottle around so he could read the label. "You guys opened the D'Alba? That's a hundred-dollar bottle of wine. We usually save that sort of thing for company."

"Ronnie's company," Bita said. She smiled at me and then took a sip of water. I'd drank nearly the whole bottle by myself. I had no idea it cost so much. Bita wouldn't have told me, unless she was making fun of it.

"I suppose," he said. He ran his slender fingers through his hair and gave me a good, long stare. "By the way, saved *your* ass today."

I'd totally forgotten about devil-child Ian, forgotten that earlier in the day, I'd been waiting to get tossed out on my ass by the Bernsteins. I'd actually convinced myself that no news was good news and that maybe there was nothing to worry about. Besides, I was about to be a published author and prove Charlie wrong. Going to school *did* count for something.

"Ian told his dad that you hated his guts and didn't want to work with him anymore. Said you called him a smart-ass."

True.

"But," Charlie grabbed a handful of Bita's thick black hair before letting it drop back down her back, "I told Richard that you most certainly had to have a job, that you were living in a tiny apartment, with a *bartender,* and that you needed all the help you could get." He smiled at Bita, all happy and self-satisfied that he'd saved her friend's ass.

"So I'm not fired?" I had one egg in my refrigerator, and Earl and I were still living from paycheck to paycheck, in spite of his okay bartending salary. That which makes you want to kill someone, namely a spoiled, self-absorbed rich kid, will make you stronger, I suppose.

"You're welcome," Charlie said. "I'm going to get me a glass. I want a taste of this D'Alba myself."

He went through the swinging door. Bita sighed, put her spoon in her bowl and pushed it away from her. She blew me a kiss from across the table and then sank down in her chair.

"Thanks for stopping by, Ron." She said it as though she had made up her mind about something. What, I did not know.

I winked at her. Bita and I have always done things simple that way. "Hey." I sit up in my chair like a shot. I felt ready to tell my good news. Charlie came through the door with some soufflé in a bowl and a big wineglass. He took his seat next to Bita and patted her thigh underneath the table. "I got news. Good news."

"You and Earl are breaking up," Charlie said.

"Shut up, Charlie." Bita glared at him. "Don't be such a jerk."

"What? I'm just saying that Ronnie and the bartending badass are quite the odd couple. You two would be a great sitcom." Charlie sipped his wine. "An interracial *Green Acres.*"

Bita crossed her arms and set her lips tight. "You don't know anything."

Charlie raised both hands in surrender and took another sip of his wine. "Fine," he said, still grinning like a know-it-all idiot.

WE KNOW YOU'RE HAVING AN AFFAIR, YOU IDIOT, is what I wanted to say, but I just changed the subject. "*Anyway,* as I was saying. I got good news. My book's being published."

"Hey!" Bita grinned, it was the biggest smile I've seen on her all night. "I can't believe you waited all this time to tell me."

"Well, that *is* good news," Charlie said. He held up his glass so we could toast. I clinked glasses with Charlie, and then Bita knocked her glass against mine, a little too hard.

"Who's doing it?" Bita asked, back to being generally happy for me. "Little Brown? Somebody like that?"

"No…not exactly…some press called Burning Spear?"

Charlie spit up his wine. "Burning Spear?"

Bita frowned at him. "What's wrong with Burning Spear?" She turned to me. "It's going to be a real book, hardcover and everything, right?"

"Yeah, hardcover and everything."

Bita gave Charlie an I-told-you-so look. But he was on a roll. He put his glass down long enough to rub his thick hands together. "We get press releases and galley proofs from them at my office all the time, from agents trying to get us to make *films* out of that crap. Hil*a*rious."

"You're just being sexist and dismissive because it's women writing these books."

"No," Charlie says, pouring himself more wine. "I'm being dismissive because that shit is *silly*."

"What about all the books written by men?" I stand up because I'm getting so mad. "All that macho Hemingway bullshit, lots of drinking and fucking and angst about the minutiae in their lives. *That*'s so important? Or what about all those books set in academia where the male, *troll,* professor is always banging the undergrad who's just dying to suck his old, shriveled up—"

"Don't even talk to Charlie about this," Bita says. "Charlie, don't you have something to do?"

But I was not finished. "They ought to call that dick lit, but they call it *literature*."

Charlie shook his head. "Well, congrats, Ron, I guess. Good for you. I'm going upstairs to catch the end of the ball game. Try not to get fired this week."

Just like Charlie to rain on my parade. Bita reached across

the table and grabbed my hand. "Ronnie. This is good news. It's the very best news. You're going to be published, and I'm proud of you. Don't listen to Charlie. Consider the source," she said nodding toward the stairs.

As I turn up Ian's narrow street and prepare myself for the latest confrontation, I wonder why I let people like Charlie get to me. People like Ian. People like Katie. If I'm going to be honest with myself, I have to admit that the main problem is me. For all my tough talk, it doesn't take much to make me doubt myself, and that's why I can't be an adult around Ian. He turns me into one of those kids on the schoolyard who finally has the guts to fight back—except I'm not a kid, which makes me pathetic. But his privilege, and alternately his cockiness and cluelessness about his privilege, that's what I can't seem to get over, so until someone gets fired—or strangled—this is going to be my life. A duel to the death with Ian.

I press the entry button at the bottom of his driveway and wait for his housekeeper, Maricela, to buzz me in. And as I wind up the driveway, I try to psyche myself out. *You love Ian. He's the sweetest. You feel sorry for Ian. How tragic to have money coming out your ass from the day you're born until the day you die. Tragic.*

I park in the circular driveway that makes a doughnut around the fountain in front and knock with the lion's head on the door. What a house. It looks like the place where tigers and mermaids and cherubs come to die.

The door opens and Maricela pokes her head around the door timidly. "Hello, Veronica," she says, nodding and smiling and I think that if Maricela has managed not to put her foot up Ian's ass after ten years of dealing with him, I need to try a lot harder.

"Maricela," I say. "How are you today?"

After closing the door she wipes her hands on her immaculate white apron. Her dress is light pink and her long, dark hair is in a bun as it has been every time I've ever seen her. "Fine, fine," she replies. "Ian is in the study." And then she leaves.

I can hear the television coming from the study, so I just follow the sound and knock on the door before I enter. Ian's got the TV on so loud he doesn't even hear me. Of course, *TV* is the cute word for gigantic, wall-mounted plasma something or other that Ian's watching. He must be sunken down in the green leather couch facing the TV because I can't see him. The channel's on *Pimp My Ride* and he's watching a van being converted to a house, basically, with a washing machine, television, bed, everything but a toilet.

When I reach the couch, I stand over Ian, who's laid out on his back, his arms crossed over his chest with the remote tucked under one of his arms.

"Hey," I say, trying to get started on the right foot. "Can you believe all they can do to cars these days? It's crazy what they can do."

"Yeah," Ian says, still not looking at me.

"I mean, a washing machine. In a car. That's wild."

Silence.

"All right. So let's get started then. Time is money. Turn off the TV, Ian."

Ian sighs all big and exaggerated like I'm asking him to do

something that's just *exhausting.* Like building the goddamn Egyptian pyramids. It takes him *forever* to finally click the television off.

"God. Are you all right? Do I need to call a doctor? Get you a glass of water?"

Ian sits up and glares at me through his scrupulously accidentally tussled and moussed bangs. I can practically hear the "fuck you" on the tip of his tongue. "Whatever," he says.

"Where's the Morrison?" I sit down on the couch—on the other end of the couch so my hand won't fly out in a spontaneous slap.

"Oh, c'mon, man. That shit was brutal. I get it. The girl wants blue eyes because she wants to be white and all that bullshit. It's a classic, blah, blah."

Not bad, actually. You have to read a bit of the book to get even that little bit of theme. So Ian had read *something.* "How do you know that? That she wants to be white?"

Ian shrugged. "I dunno. The book opens with that stuff. That stuff that's all the American dream stuff run in together. See Dick and Jane…"

"So why does Morrison run it all together, then?" This kid, as big a jerk as he was, was actually smart—if he half got off his ass.

Ian picked at his black fingernails and blew air up toward his bangs. He watched them rise and fall for a while before he answered me. "What about that stuff you mentioned last time? That stuff about work songs and Gil Scott Heron and hip-hop. I looked up work songs."

He *did?* "You *did?*"

"Yeah? So? Like that's so hard? To look shit up?"

"It's not hard. I'm just saying." *Just saying that you're usually too cool for school and too damn lazy to care about anything or anyone other than yourself—unless it's music.* "So what did you learn then?"

Ian sighs. Everything is such a gigantic pain in the ass to him. So exhausting, dealing with me. The biggest tragedy of his life. He sits up and faces the TV, refuses to turn his head to look at me. He's going to turn to stone or something if he does. "It's not like I *learned* so much." He glances sideways at me, turns his head ever so slightly. "But the stuff I looked up talked about how slaves sang songs to help them get through their work, and then out of that came jazz, and then rock and roll and then hip-hop."

That was the *very* short version, yeah. In grad school, my students would rather kill themselves than actually set foot in the library and so I would get these goofy "research" papers that had "facts" from whatever came up on the Internet. Stuff that quoted the Bible or some random dude as part of their argument and analysis for a comparison between *Dude, Where's My Car?* and *American Pie.* But whatever Ian had found was pretty good. I stretch out my legs in front of me, put my hands behind my head and lock them so I can rest my head on them. "Where did you read all of that?" My legs keep sticking to the leather on the couch and I continue to be totally at a loss for why people blow money on leather for furniture. Tacky, one, and disgusting, two. Like sitting on skin all day long.

"I found this article that came from the Library of Congress. All this history stuff was at this one link."

"Cool," I say, casually, as if I don't care. But the Library of Congress? Ian was an impressive little shit. "So, you knew all this stuff already? You said you didn't learn anything."

"I mean, I guess I didn't *know* it know it, but I kinda did. Like I knew all about rock coming from the blues and stuff. Any idiot can listen to the Rolling Stones or Led Zeppelin and hear that."

True.

"But if you didn't *know* it know it, but now you *do* know it know it, then you learned something." I don't know what's wrong with me. It's like I want to make the both of us miserable by having us go around and around. I can never leave well enough alone. When it comes to teaching and learning, even in its *way,* like *seriously,* loosely termed variations in the form of me and Ian, I'm like a sports coach. Nobody ever told Shaq, *that's good enough, that you sorta kinda know what you're doing. Don't practice as hard today. Just shoot a couple of hoops, as long as you sorta kinda have a feel for it. Whatever.* What the hell kind of coach is that? And so even though I fled academia and Indiana, it's in my goddamn blood, the pushing-teaching thing. Followed me all the way to L.A.

"Whatever," Ian spouts.

Whatever. Whoever started the whole "whatever" thing should be drop-kicked. It's so final and perfect, unless you're the one hearing someone end a conversation with it.

I decide to give Ian one more nudge because I'm a glutton for punishment, and I do have to feel as though I'm earning my money and not robbing his parents blind by just babysitting. "You did really good research."

Shrug. Yawn.

Hate him. "But one more thing. How does all of this relate to Morrison, to the context of her novel in the context of the times in which she's setting the novel?"

Ian finally turns to me and levels his light brown eyes at me. "You're kidding, right? How does *music* relate to Morrison? That's the most random shit I ever heard. Like how work songs and hip-hop relate to Morrison?"

I use one of Ian's smart-ass lines. "Did I stutter?"

He rolls his eyes at me. "Oh my *God,* I wish you'd get fired or leave me *alone.*"

"Yeah, well, you know what they say, you can't always get what you want." And I stick my tongue out.

He doesn't mean to, but Ian laughs. A real, amused laugh. And then he recovers, replaces the laughing eyes with the sullen again. "Very funny."

"Seriously." My thoughts wander for a bit, thinking about a good way to get Ian onto stuff without being preachy. "Seriously. All of this stuff is connected. Books and music and film and art and the world and politics and why you want to produce hip-hop, even. It's all related."

"Whatever," Ian says and then it's *my* turn to sigh. But then he stands up. "Listen, I know all of this stuff is connected because I'm not a retard. I get stuff. You think you're, like, *tricking* me into learning and stuff, but you're not."

"So tell me how it's all related then."

"I will, but not right now. I'm hungry. I'm going to ask Maricela to fix me a sandwich or something. You staying?"

That was his elegant way of asking me if I'd like to join him for lunch.

"No, as much as I can't tear myself away from the good times we're having here, I should go. But next time I'm staying a full hour."

More eye rolling. "See you Thursday, then."

I make my way toward the door and Ian follows me until he hits the kitchen. "Later," he says, and then he's gone.

My flip-flops make loud slapping sounds as I walk down the hallway. When I get to the door and pull it open, I'm yet again amazed by how heavy it is, that Maricela has to come open this damn thing every time she's near. I close the door quietly behind me and unlock my car, which now strikes me as ridiculous. What was I thinking? That some millionaire, desperate for a shitty, dented Honda, would hot-wire it and jet off to Bel Air? Dumb. I get myself settled in the car and turn the key, but only get a sickly, throat-clearing kind of sound. "Do not play," I whisper to my car. "Do not fuck with me today." I try again. More screechy throat clearing. I try again and again for five minutes until I accept the fact that my car is not going to start. *Shit.* I sit for a moment, running through all my options. I could take a cab home—if I were rich. From Beverly Hills to Echo Park. *Please.* One-fourth my rent. I could ask Ian to give me a lift home. He-larious. I could call Earl to come get me. The only real option.

I get out of the car and knock on the door with the lion's head. Ian opens the door and eyes me suspiciously. "I thought you left already."

"Yeah, well. My car won't start." Ian studies me, and then spots my car. "Nice ride."

"Just, can I use your phone, please?" Ian stares at me as though I'm speaking French all of a sudden.

"What do you mean? What's wrong with yours? Your cell's not working?"

"I don't have a cell phone."

"Wow." Ian shakes his head and turns up the corner of his lip. "Please tell me you lost it or something."

"I never had one, okay? How long do you want to chitchat before you let me use your phone?"

"Man, you should be treating me *so* much nicer. You *so* need this job, like a lot you need this job. No *cell*. You have running water at your house, at least?"

I raise both my eyebrows at Ian. "Phone. Now."

He opens the door wide, exaggeratedly, and gestures me through, like Vanna White displaying letters on *Wheel of Fortune*.

"Thank you." I use the phone propped up on one of their many elaborate marble tables in the foyer and call Earl, who happens to pick up. Like the sweetheart he is, he says he'll be right over and so I tell Ian I'll wait in the foyer for Earl. He shrugs and takes his sandwich back to the gigantic TV.

I don't know what to do. Sit on the steps inside the foyer or wait outside? I decide it would be boring just to sit around, and so I follow the sound of the television and sit in a chair next to Ian, who's sprawled out on the couch.

"What are you watching?"

"Laguna Beach," Ian replies, mouth full of sandwich.

"Never heard of it. What's the premise?"

"The *premise?*" Ian smirks. "The premise is that these kids hook up with each other and the girls are total bitches and the dudes are dumbasses."

I watch TV for a while and then I watch Ian watch TV. He's right. It's a reality TV soap opera and the kids aren't likeable, really. At least that's my geriatric thirty-one-year-old's perspective. They're pretty to look at though. One group of girls is torturing another group of girls and the dudes are all players. They all have a ton of dough and live in ginormous houses, not unlike Ian's. The camera follows them and all their little dramas and the more I watch, the more I miss the early days of *The Real World,* before hot tubs and threesomes.

"So, why are you watching them?" I ask after a while.

Ian shrugs. "It's so dumb it's genius. I can watch this crap for hours. It's like watching two stories. There's the dumb one, which they totally rig to be *reality*—" Ian rolls his eyes at this "—and then there's the show that's actually reality. Like, these people, they totally look like tools, but then they're acting like tools on purpose because they're total whores for the camera."

Ian is *looking* at me when he's telling me all this. My little culture critic! Bravo! I get an idea for an assignment for Ian, something that, hopefully, he won't think sucks. "You want to write a paper on *Laguna Beach?*"

Ian puts his empty plate on the table in front of him and gapes at me. "What?"

"A paper. On *Laguna Beach.*"

"Seriously?"

"Yeah."

"Instead of reading a book?"

"In addition to."

Ian snorts.

"C'mon," I say. "Write a paper about what you were just arguing, that the show works on two levels or however many levels you think. Take notes the next time you watch the show and form your argument."

Ian stands and picks up his plate to take to the kitchen. On his own! "If you leave me alone about Toni Morrison for like, two seconds, then I'll do it."

"One second."

"Jesus," Ian says. "You are so, like, *annoying*," he tells me before he leaves the room.

And because I can't take another moment of *Laguna Beach,* I go wait for Earl outside.

I listen hard for the sound of Earl's hog so that I can buzz him in. His bike is so loud, though, there's probably no avoiding it. If I find it strange that I'm pulling up here in my Honda two days a week, Earl looks positively *surreal* sitting on his Harley with a big grin on his face and a blue bandana wrapped around his head.

"Fancy doin's," he says after he turns off the bike. "I *mean,*" he says, and whistles slow and long.

"I know." I come down the steps and give him a kiss. "My shitty car," I pout, pointing at it.

"Now you ought not talk about your baby that way," he says, grinning. "We'll get it working and acting the way it ought to. But we're going to have to leave it here for a bit."

Leave it here? Hmm. I hadn't thought of that. I don't think the Bernsteins would dig my car junking up their driveway. "I don't know about that, Earl. I don't know if I can."

"'Course you can." Earl gets off his bike and pops the hood of my car for the cursory "look-see," as he calls these sorts of things. "I can't quite see what all the trouble's about on my own. We're going to have to tow it."

Goodbye money. "Damn, Earl, that'll cost a hell of a lot of dough."

"Cain't be helped, baby, unless you got something else on your mind to do."

Can't say that I do. I keep looking at Earl, who keeps looking at my car and chewing on his bottom lip. I get distracted by his dimples. They take the edge off a lot of things, those dimples. But then Ian comes to the door that I forgot and left wide-open.

"Hey," Ian hollers. He looks at me, and then at Earl. "The mechanic came already?"

Whoa. Earl looks Ian over, cool and even. Then he says, "I'm Earl."

"My boyfriend," I blurt, so Ian doesn't say anything else that's fucked up. Earl's not too touchy a guy. However, he's already noted, I'm sure, that Ian doesn't put him with me, and that's irked him some, no doubt, now that I know that he's much more sensitive about this stuff than I thought.

Ian squints his eyes at me as though I'm trying to sell him

something he's not interested in buying. Then he notices Earl's bike, admires it really, and then I see him take in everything Earl's wearing. The bandana, the biker boots, the black T-shirt and the leather bracelet I gave him when we went to the bluegrass festival in Bean Blossom, Indiana. It has EARL burned into the leather.

"Your *boyfriend?*"

"That's right," Earl says, no smile on his face. He's heard me complain about Ian, like, every day since I've had the job, and so he's not having any of Ian's cuteness. I want to warn Ian, in a way, but every man for himself. If he wants to talk shit with the big boys, he's got to get shit from the big boys.

But, as Ian so delicately put it, he's not mentally challenged, so he plays it cool. "Nice to meet you," he says, coming down the stairs and shaking Earl's hand.

"Likewise." Earl grips Ian's hand and Ian winces just a tiny bit. Earl gives Ian's hand a couple of good pumps that throws his puny sixteen-year-old body around some. Makes me unreasonably happy, I have to say.

"So, I'm going to have to leave my car here, only overnight. I hope it's okay." And then, because I hate that I sound as though I'm asking *him* for permission, I say, "I hope it's okay, with your parents, I mean."

Ian keeps his eyes on Earl. "They'll live."

"All right, then," Earl murmurs, and then he gives me the helmet that he was *not* wearing. I'll remember to holler at him about *that* later. L.A. is no two-lane country highway like the ones Earl was used to riding on. He could get killed by some Escalade-driving, cell-phone talking, TV-watching moron not paying attention to the road.

"So thanks, Ian. Please tell your parents what the deal is?"

He nods. "I'll tell them." And then before Earl starts up the bike and pulls away, Ian gives me a shit-eating grin that means he's up to something—or going to be up to something.

Later that night I complain to Doris on the phone about Ian and how amused he seemed by me and Earl—together.

"He's a child," Doris argues. I can hear the TV in the background. "Like you care." She pauses. "Do you care?"

"Of course not," I reply, maybe a little too quickly. "It just bugs me, all this assumption about who belongs with whom. What happened to the melting pot and all that bullshit?"

"It's a salad now. Not a melted pot of soup or whatever. You're supposed to enjoy all the separate tastes, not blend them all together so that it tastes like some ass-y vegetable smoothie."

"Smoothie, salad, dim sum. Whatever the hell, it's all tedious. Speaking of such nonsense, I told my Burning Spear editor that I'm accepting their offer and that I'll do the changes they asked for."

"Shut up," Doris says. I can tell she's lowering the volume of her TV. "Are you sure—"

"Do you want cornrows or dreadlocks?" I get up to pour myself a glass of Charles Swab, a $1.99 bottle of wine from Trader Joe's. It's a far cry from Francis Coppola, but broke asses can't be choosers. I guess Doris hears me pouring.

"What are you drinking, anyway?"

"Two buck Chuck."

"Damn. You and Earl have got to make more money."

"I get six thousand dollars for the book," I say, sipping on my wine.

"Afro," Doris says. "Give me an afro. And cash that check as soon as you get it."

doris

The Transcendentalists: A still-influential and deeply counter-cultural group of writers from the mid-nineteenth century. Ralph Waldo Emerson and Henry David Thoreau being the two most famous transcendentalists, influenced a whole wake of writers from Melville to Nietzsche. Emerson advocated that the individual, instead of looking to the outside world for models and advice, should look inside and trust the "core self." Inside each person, he believed, was a touch of divinity, accessible only to those who shut out the clamor of the present day's fads, and instead, trust their own interior truth. Father of today's dreamers and tree-huggers, God bless him.

The nice thing about teaching is that for every Paige Prentiss there is a Tommy "T" Evans. T. not only enriches class discussion, but has become the closest thing that I have to a friend on campus. He busted me the second week of classes, during office hours, reading my favorite style blog, "GoFugYourself," and rather than thinking less of me, we now talk equally about Emersonian ideals and Britney Spears's fashion choices. I'm not sure Emerson would approve, but it does make my life easier.

T. sticks his head in my office and says, "loved the essay," before disappearing for his next class. I give him the thumbs-up, and return to my class prep.

I love to teach Emerson because he stands so staunchly in contrast to much of what Americans value today. In fact, I venture to say that, while Franklin might have a grand old time were he zapped back from the 1700s to now, Emerson would probably build a compound in the Montana woods, only to be rooted out by the government as dangerous and incendiary. When Emerson warns us that consistency is bad, I think, ha, the original flip-flopper! And when he holds up the truly successful individual as one who shifts careers and interests his entire life, I think, job jumper, never gonna have a career! Everything about Emerson runs so counter to our present way of thinking that it's no wonder my students look at me as though I've presented them with stone tablets when reading one of Emerson's most famous essays, "Self-Reliance." And I just love him for it.

My favorite Emersonian moment, though, came today when

Paige claimed that Emerson is the sort of man who made terrorism possible. T. turned ten shades of purple, and I decided that now I had, in fact, officially heard everything. Driving home from work, I call Ronnie to let her know about my latest run-in.

"Long time," I say. "What's the news on Bita?"

She fills me in, and I feel temporarily grateful that I am merely single and alone.

"How's the chilrens?" Ronnie asks.

I tuck the cell-phone under my chin and try to find an opening in traffic.

"My favorite conversation. Paige Prentiss informed me that if one were to take Emerson seriously, then one could justify terrorist action, if it were one's internal truth."

"So it's true what they say," Ronnie banters, "A little knowledge is a dangerous thing."

A BMW convertible swerves in front of me, passing on the right and almost causing five kinds of accident.

"Good lord. I think I should start practicing at the local arcade to survive the streets of Atlanta. The way people drive here is simply not normal."

"Try L.A."

"No, thanks. I think my poor Corolla would be laughed right off the Hollywood Hills. Anyhow, because I'm evil, I just let Paige believe that Emerson, indeed, might support terrorist action, because it's not totally far from what he's saying. It's just sort of a misrepresentation. Gives her something to report back to the junior fascist league of America, get another bar on her swastika."

Ronnie laughs. "Any more word from them?"

"Not for me. Evidently, I'm behaving, but my colleague, Asa, got a pretty creepy note. Same creepy lettering, but it just said 'THAT'S TWO. YOU'RE ALMOST OUT.' It wasn't even so much what it said, as that she was out in the parking lot, and started looking for her keys, and somehow between her looking for the keys and opening her door, the note appeared under the windshield wiper. She said there were plenty of people around, and she couldn't believe that she didn't notice. Creepy, creepy, creeepeeeee. She was really shook-up. I don't think she even knows what she did."

"Does the administration do anything?"

"No," I say, flipping on my turn signal and pulling into my apartment complex. "You know that they're not so much students these days as paying customers. If they want every hour to be the children's hour, so long as they're not waving machetes, the administration acts like we're overreacting."

"How depressing."

"It is. I'll call you tomorrow. I'm supposed to have wine with Toni tonight, she's going to help me with my Internet profile and following up on my speed-dating matches."

"So no word from Zach?"

"You mean other than 'goodbye,' and 'I have to change Lolita's diapers'? No, not much follow up. It's really too depressing to get into. I hate him and I miss him at the exact same time, and probably in equal parts. I've decided instead of just sitting around and wallowing and getting fat, I'm going to date. I might even get fat on dates, but at least it's social obesity."

"That's great, Doris."

"Oooooh. And I almost forgot. I got a call from one Dr. Antonius Block, asking me if I'd like to have tea with him at his home in Virginia Highland. Doesn't that sound so Southern and civilized that you can barely stand it? I haven't even seen him this semester, but I do gaze fondly at his Anthony Hopkins-esque picture looking down on me as I enter the building. Do you know how much I worship that man's work?"

Ronnie musters an unenthusiastic, "Yes."

"I know you hate him."

"I don't hate him. I don't know him. I just don't connect with his work. I think he'd be writing about the darkies loooving old Savannah if Martin Luther King hadn't come around."

I almost run off the road pretending to cover my ears.

"No. That's just speculation. He could be secretly and totally progressive now. Maybe he's had a change of heart."

"Because that happens so frequently."

"I'm not talking to you. And what was it that woman said in *Miss Lonelyhearts* by Nathaniel West? That you're the nastiest kind of woman, one who won't let me cherish my illusions."

"Okay, Doris. I'm wrong. You and Block are going to sip mint juleps and talk about third-wave feminism and then at the end of the evening sing *We Shall Overcome*."

"Har-har," I say. "Back to the demon child for you."

* * *

Here is one of the secret, true confessions of Doris Weather-all. You know when you read those articles about high-powered folks who've spent their whole lives gaybashing and whatnot, and then you read some tabloid that details how they've been found dead in women's stockings with an orange in their mouth and leather chaps on the bed? You know those articles? Well, I never read them with surprise, and not only because I'm a cynic, but because I understand inconsistency. Yes, as I've said, God bless Emerson. So as I approach the doorstep of Antonius Block's outrageously beautiful three-story Tara-esque mansion, I am fully aware of my own hypocrisy. I'm like Jodie Foster's character in *Silence of the Lambs,* hypnotically drawn to the ever so slightly evil genius of the oh so talented if slighty misogynistic Antonius Block. And did I mention, to further dig my own grave, that he's kind of hot in a Kevin Spacey, *Midnight in the Garden of Good and Evil* kind of way? I have dolled up extra-girly and extra-pretty for tea today. Pink lip gloss, a yellow-and-red sundress with a three-quarter-length sweater—the way I always imagined Southern sorority girls dressed before I knew they mostly dress like every other teenager.

I bang gently on the oak door, and marvel at the minigarden growing on the porch, when a girl who looks my age, maybe younger, opens the door and lets me in the house.

"Hello. You must be Doris. We've been expecting you. Come in."

She's pretty in an androgynous way, with a pixie haircut and Katherine Hepburn–style trousers hanging off her hipbones. "I hope you're settling into the department. I know that it can be a real snakepit."

"It's okay so far," I tell her, fanning my dress beneath me and perching myself at the edge of a large leather chair.

Antonius Block enters the room and kisses the woman on the mouth. She gives him a playful pat on the ass (I am not making this up), and he says to me, in a matter-of-fact Southern drawl, "Now, you've met Vera. She was my student, she's now my wife. And you're among the first to hear that piece of news, although I've no doubt you've heard rumors of our involvement."

Both of them are grinning like the cat who caught the canary, and I am thinking three things at once: 1) Please, God, let him mean his ex-*graduate* student; 2) how totally and tragically obvious; 3) Dammit, now I don't get to be child bride number four. Curses on the pixie!

"Congratulations," I say. "That's wonderful."

He gives me a smirk that's half self-congratulatory, and half lets me know that he knows that I'm probably judging him. Which I totally am.

"Love is a wonderful thing, Doris. Don't let too many years teaching English teach you otherwise. Love and the other humanistic virtues. I know it's not in favor, but I do believe that the universals will prevail. Long after the fad for sub-par voices from the fringe falls by the wayside. I do hope that you'll continue to incorporate some of the classics into your reading list. I worry so when I see that a class contains only voices from this last sad century. So much is lost dwelling only on the recent past."

Now, if Antonius Block were one of my students we would be about to engage in a heated debate about what, exactly he meant by "sub par voices from the fringe" and "this last, sad century" as opposed to those other *fabulous* centuries of slavery, war and imperialist conquest. However, PC-Doris knows that Antonius Block is super-senior faculty, and therefore at the absolute top of the list of people not to piss off if one knows what's good for one's nontenured ass. She is also two percent seduced by the lulling surety of his voice, falling, Eva Braun style, for the charisma underneath the evil. Bad, bad Doris!

I almost hear myself say, "I don't know *nothin'* 'bout teaching no *commies,* or *dahkies,* or *silly bitches with pens,*" but quell the cry for sarcasm deep within my soul. Emerson would be very ashamed. Instead I say, "I always try to teach Keats and Dickinson. You can't go wrong with Keats and Dickinson."

"And Byron, for chrissakes," Antonius chimes in. "Do you know what Byron can mean to a young mind? Honey," he says, not quite looking at Vera, "would you mind bringing us some bourbon. Neat. Two glasses."

"Midafternoon boozing," I say. "Gotta love the South."

"Doris," he whispers, all but leering in my direction. "We are going to talk about poetry. Poetry until the darkness swallows up our tiny pinhole of light in this godforsaken city."

For some reason, I can only imagine Zach standing behind him, sticking a finger down his imaginary throat and mouthing *poets,* like the word held all the toxicity of anthrax. Antonius

Block is one bourbon shy of becoming a total parody of himself—the old dude who watched *Dead Poet's Society* about ten too many times, and doesn't quite get that it's the voices from the fringe that are around to stay, and that he's the fading part of the canon. Or maybe he does get that—thus the bourbon, thus the child bride.

But since Zach isn't here, and I actually enjoyed *Dead Poet's Society* the first two times I watched it, I tell myself, "When in Rome…" and make the next bourbon a double.

It's a good thing that I don't teach on Fridays because the next day I am tragically hungover, with all the postalcoholic gloom and doom that said state occasionally entails. I knock on the walls, which is now code for Toni to come on over if she likes. I think we're developing a Mary Richards, Rhoda–type bond, but I am unfortunately and definitely the Rhoda of the equation.

"I spent an evening with a sixty-year-old," I tell her. "And I thought, good freaking lord, in his mind, I'm probably already too old for him. Not that I liked him. I mean, he's a total fascist, he's just kind of a hot fascist."

"Age ain't nothin' but a number," Toni says, sidling beside me and pointing to the ad for singles on Match.com flashing across the screen of my laptop.

"Spoken by some deluded soul who clearly never dated on the Internet," I say, looking at the hagged-out, forty-five-year-old, grinning, hairless, across the screen, who will only date women aged twenty-two to thirty-eight. Priceless.

With Toni's help, I've gone from an Internet dating virgin to veritable savant in a few short weeks. And let me tell you, ladies-over-a-certain-age (puberty), in case you don't already know, the cyber-landscape isn't always pretty. Given, I am probably overly sensitive about this issue because of Zach and Toni, and Antonius and Vera, but unless you're practicing kabbalah, there's not a whole lot of Harold and Maude out there. It never occurred to me that I, at thirty-two, might be considered too old for men my age.

"That's him," I say, when we get to Andrew. We responded "yes" to each other on our speed-dating sheets, but Toni is still too caught up in Tino to want anything to do with him. I, on the other hand, am up for anything to get my mind off my own present situation.

"I guess that's him," Toni says, squinting at the screen. "The problem with these profile pics is they're like the hamburger advertisements on TV. They show you a big burger on TV, and it's like, wow, great, get me one of those, then you see it in person and it's like, yeah, I guess that's lettuce, and I guess that's the meat they told me about, but it sure doesn't bear any resemblance to that thing you showed me to get me in the place."

I laugh, and Lotto lets out a catcall through the walls. Toni walks to the wall and bangs against it, shouting, "Shut up, you crazy white-trash bird. Shut up, shut up, shut up. God, Doris, you're a saint for not calling the management on me. Have I thanked you again?"

"Please," I say, scrolling through Andrew's information, "you forget what I lived with through the walls in Indiana for six solid years. Noisy undergraduate sex and accompanying pot-patchouli scent."

"Dear God," she said. "Indiana."

"Okay. You have to read this. More material for your study."

Andrew's profile pegs him as a thirty-five-year-old psych grad student who is looking for a toned woman aged twenty-two to thirty. His e-mail to me reads: "Doris, great to meet you. Hard to find smart women with a sense of humor. Would love to catch up. Here's my cell number if you'd like to take coffee one of these afternoons."

"You've got to be kidding." Toni laughs. "Seriously. He sent me the exact same e-mail, word for word."

"And not even good words," I say. "Who says 'take coffee.' I mean, coffee is fine, but it's not like 'taking heroin' or 'taking a vacation.' It's just another of those drinks that falls above water and below martinis in the great chain of being."

"Probably some pretentious turn of phrase he'll attribute to a summer traipsing around Europe," Toni speculates. "Probably Prague in the early nineties, where he was going to be a great writer, but ended up with the sad, rich, white boy's version of a long 'dear diary.'"

Also, while I don't know what he and Toni talked about, I know full well that I acted like an idiot, so it seems clear to me that Andrew is pulling that age-old trick of telling a woman he finds pretty that she is smart, in the way that he would no doubt have emphasized that he found me attractive had I sold myself as an academic. Or, he could have thought that I *was* smart and just be flirting. But I am in no mood to give anyone the benefit of the doubt.

So with Toni's approval, I write back: "I would be glad to take coffee with you, but alas, I'm out of your age range. But who knows, maybe I'll serve you coffee one of these days if you fly the friendly skies." Because it's the Internet, and my chances of seeing Andrew again in a city as large as Atlanta are zero-to-none, I send said bitterness into the world.

After almost a bottle of wine, Toni is ready to talk about Tino. She's stretched across the floor of my apartment on the faux sheepskin throw that seemed retro-sexy at the time I bought it. I have since downgraded it to frightening, but comfortable.

"So I still haven't told him," she says. "And it's not like he's said anything crazy, like 'hang them coons,' but it's like I have this thought bubble written over his head, and I'm waiting for the crazy thing that he's going to say that I'm going to have to write in it, then write him off."

"But maybe he won't," I hazard. "Maybe you should give him a chance."

"When I was a full-out white girl, I dated guys who would say things on occasion. You know, without even thinking about it, a 'those people,' or a 'that kind of girl,' or a 'well, what do you expect,' and I knew it was racial, even then. But it hits me differently now."

She flips over onto her belly and pushes herself up into a seated position.

"Here's a crazy and true story," she says. "I thought I was white for, like, sixteen solid years. My mom, she never knew she was biracial, because her mother was white. And her dad died when she was really young. So she just up and moved, and told me that my father had had no family to speak of, married my stepfather, and had two more full-out white babies."

She pauses and lets out a long sigh.

"On my sixteenth birthday it turns out my great-aunt, my father's sister, has been trying to track me down for years. And she's black for sure. So black I am. I took off and didn't speak to my mother the entire summer. Then when I went away to school, I guess I got sensitized to it, but it felt like race was everywhere. All the places people think it isn't, with who gets carded for ID at the video store, or whose house gets rebuilt, or all those other light-skinned women like me, who chose to pass or not pass as white, and me, passing without even knowing it for most of my life. So I feel, being with Tino, like I'm sliding into this bad, awful, sick, diseased habit, and part of me just hates myself for it. And then I consider whether if I'm not punishing myself for sliding by for so long, and I don't even want to tell Tino the truth because even if he thinks it's okay, I'm going to think it's because I still look white, and he can make it exotic and a little trashy, and maybe a little more sexual like some old-school massah before the wind done gone."

All the joy had gone out of her voice by the end of her story.

"I have to tell him," she said, resigned. "And then I have to break up with him. That's all there is to it. Any man who will only date white girls is never going to date this girl."

And though the anger and bitterness all but seep through her voice when she says, "white girls," I don't take it personally.

* * *

After Toni leaves, I turn my music down lower so as not to disturb the neighbors (nor agitate the parrot), and return my attention to my laptop, to which I have developed a sort of Internet-fantasy addiction. A fantasy that is shattered each time I really read what folks have to say about themselves.

Part of the problem with Internet dating profiles is that they all sound alike. Everyone loves the outdoors, wants a woman who "looks as good in jeans and a baseball cap as out on the town." Everyone's last favorite book read is *The DaVinci Code*. Everyone has a good sense of humor and is looking for someone who makes them smile. Everyone is "living life to the fullest and looking for that special someone to make me complete." And grammar? Spelling? Forget about it. If I decided to be snobbish about English usage, I would never leave my house again.

Then there are those who dare to be different. The handsome, six-foot-four African-American man whose profile stated that he is LOOKING FOR A SOCCER MOM, SOMEONE WHO LIKES DOING CRAFTS OR SOMETHING OUT OF THE HOUSE. ALSO I'M A TWO TIME A DAY GUY SO IF YOU'RE NOT PASSIONATE.... I was surprised his tagline didn't read: "Stud seeks local concubine with eye for macramé." There's also the gentleman who likes WOMEN WHO WEAR PANTYHOSE AND LINGERE (Together? Please, God, NO!), and the one who advertised himself as GOOD HUSBAND MATERIAL. (Yikes! As scary in men as GOOD WIFE MATERIAL would indubitably be in women.) Furthermore, having surveyed the sheer volume of men who list brainiacs as a turn off, I have now concluded that when a man says he wants a "smart woman" what he means is "smart enough to unzip my pants." It was sort of like taking a trip to the Designer Shoe Warehouse where there's lots of material, the promise of a great find, but lawdie, lawdie, the junk you had to sift through to find one decent sole (or soul, as the case may be).

I also had a "yes" from Maxwell-the-speed-dater, and I'm anxious to look him up and see if he's sent me an e-mail. I shied away from doing this around Toni, as I'm not yet sure whether or not she'd approve of my own cross-race dating, white girl that I am.

Maxwell has a nice tagline: "Where are all the brainy beauties?" His self-description is written in a recognizable version of the Queen's English, and nothing stands out as terribly different, nor does anything strike me as terrifying. The veganism is a little troubling, only because it's one of those lifestyles that cannot help but make the nonvegan feel like a worse person. I read an interview with Billy Bob Thornton saying that being with Angelina Jolie made him feel bad because she was off saving the world while he just wanted to stay home on the couch and watch *Green Acres*. To paraphrase Melville, call me Billy. That, and the slightly kooky sandals (no matter how humanitarian, I cannot call plastic masquerading as cow a step forward), are the only strikes against Maxwell. Puny little strikes. Ostensibly, he's what's known in urban parlance as a catch. I mentally calculate ways of getting him into my bedroom without seeing that non-PETA friendly chamber of horrors—

my shoe rack. I could give up eating meat in a New York minute, but a beautiful pair of leather pumps, of python (God forgive me) high-heel sandals? I'm sorry, but vegans haven't mastered the stiletto to my satisfaction. Pleather with a three-inch heel is like a piece of nonfat chocolate cake, or your favorite song set to elevator music.

I start to write Maxwell an e-mail.

My subject line reads: "Are you an actual crackhead?" Not flattering, but one must hope that he can take a joke. And, in fact, *crackheaded* is the word that came to mind when I finally got a hold of a picture of Maggie Mae Mischner's mother—Misty Lee Mischner—who is about two surgical procedures from looking as if she should be a fixture at Madame Tussaud's wax museum. I even made Ronnie look up Misty Lee Mischner on the Internet, and Ronnie concurred that while there was something in the nose, the deadened Stepford-esque glaze to the eyes and over-toxed forehead canceled out any true resemblance.

"Read your profile," I begin, "not sure I'm gorgeous, but am fairly certain that your lenient definition of *fox* leaves some room for discussion. At the very least, not a hag."

Hmm. Not in love with how that reads. Clunky. I know Maxwell has met me before, but I worry that he'll mentally substitute "hag" for "not quite beautiful." Modesty, not hagdom, is the desired effect. I call Ronnie to get some advice, but Ronnie is unavailable. I knock on the wall, and Toni materializes five minutes later, wearing her pajamas and thick Buddy Holly glasses.

"Oh no," I say. "You're doing work."

"True. You have five minutes."

"Okay. I'm sending an e-mail to a man that I saw on the Internet, one that I actually like, and I don't want to screw it up."

"Fine," she says, pushing her glasses farther up the bridge of her nose. "Do you want feminist, sensible Toni's advice or the advice of Toni the professional dater who knows how to get you laid?"

"Please. I'm recently broken up. Do you even have to ask?"

"All right. But you may never judge me for what you are about to hear."

I love it. Un-PC advice is about to be divulged!

"Okay," I say. "I want to sort of sound modest and acknowledge the fact that I'm not a model, but I also don't want him to think that I think I'm a hag. How about 'not beautiful, but not haggy.'"

"Are you completely stoned?" Un-PC Toni asks. "Saying 'not a hag,' that's like saying 'don't think of elephants.' Men are visual. Mentally visual. Only emphasize the positive. Men are also highly, *highly* suggestible."

"So I should *suggest* dinner and potential nakedness?"

"God, no!" Toni blurts. "You should *suggest* that you are far too busy for dinner let alone nakedness. Men want what they can't have."

"Oooh, that's *such* a cliché!"

"But like most clichés, it's also true. I went to college, too, remember? I know what you like to think in the little liberal bubble of academia, but in the real world? Men? Women? Different. You must stroke their egos and bat your eyes. Get used to it—you might even find a boyfriend with a job who treats you like an actual *woman*."

"Zach had a *job*," I say. "The same *job* I had for near on a decade. And you know as well as I do that gender is largely a social construction. That we are what we're socialized to be. If there are differences between men and women, they're far more cultural than biological."

"And what is your beloved Zach doing now?"

"Dating a twelve-year-old."

Toni gives me an I-rest-my-case smile.

"Doris, as your un-PC advisor, whom you will never acknowledge that you even met after this evening, let me give you a piece of advice. Do not under ANY CIRCUMSTANCE say that gender is a performance or whatever crap you're selling at work to a man you're dating. I'll bet that twelve-year-old of Zach's is a major ego-stroker. Repeat this to yourself—I am in the REAL WORLD."

Possibly the most frightening part of this conversation is that Toni now sounds far more like a Langsdale local, or Paige Prentiss, than the Atlanta-based woman-of-the-world I know and love.

"You're kind of scary like this, Toni."

"You have no idea." Toni smiles. "I didn't say it was pretty or true, I'm just trying to get your overly analytical little academic arse in the nude condition as quickly as possible. It's called friendship."

I give her a hug, and she leaves to work on her writing. That she used the word *friendship* makes me happier than just about anything that's happened to me since I arrived in Atlanta.

I decide to take Toni's advice, but instead of writing Maxwell back immediately, I decide to do a reverse search of sorts, and check to see what other women my age—my competition as it were—are looking for in a man. Could it be that my brain has been seriously warped by years of gender theory and dating of the über-politically correct? I know from my conversations with Paige that it's entirely *possible* for young women to reject feminism, and not just the name, but the actual ends. If scads of women view marriage as the chance to sit on one's ass and be cared for, who's to say that women aren't devolving, putting Gloria Steinem and Betty Friedan, not to mention Naomi Wolf and Susan Faludi, to shame. It hurts my head to think about it, since women disidentifying with feminism seems to me the equivalent of African-Americans looking at the civil rights movement and deciding that it really didn't do that much.

Here is what I learned about single women and Internet dating in general.

1. These ladies have gone to Glamour Shots. Seriously. I will be changing my cute and candid picture in the very near future.

2. Toni has clearly done her research. Passivity in the female subject is alive and well. It's not so much the occasional girl who says she "wants a prince," as the sheer volume of girls who describe themselves as "down to earth," who want a "nice" man who likes "to treat a

woman right." There are ladies aplenty who announce up front that they'd like to settle down, or they like to party, but very little that reveals a sentient being with unique and independent thoughts. And women, too, love that *Da Vinci Code,* though there's a healthy smattering of Oprah book-club picks for variety's sake.

3. Overall, the women are pretty much EXACTLY like the men in most respects. Generic and slightly depressing. Testament to the self-Stepfordization of America. I will no doubt be haunted and horrified well past this moment by the woman who "loves the news, but only FOX News." It's like thousands of versions of the exact same person looking for the exact same things. Scary. Very, very scary.

4. And perhaps this goes without saying: it will be a miracle if I meet anyone through this venue.

Mid-September in Atlanta is still summer. If I ever deigned to visit the gym near my apartment, I have a sneaking suspicion this is how the steam room might feel. In the short time it takes for me to cross the two blocks from the parking garage to my office, I can feel the back of my once-crisp white blouse (button-down with a Peter Pan collar—thank you, Anthropologie sale rack!) plastered against my back, sweat dripping beneath my cropped brown pants. The outfit would be women's-club conservative, but I'm wearing a no doubt inappropriate pair of red shoes, a half inch too high to be strictly professional, but not so high as to be overtly trampy. At home, I thought the outfit screamed sex and money. Now it simply screams for antiperspirant.

On the way to teach world literature, I pass Asa in the hall, who is wearing a similarly conservative outfit, but with well-worn, beige leather sandals that scream professional and practical. She gives me the once-over, but withholds comment. This is the single tangible advantage to being the resident poet, from those Byronic blouses to the always-in-season Dickensian white: no one has ever expected those skilled in verse to dress like normal people. I vow to stop by her office later and make a second pass at making friends.

Making the transition from graduate student to professor is similar to moving from engaged to married. Everything about you is technically the same, but somehow the formalization makes everything different. It's not that I know more than I did a scant four months before, but my students treat me with respect. No more of that "where's our real teacher" nonsense that so riddled my experience at Langsdale. In Atlanta, it's all polite smiles and "okie-dokie, Miss-I-mean-Dr. Weatherall." I take that back. Aside from Paige Prentiss, it's all okie-dokie.

Paige is now in all three of the classes that I'm teaching this semester: advanced poetry writing, American lit and world literature. Initially, she was only in two, but I think she's become the Lex Luthor-ette to my Super-prof—she hates me, but it's clearly a fascinated kind of hatred. In poetry writing, she's a regular shark and on her way to becoming the real deal. She's what teachers call "gifted." In possession of a turn of phrase that seems almost beyond her control. Her metaphors are consistently surprising, her critical eye astute, and yet she refuses to write about anything more troubling than an unweeded garden and a slightly untrainable boyfriend. In world lit, she plays dumb. This is almost entirely due to the presence of Jack Moynihan, a generically handsome, deeply mediocre but good-hearted student whom Paige seems desperate to impress. Jack reminds me of the young version of every half-datable man with a profile on the Internet. He all but cries for a women who loves her dog, country, God and man, but not necessarily in that order. And Paige is far more interested in impressing him with her awe-gee-shucks stupidity than she is in stunning me with her smarts.

Today we are reading *July's People,* a provocative novel by Nadine Gordimer about the dissolution of a white South African family in the wake of some fictitious revolution that reverses the terms of apartheid. The white "masters" find themselves at the mercy of their black African servant, July, and the identity of all is in flux. I came prepared with a timeline of South African history, and an explanation of the roots of apartheid, as well as its perpetuation well into the 1990s. I've long since given up on expecting students to know history when they arrive in a college classroom. Hell, Ronnie taught a class at Langsdale where not one student knew what the color lavender looked like. Out of eighteen students, nary a soul had heard of lavender and associated it with a pastel blue-purple. In fact, one of the students finally ventured, "It's like the color of blood, right?" To which Ronnie responded, in one of her few losing-the-cool moments, "Do you all live under rocks?" That was the only semester that Ronnie had less-than-stellar teaching evaluations. No one likes feeling stupid. *Especially* stupid people.

Out of my class of twelve, one student had heard of apartheid before reading the book. James Jackson, a deeply Republican African-American student, who objects to any swear words he finds on the page. Asa taught him in American lit, and evidently Jean Toomer's *Cane,* a Harlem Renaissance classic, was too sordid for his taste. Paige Prentiss kept her mouth shut, and the rest of the class scribbled notes as I gave a general overview of colonialization in Africa, and the legacy of apartheid in South Africa today.

"When I was in college, not quite the Stone Age, as you might imagine, all of this was still taking place. People wore T-shirts that said 'abolish apartheid, divest now,' and there was a famous video where a number of musicians sang a song where the refrain was, 'I ain't gonna play Sun City.'"

James nods. Paige looks at her nails. Jack Moynihan seems oddly engaged.

"What do you mean by *divest?*" he asks.

"Good question. It means that countries like the United States, which tacitly supported the white South-African government by investing in the country, were encouraged to pull out their financial assets, thus weakening the country's economy, and also sending out a moral message."

And maybe this is where I should have stopped. Looking back, perhaps this was the moment to leave it at a history lesson, but pre-Marc-Jacobs-obsessed-ex-college-commie in me just couldn't help herself. I wanted to make some link between the past and present, or as I was to learn later, "to bring politics into the classroom."

"In fact," I say, "a number of people in this last election objected to Dick Cheney, our vice president, because he not only supported investment in South Africa, but opposed a bill supporting the ANC, or African National Congress, and voted against a resolution to free Nelson Mandela from imprisonment." And now I was getting pissed. "He even went so far as to call Nelson Mandela a terrorist, which in my book is tantamount to calling Martin Luther King a terrorist."

Jack pursed his full lips and ran one hand across the front of his too-tight blue T-shirt. "Is that true?" he asked. "About the vice president?"

"Look it up," I tell him.

Paige Prentiss made a tsk-tsk sound. "Maybe it's true, but I don't see how it relates to anything going on in the book. I think we're supposed to be talking about *July's People*, not Dr. Weatherall's liberal agenda."

"It's not my liberal agenda," I said, equal parts shocked and awed at her nerve. "It's history, and it's relevant. There's not always a clear separation between literature and politics. Look at the former Soviet Union, heck, look at America today. Poetry teachers at public high schools have lost their jobs for allowing students to write anti-war poems. Sounds awfully like fascism to me. And it's not like I'm making this up about the vice president, he's gone on record to say that if he had the chance, he wouldn't have changed that vote. I don't know about you, but that infuriates me. Now maybe *that*'s not relevant to this class, but where are we if we can't have an open dialogue, if we can't start on one place in the world, say South Africa, and investigate how it is or is not analogous to other situations? Civil Rights and black consciousness weren't such unrelated movements."

Maybe Paige was just trying to goad me, or maybe she really was Satan in cutesy-wear, but next thing I hear out of her mouth is...

"Well, we weren't there, so maybe the vice president knew something about Nelson Mandela that we didn't. Maybe the ANC were plotting some terrorist attack that none of us knew, and the vice president was looking out for Americans. Just because Nelson Mandela is popular now, that doesn't mean he couldn't have been in jail for a very good reason."

I could barely believe that I now had to explain the relevance, necessity and generally goodness of Nelson Mandela.

"Nelson Mandela is one of the great leaders and peacemakers of our time. If you knew anything at all, you'd know that the ANC was actually considered conservative. Like Martin Luther King in America, as opposed to a Malcolm X."

Paige shrugged. The rest of the class was silent, and I calculated the time it would take to get two Excedrin in my system and stop the headache threatening to move from the back of my head straight through my eyeballs. No, there was no joy in Georgia that afternoon. And I could only imagine there would be a note waiting on my windshield in the not-so-distant future.

Age may be nothing but a number, but there is a divide between youth and maturity that teachers are constantly called upon to negotiate. For instance, as much as I'd like to rip Paige's head from her tiny frame, as much as she's flat-out incorrect in many of her statements, I'm better off engaging with her than silencing her. Yet sitting in my office, the small bastion of kitsch in my newly adult lifestyle, surveying the Felix the Cat magnets on my file cabinet and Dukes of Hazzard lunchbox with its less than ironic confederate affiliations, I can't help but wonder what's happened to the youth of America. When I was in college, a liberal arts education meant challenging the ideas you'd been handed by your parents. I remember a class on social theory that I took where the professor announced, as though he'd received a memo directly from the source, that God was a myth, and wasn't it nice that we'd all evolved past believing in such an antiquated archetype? This incredibly well-educated and authoritative man challenged what I believed. But at the end of the day, it was my job to weigh the different evidence and sources, and my beliefs were still my own. And if college was a place of same-sex kiss-ins, protests against U.S. policy in Africa, rabid vegans and sweatshop consciousness awareness, wasn't that the point? To shock you out of complacency and challenge what you believe, so that when you left you could think critically and come closer to calling your ideas your own?

"That bad?" Asa asks from the doorway of my office. "You look like they really put you through the wringer."

I motion her inside and she sits down, wrapping both legs beneath her, and stretches back into the leather armchair that I'd bought at a surplus store over the weekend. "Atlanta

State's a conservative school. I assume you're used to that from Langsdale."

"I guess. I just always felt that in Langsdale the kids had an excuse. I mean, it was rural Indiana, for God's sake. Half of them hadn't even seen a black person live and in person until they got to college, and if they'd met a gay person, you can bet he was in the closet. These kids are bossy and...intractable. They won't budge an inch from what they come into the classroom thinking. What's that about? It's like they arrived at college intent on *not* learning anything we have to say."

"I'd finally gotten used to the kids," Asa says. "But now there's this policing in place by the university, and it's both distracting and offensive. I was telling my partner, David, about this the other night. Did you know that the university is actually allowing parents to monitor the classrooms? The rationale is that parents are paying for a product and they deserve to see where their hard-earned dollars are going. So not only do I have no one in the administration backing me up, I have to contend with hostile students and hostile parents. I'd have taught high school if that were my goal."

I grunt in solidarity.

"I really don't know what I'd do without David these days. He's coming by to walk me out to my car this evening. The note on the windshield left me quite shaken. I hate to say it, but there are times when having an evolved, loving man in one's life makes all the difference."

Maybe I'm just paranoid, or lonely, but the "evolved, loving man" line from a smug partner makes me want to leave the room. I silently vow that if I am ever involved with an "evolved, loving man" I will have the sense and kindness not to rub it in the faces of those around me.

"I wouldn't know," I say, trying to joke about it. "I seem only in possession of the broken-up-with and virtual kind."

Asa gives an ever so slightly condescending nod. I know this nod. It is the nod of the person who secretly believes that single women are immature and unable to figure out what they really want. Did I mention that I might be feeling paranoid?

"Doris," Asa says, gesturing behind me. "I want you to meet David."

I turn to face a tall, good-looking boyish man whose broad smile deflates within seconds of my facing him.

"David," I mutter, repeating the name to myself. "David."

"Uh, yeah," he says. "Nice to meet you, Doris."

"Nice to meet you, David. Always nice to meet a David."

Asa gives me a look like I'm out of my mind.

"But you know what," I continue, "it's funny, but to me you almost look more like an Andrew. Has anyone ever told you that?"

"Spooky," Asa says. "Andrew is David's middle name."

David is giving me a look that's hate mixed with loathing and a side of "ha-ha—you think you're a funny little smart-ass."

"You know what's weird," he says. "You look just like this flight attendant that I had when I traveled home the other week. I mean, you're a little bigger than she was, but similar."

Asa hits him playfully in the stomach. "David," she admonishes. But I can tell that she likes this gesture of complete and overt un-attraction for me.

"We must both be psychic." I smile and give a more than knowing gesture in David's direction. "People are always telling me that I look like the fat version of some flight attendant." Now Asa is looking at me as if I'm truly, totally, out of my mind, but I avoid meeting her eyes and stare straight at him. Because he and I both know that I'm way more than psychic, and what I know and Asa doesn't is that this so-called "David" of hers (he'll always be Andrew to me) is way, way less than evolved.

ronnie

I miss Doris. It's great to be home, to be near old friends like
Bita, but Bita's married, which makes her a different genre of
woman. To my mind, there are four genres of women:
single/hetero, single/gay, married or mommy. And gay or
hetero, once you're in the married/mommy category, the
single-with-no-kids category is a distant, *distant* memory. So
Doris feels my pain. And I feel hers. We're also two people who
see eye to eye about a lot of things. We're both pains in the asses
when it comes to books and learning something, for God's sake.
If you're a man, they consider you an intellectual. Well-read and
well-informed. If you're a chick, you're better off keeping a lid
on all that knowledge and keeping your mouth shut—unless
you're talking about looking for a man. Unlucky for us, we're

both too political for our own good; we're both in charge of folks who do not give one ounce of shit about books or politics, and both of us are pathologically determined to make them give an ounce of shit.

So the next time we talk, a few days after I've given Ian his TV-watching assignment, we trade war stories. I wasn't surprised that she was having a hard time. Okay, really, I'm just using "hard time" as a euphemism for "flipping the fuck *out*." Teaching is hard and underappreciated. Newsflash.

"If there's a God, I would like him to give me actual students who actually care, and if they don't, they should just sit down, shut up, and do everything I say, anyway," Doris rants. She has just gotten home from work, so the good times are still fresh in her head.

"D." I'm thinking about my own special hell with Ian. Who, as annoying and trying as he is, is a smart, interesting kid because his little demented wheels keep turning, even when he doesn't want them to. "That's not true. You'd be bored out of your mind teaching kids like that. Kids who'd agree with you in a robot monotone." This Paige Prentiss sounded like a doozy. I imagine she and Ian getting together, towering over us, and crushing us with their thumbs. If you're a teacher, kids who don't care worry you about the future, but smart kids who could really do something with their smarts, but choose mediocrity, those are the ones who are really scary. Paige and Ian were scary, but they weren't hopeless.

"Maybe I'd be bored," she admits. "Okay, yeah, I would, but it would be so much easier. I do have this one awesome student,

Jack Moynihan. Not T., my gay fashionisto, but an honest-to-goodness frat boy with a conscience. Anyhow, he came to my office the other afternoon to tell me that he's switching to English as his major. From business, so his parents might hunt me down and kill me, but it's a small victory for critical thinking."

"Yeah, well. A drop in the ocean."

"True. I miss you and Earl. The new friend thing is stressful. I keep waiting for the crazy-bomb to drop with all these new folks."

"Why don't you come to L.A.? Come have a little vacation with me and Earl."

"And sleep where? Between the two of you? That'd be cozy."

"Earl wouldn't mind." Earl would turn at least three shades of red if he heard me joking about this. *You ladies,* he'd say and shake his head as though he didn't know what in the world to do with us.

"No offense, but ew," Doris says. "Not funny. Like sleeping with my sister's husband, that would be. Besides, I've got my own man, kind of."

"Details," I demand, and pour what has to be my fourth Diet Coke of the day. "I have a Coke habit. Ha-ha. I drink like, six a day."

"Well, quit it for a minute and maybe I'll confess to meeting Mr. In The Meantime, this Maxwell I told you about." I hear Doris opening and closing refrigerator and cabinet doors.

"What are you eating?"

"What am I *not* eating, is really the question."

"So vegan is okay, then?" I remember Doris telling me *that* little detail. I, personally, wouldn't know what to do with a vegan. It'd be like dating someone who said they much preferred water to eating, and potato sacks to clothes. So much for my liberal "tolerance."

"We'll see what the deal is," Doris says, changing the subject. "Let's just say my expectations are low, low, low." I catch her up on Earl finally cracking, Bita possibly dumping Charlie, and my conclusion that Ian is a smart, smart little nightmare. She says, after hearing more stories about Ian, that she'll never complain about her sweet angels in Atlanta again and that she had a spare crucifix she could put in the mail for me.

"Promise you'll think about L.A.," I insist before we hang up. "Our couch is comfortable, I swear. Good to sleep on."

"You've already slept on your couch? Who pissed who off?"

"No," I said. "We've not *slept* on it."

"My second ew,'" Doris moans. "Time to hang up now. And you think about Atlanta. There's lots of good food and not a hipster-with-a-screenplay in sight."

On the tip of my tongue was the makeup smear on Earl's shirt. But I didn't want to get into it, not really. Doris had already yelled at me once, had convinced me that I was being silly, that it could have been anyone who brushed up against Earl. But I've seen Earl bartend many, many times and he's a stand behind the bar, strictly business kind of guy, not a mingle among the crowd, touchy-feely bartender. The obvious answer is that it's Katie's makeup smudge—he's been fighting her off. But still. It's my Lady Macbeth-like obsession. I can't get it out of my mind. Out, out, damn spot!

"Hey. Did you hear me? I'm hanging up."

"Yeah. I heard you."

"What's wrong over there?"

"I saw something on Earl."

"What. Warts or something?"

"Doris."

"Well? What then?"

"Lipstick and makeup smudges on his shirt."

"Okay. That is a little weird. But that's not Earl's style. I know we're both a bit kooky now, being uprooted and all that, but let's not flip out completely. He could have an explanation, right? Maybe there was a bachelorette party or something."

"He was just so worked up the night I noticed it."

"Earl's a big boy. Give him some credit. And don't be such a girl. What are you, going to start digging in his pockets now, looking for clues?"

"When did you get so strong and reasonable all of a sudden?"

"Since you and Earl are the only couple in both recent and distant history that are making a shred of sense. My head will explode if you guys start any nonsense. So cut it out."

"All right," I promise. "I'll cut it out." And I try. I really try.

Bita's a hard-ass. When she decides to do something, you can't talk her out of it, no way, no how. And I can tell she's had enough of Mr. Charlie. She's not a blabber, though. She thinks a thing through before she says anything about it, but by then, she's already made up her mind. I bet she's thinking of divorce, she's thinking of *half,* as spouses get here in California. She snapped when Charlie didn't even bother coming home a few nights ago, thinks that's just being too careless with her feelings and she's right. About a lot. It'd be time to go, if I were her. But I haven't told Bita any of that, not until I get her e-mail. It's a rare quiet day. A Monday. Earl is down at the bar getting ready to open, and I'm at home trying to come up with ways to tutor Ian so that he won't be bored and difficult. I could tell that he liked that TV assignment and he did crazy-good analysis. It was sloppy and full of grammatical errors, but at the end of the day, I loved that paper. Typos or not, Ian is a kid who's willing to open his eyes and look at the world. True, I had to pry open those eyes, but his ideas are all his own. I'm still considering having Ian watch more television for analysis, maybe some films, too. I'm not making books play second fiddle, but you have to draw in your student in any way you can. I sit at the kitchen table with our one electronic luxury, my seven-year-old laptop, and read what Bita has written:

Ron,
You know what I know about Charlie. I think I'm going to leave.

I'm thinking, oh no, *you* don't leave that house. Somebody else named Charlie Asshole should leave the house. I log off and pick up the phone to call her, but hear a knock on the door. When I open it, Bita is standing there, looking overly cheerful. Weird.

"What's this? What are you doing here? I was just going to

call you. And don't say you were in the neighborhood because you are never, ever in this neighborhood." I grab her hand and pull her into the apartment. She's been to our place only once before, when it was supposed to look small because of all the boxes and junk piled everywhere while we were moving in. Now, though, it looked…small. Bita lied, though, and said, "Hey! The place looks great!" She sat down at our little wooden kitchen table and tried to look comfortable.

"Just getting out of the house," she says, still looking around.

"Bita," I say, "for real. What is going on?" It seems like I'm always pulling something out of someone. Ian, Earl, now Bita.

"I kicked him out," announces Bita, sounding surprised at herself.

Yay! "Wow, Bita." I don't know what else to say. "Are you okay?"

"No." She brushes some stray salt off the table, and then wipes her palms on her skirt. I have to be a better housecleaner.

"You'll be okay. You did the only thing you could do."

"I don't want to go back to my house," she says loudly. She stands up and hugs herself. "It feels very big now… I want to go driving in my car and shopping and laughing and talking shit like normal, so can we please do that?"

"Of course we can."

"And can I please have some water or something? It's hot as hell."

"All right. Take it easy. You going to crack a bottle and hold it up to my neck or something?"

"I might, if you don't straighten up." Bita's finally grinning at me. In the end, I get her a can of Diet Coke and we hop in her car and drive all the way from Echo Park to Melrose, where Bita buys a ton of overpriced clothes and I buy nothing because (a) I'm broke and (b), even if I weren't, in spite of the fact that I've dropped a pound or two, I'd *still* be unable to fit into anything Fred Segal would be selling. And I don't ask about what happened, exactly. I save that for later.

Once upon a time, Charlie was a prince and a knight in shining armor and all that bullshit. When we were undergrads at UCLA, and Bita first met him, he was all right. Not *my* type, but still. He was in a fraternity (strike one), the fraternity known for having money, and though Charlie didn't really come from money, he really, really wanted to be in that fraternity (strike two) and so he rushed it and got in for being an overall good guy. That's what they used to say about Charlie. As the years passed, though, Charlie became more and more "carried away" with himself, as Earl says. Once—just once—I actually went to one of those fraternity parties because Bita begged and begged, and I overheard one of Charlie's "brothers" talk about how they'd really like to bang the curry out of Charlie's "Indian chick." When I told Charlie about what I'd heard, as I was getting the hell out of there after a night of feeling slimed, Charlie said he was sure it was just some misunderstanding, and kept drinking from his beer (strike three), even though he was already *amply* hammered. It's not as if I expected Charlie to conjure the guts to give his buddies an ass whipping and a lecture on feminism and race relations. But *damn*. If you ain't part of the solution, then you're part of the problem, as the militants say.

In my mind, from then on, Charlie's shining armor got really, really rusty. But one thing used to be true. He loved Bita, no matter what, and she loved her Charlie—even though in their ten years together there has been a lot of that "I'm sure it was just some misunderstanding" business from Charlie. Totally clueless, he is, about that sort of thing—when he wants to be, anyway.

I truly believe that Charlie's determined to make himself as bland and blendable as possible. He's a much bigger fan of the melting pot, not the salad. Hell, if he could turn back time and show up on Ellis Island, he would have *requested* that they fuck up his family name. I can see it now: "Look, I'm fresh from Ireland and I don't want any trouble. Would you please change my name from Flannigan to Jones or something?" And he's the love of Bita's life.

As for Bita's part in all of this, I'm at a loss. In her case, love wasn't blind. It was lobotomized. In the years since they've been together I've seen signs that would have been clear to anyone. I will agree though, that you never know what goes on between two people. As close as I am to Bita, there are things that I will never know about her and Charlie, because it isn't my business to know. And all these things likely add up to reasons why a smart, beautiful woman like Bita was willing to put up with Charlie's shenanigans. I should have been a better friend. I should have talked more trash about Charlie, but I thought it best to stay out of it—at the time. After all, Bita didn't bat an eye when I got off the plane with Earl, who was wearing what he always wears: his tight jeans, his black T-shirt, a gigantic belt buckle and black biker boots. And a hat. He came off the plane at LAX wearing a huge black Stetson.

What can I say? I was used to all that by then.

Even Doris, Earl's biggest fan, was, at first, not into Earl. He looked odd to us. We were bicoastal city chicks who had little experience with dudes who looked and talked like Earl. And I think that's why Doris and I are close, despite our differences. Talking is the thing. Even if you don't want to hear it, even if it hurts you, makes you sick to your stomach to hear it, talking is good medicine. Nasty going down, but you feel so much better later. True to form, Doris, later, when I was still running from Earl, kept talking to me, telling me I was a dummy for holding his accent and ZZ-Top beard against him. Bita and I, though: we don't always talk the way we should. When she met Earl, I knew she liked him, sure, but we never talked about the complications.

When Bita met Earl, she parked the car (which is a be-yatch at LAX) and met us down at baggage claim, where she gave me a hug, held my face and said that I looked fantastic. When she turned to Earl, he took off his hat and extended his hand. He knew Bita was my only other dear friend in the world besides Doris. He wanted to make a good impression, even though all he did was be himself. "Hey," he said, and when Earl says, "hey," it sounds more like "haaay," all long and drawn out. "I'm pleased to meet you, Miss Bita," he said, grinning and killing me, at least, with those dimples. She went to Earl and gave him a big hug, and when she pulled away, he put his hat back on. He blushed and was happy, I could tell, that she was so warm, what Earl would call "down home." She looked at me and then looked at Earl and said, "I like him."

It was only earlier, when I still lived in Indiana and Bita hadn't met Earl, that she seemed a wee bit dubious, thought I was being like one of those women who traipses off to some island and gets enamored with one of the locals and gets it in her mind to bring him back home with her. After she met him, though, she said it was something about the eyes, the way he really looked at her, the gesture of taking off his hat and calling her Miss Bita, that charmed the hell out of her. And when I worried, at first, about how hard living with Earl in L.A. would be, what the nay-sayers would say and all that insecure bullshit, she said, "Ron, only a man and woman really knows what goes on between them."

"Also, only a man and a man and a woman and a woman knows what goes on between them," I said, out of habit.

"Jesus. What grad school has done to you," Bita admonished. "Have we got everyone down now? All the combinations covered?"

Very true what Bita said about two people being the only ones who know what the deal is. Now, Doris and Bita think Earl and I are perfect together, but for me, there's that Lady Macbeth spot I just can't rub off.

So the moral of my meandering fairy tale and Shakespearean digression is unclear, even to myself, except that I'm dreading tutoring Ian today. Still, he's making me feel like a kid in the schoolyard, and like a kid in the schoolyard, I don't think Ian can grasp the subtleties of the whole goings-on between a man-woman business. He'll just want to give me shit about Earl. We've had a little more than a week off because of his family's vacation, and the last time I was at the "crib," as Ian calls it, I was there with Earl just to pick up my car. Even Maricela seemed glad that I was removing my unsightly junk heap from the premises.

Today, she buzzes me in like always, and I find Ian in the study, farther down the hall from the entertainment room with the gigantic TV. I've brought Toni Morrison's *Jazz,* Salinger's *Catcher in the Rye,* which they're apparently not asking kids to read anymore, and *White Boy Shuffle* by Paul Beatty, because I think that it'll strike some kind of chord with Ian. It's funny and smart-ass, a book on identity. It's contemporary, so Ian won't, I hope, complain about the other two books. When I enter the room, it's eerie. Ian is sitting at the table with pen and paper, all ready to work. *The Bluest Eye* is cracked open and laying face down. Ian looks at me with no expression I can read, and so I sit down across from him at the table.

"Okay, man. What's up?" I say. I remember his satanical grin when I last saw him, when he met Earl, and I'm waiting for him to fuck with me in some way or another.

Ian shakes his head and holds him palms up. "Nothing. Nothing's up."

"All right, then. I brought some books that I think you'll like. There's one classic, *Catcher in the Rye,* another Morrison, *Jazz,* and this guy, Paul Beatty." I hold up the books as I tell Ian about them, and his eyes linger on *White Boy Shuffle*. When I put it down, he slides it over so he can take a look at it. Paul Beatty's black. I see Ian linger over that detail when he spots the author's photo at the back of the book.

"We're reading a lot of books by black people," Ian says after a moment.

I'm not sure what Ian means by that comment, so I say nothing and organize the study guide notes I made up for him. We'll read *Catcher in the Rye* after Morrison, my little gift to Ian. How can he complain about a kid who leaves school because he thinks it sucks?

"I mean, like a *lot* of books," Ian repeats, and crosses his arms so that his hands are tucked under his armpits. He's wearing a brown Run-D.M.C. T-shirt. Cool, I have to admit. I wouldn't mind wearing it myself.

I stop organizing my notes and place my hands carefully on top of the table. Here we go. "Is this troubling to you in some way, Ian? Do you have something you'd like to say to me?"

"Maybe," Ian replies. "But I don't want to break your achy-breaky heart," he says, the corner of his lip turned up. He must have spent the whole week thinking of that one, but I play it off.

"Am I supposed to get what you're talking about?" I speak slowly, patiently. I don't have the energy for any showdowns with Ian today.

"Isn't that what guys like that listen to? That country crap?"

He means Earl, I know, but I want him to say everything he means to say. "Guys like what?"

"That guy the other day. Your *boyfriend?*" Ian says it like he still can't quite believe it.

"Yeah? So? He's my boyfriend. Your point is?"

"My point is that you're all into this black stuff and you're dating *him*."

"Again, your point is?"

Ian props his legs up on his chair and rests his head on his knees. "You're just totally random," he says and picks at a hole in his expensive jeans. "You sound like my *grandmother* most of the time, and then every once in a while you'll get all ghetto on me."

I let the whole ghetto thing pass. Everybody is saying that now: ghetto booty, ghetto fabulous, and not just black folks, either. There's a whole lesson/discussion in that phenomenon, if you ask me. But Bita would just say, *What has grad school done to you?* Still, I get all teacher on him, not ghetto. "So people are complicated, Ian. There are all different kinds of people, right? Every black person you see hasn't wandered off the set of some ridiculous video on heavy MTV rotation. I don't kick it with my bitches and hos. I'm not busting caps in people's asses. And no, contrary to nearly every black film that comes out these days, I don't work in a beauty shop *or* a barbershop. I read books, and I write books, which, I'm sure, you think is a very white thing to do."

Ian shrugs.

"Anything else about me or my life you'd like to critique?"

Ian shakes his head, but then says, "Is he for real, talking like that? Only dudes on TV talk like that. Dudes on TV who talk like that don't end up with chicks like you."

"And what is a chick like me?"

"Insane?" Ian quips. "You know what I mean."

"Well, anyway, according to your paper, what we see on TV isn't real, is it? And what about you, Mr. Hip-Hop? Have you ever thought about how absurd someone in the so-called ghetto would think you are, with your four-million-dollar house and NWA on your iPod?" This is getting mean, but Ian started it. That's what I'll say when the Bernsteins toss me out on my ass once and for all. *Ian started it.* I'm so mature.

"Whatever. Music is universal. It's for everybody. It's about how it makes you feel."

I put my elbow on the table, and rest my chin on my hand. "But people? It's not about how people make each other feel?"

Ian says nothing. He picks up *White Boy Shuffle* and flips the pages over and over. I have an epiphany that weeks and weeks more of this is just not going to work. Maybe Ian, in all of his sixteen-year-old tenacity and stubbornness can do it, but all of a sudden I'm thirty-one and exhausted. I reach out and take the book from Ian, lay it all out on the line. "Look, Ian. If you've seen enough bullshit Hollywood movies, you know that there's always the movie where the black person comes in and shows all the clueless white folks how to change, how to really see things in their lives, and all of that horseshit. Well, this ain't that movie. You need to get a good grade in your lit class because your parents want you to, A—and B, you just should. You should pay attention in class, pay attention to literature, because I promise you, it helps you to make sense of the junk we all have to go through before we live our crazy lives and die. So you and I, let's just stop it. Let's make it easy on ourselves. You and I both know that you are smart enough to pass the class in your sleep—if you actually gave a shit."

Ian picks at his nails, which are metallic blue today, and then says, "In *The Bluest Eye?* Morrison was looking at how hard life is, how life grounded those people down, but that there's, like, I dunno, some hope still. Kind of. Like, you can just get all fucked up and stay that way or climb out of it. And Pecola's like a, like a..." Ian looked around his huge study. "She's like a symbol of how the whole black and white thing and being poor messes with people. And that's how work songs and hip-hop are. Like that."

This is why teaching is so damn cool sometimes. The cobwebs get cleared out and wheels get to turning. "What do you mean when you say, 'Like that'?"

Ian picks up *The Bluest Eye* and flips through the pages. "I guess...I guess I mean that without work songs or hip-hop, people would have really fucking freaked out."

I want to ask Ian what he means by "freaked out." I want him to be more specific about "people." But that would be really, really pushing it. I've had my breakthrough moment today, my moment where Annie Sullivan spells out *W-A-T-E-R* in Helen Keller's hand and Helen Keller finally gets it. Okay, maybe not that dramatic, but damn near. Pretty damn near.

"Good, Ian. Those are very cool connections to make. Let's get started on Salinger."

"Fine," Ian argues. "I'm going to get a Coke. You want one?"

"Diet, please."

Ian heads for the kitchen, but then turns around. "That dude's bike was cool, by the way. Sa-weet."

"Earl. His name is Earl."

"Right," Ian says, rolling his eyes.

That dude. There's a voice in my head, but I try to push it out. *Hey, Ronnie. When Ian talked about Earl, you were embarrassed, just a little bit, weren't you? No, I wasn't. Shut up. Oh yes, you were. But embarrassed for who? Earl or yourself? What? Why would I be embarrassed about myself? Come on, now. I'm talking to you, don't you hear me talking to you? No, I don't hear you. Shut up, shut up, shut up!*

It's rare, but sometimes I catch the Bernsteins on my way out. Mrs. Bernstein arrives as I'm packing up my stuff. They've never been anything but polite and nice to me, desperate for someone to help their kid actually learn something in school. And I get the sense that they understand precisely what a pain in the ass their kid can be, because they give him as much shit as he shovels out to them. In *my* house when I was growing up, if I *ever* talked to my parents the way Ian talked to his parents, I would have had a hand across my face and a foot up my ass, but they call that child abuse now.

Both the Bernsteins are writers for television, but I try not to hold that against them. They work on the same show together, some tug-on-your-heartstrings drama about a poor teenage brother and sister from Kansas, who happen to be perfect-looking in that boring, Hollywood kind of way, who happen to be homophobic, but get dropped on the doorstep of their gay uncle who happens to be loaded and living in Malibu. I watched it once and howled with laughter.

"Veronica," Mrs. Berstein says, putting her briefcase down on the table in the study. "I saw your car outside. We've not seen you in a while." She smiles a genuine smile and takes my hand in a half hold, half shake. She was an older woman in Hollywood who looked great. Everything about her face looked natural and nonfrozen. She was skinny in that rail-thin, vein-y way that women who don't eat sometimes get, but at least she hadn't crossed over to the dark side, the land of plastic faces. She was lanky like Ian and had wild brown hair that surrounded her face in tight curls, and green eyes. Ian's eyes.

"Yes," I say, trying to figure out if her comment's meant to mean something about the fact that Ian and I sometimes knock off early, depending on how much abuse he and I are willing to take from each other. "Ian and I worked late." I smile, already out of small talk for some reason.

"Yeah," Ian argues, "it was a party. The best time of my life."

"Ian has told me some of the things you talk about," Mrs. Bernstein confides, sitting down at the table.

Uh-oh.

"And I don't think he could have a better teacher."

Ian sneers *and* rolls his eyes, hard to do, but the little bastard does it.

Mrs. Bernstein catches Ian's expression and points a finger at him, but looks at me. "Don't take any of his bullshit. He can be a real shit sometimes, but don't take it."

I raise my eyebrows and grin at Ian. I've been given permission to break his tiny balls with no fear of getting fired.

He tries to stare me down, but turns to his mother. "Thanks, Mother *dear*," he says, and saunters out of the study.

Mrs. Bernstein runs her hands through her unruly hair. "My bundle of joy," she quips. "After him, one bundle was enough."

doris

The Romantics: A group of poets writing largely between 1785 and 1830, immortalized by Julian Sands and
Gabriel Byrne in bad mideighties film. Progenitors of the
puffy sleeve poet blouse. The Romantics were lovers of
the individual, believers in spontaneity and freedom, and,
most importantly, an all but disastrous influence on both
people and poets of the early twenty-first century.

What does it mean to be a romantic in the early twenty-first
century, and really, is such a thing even possible? A question I've
been pondering from my less-than-romantic apartment, having
read at least seven horrible poems this week, defended in class
by their authors with the rousing cry of "but it's how I feel,"

coupled with the inevitable chorus of some equally under-read soul saying, "I could really identify with that. I've felt that way, too." No doubt, Byron was able to translate feeling into prose with greater facility, not having been raised on MTV, instant messaging, comic book renditions of *Anna Karenina*, and E! Online. Personally, I can identify with the occasional letter to "Dear Abby" and any Lifetime movie that involves a single woman dating a string of lunatics, but that does not make either of those media art. Try telling that to the bulk of my students, who prize feeling over craft, emotions over practice and control.

Yet in my so-called real life, I confess to being no better at all. After exchanging three e-mails with Maxwell, the technically perfect man, I worry that my so-called feelings seem to be winning sway over my far more clever (and definitely more on-my-side) mind. I worry that while I am perfectly capable of having Maxwell on the brain, I feel a deep emptiness, a bodily sadness when I think of Zach and the zygote. Even macaroni and cheese can no longer fill the void. To complicate matters, Zach did some drunk dialing of his own last night, and the whole useless exchange has left me nothing but confused. Yes, he misses me. Yes, he still cares about me. No, he doesn't want to move to Atlanta. Yes, he understands that I can't go back to Langsdale. We'd gone from love, to animosity, to détente. The reality of relationships: real feelings, real confusion, real pain, and no real resolution—romantic or otherwise.

When Ronnie calls, I am grading the last of my world-lit papers and feeling genuinely blue.

"What's wrong with me?" I ask Ronnie. "Maxwell and I are going out on Friday. He's cuter, better employed and cruelty-free, has never dated a lesbian or a prepubescent, both of which are inexplicably attractive to Zach. Maxwell is geographically desirable, probably even likes his mother and small children and all that Hallmark crap, and still, I just want my smelly hippie ex-boyfriend to chuck his life and come be my man-pet. Is this a new manifestation of intimacy-phobia? And if it is—is it for Zach, or for Maxwell?"

From through the wall I hear Lotto whistle, "Oooh, baby, baby…oooh, baby, baby," a slightly off-tune holdover from the Salt-N-Pepa "Push It" days. I'd bang the wall, but Toni has enough problems already.

"Crazy freaking parrot. This whole starting-a-new-life thing is completely overrated. I'm going to vanish one morning and no one will even notice. Zach will probably bring his kinder-whore to my funeral. He probably won't even wait for me to be declared legally dead before getting on with his life."

"I don't know," Ronnie says. "Things could be a lot worse. You could have some fucked-up demon child like Ian, or your own personal jackass like Charlie, then you'd really be in a mess. You've got a nice date lined up for Friday, and you're making it into a bad thing. And unless Zach has a real change of heart, you've got to see the Atlantans as your future. Not Zach."

The number-one reason I am friends with Ronnie: no romantic delusions, just the facts.

"Do you promise that if I drop off the planet, you'll send the police out looking for me? You have to check in on a semiregular basis, even if you become superfamous from your Burning Spear celebrity."

"Seriously doubt it, black Dottie," she scoffs. "The book's awfully and purposefully schizophrenic, both tongue-in-cheek and knife on wrist."

"So come to Atlanta and meet your editor. Please. I'll meet her, too. I'll wear my afro."

Ronnie laughs. "You need to come out here first. How's tricks otherwise?"

"Well, aside from accidentally almost dating my colleague's boyfriend, and the fact that I now avoid her pathologically when she's one of only two half-friends that I have here, and the fact that since Toni broke up with Tino, she is officially far more interested in her couch than human interaction, and I think I heard her muttering something about 'white people' under her breath so I still haven't figured out what I can talk to whom about, there's the fact that I got a letter from the administration giving me a warning about how I conduct my class, content wise. Otherwise, life is just Georgia peachy. What's that saying? That you're not paranoid if they're really after you?"

"What kind of warning?"

"I had the nerve to say something truthful about the administration in class. I get this letter telling me that… Wait I have it, I'll read it to you."

I unfold the piece of paper, which is short and to the point. "Here goes:

Dear Dr. Weatherall—

It has been brought to our attention that your World Literature class is being used as a forum for political discussion not necessarily related to material covered on the syllabus. We ask, in the interests of accurately representing courses to our students, that you stay focused on the syllabus, which was previously approved. We also request that you allow a follow-up visit from one of the volunteer steering committees to observe, to provide an outside assessment."

"Whhaaaattttt?" Ronnie says. "You're making that up."

I toss the letter back on the coffee table.

"No. And here's the even sicker part. 'Volunteer steering committee' is code for a bunch of mommies and daddies who have enough time on their hands to come in and harass teachers about their teaching. You know, I don't go to people's workplaces and tell them how to do their jobs, *especially* when they've had ten years of professional training."

"I can't even believe that's legal."

"Ronnie, I don't know if it's legal, but at the end of the day, I'm a first-year junior faculty member. I am as disposable as toilet paper. If it's the biggest load of crap in Georgia, I still have to go along with it."

"Until you have tenure."

"That's a long road. Okay, let's change subjects because this just depresses me. Tell me again how I'm supposed to conduct my dating life?"

I switch on the TV and turn the volume low.

"Doris, just go out. Resist the urge to compare Maxwell to Zach. Give the vegan a chance. You might actually like him."

"Yes, Mom," I say. "How's Earl? Is he superproud of you?"

"Best part of Earl is that I think Ian is as confused as I've seen the child. Can't make sense of me with Earl. Didn't come in the appendix to his 'how to be black' handbook."

"But really, can't you translate it into Hollywood terms for him? Tell him that Earl has that Justin Timberlake cross-racial kind of cache. How *is* Earl?" I ask.

"Fine," Ronnie replies. "Fine."

I hear something in that "fine."

"Are you sure?"

"Yes."

Ronnie says yes, and so I leave it at that.

"I miss you. Really, I'm not this negative about Atlanta, not usually, but you have to admit that it's a little weird that I've already accidentally almost aided and abetted an infidelity, come down on the wrong side of the thought police and learned that being alone is being alone no matter where you are. It sucks."

Ronnie pauses. "Well, there are worse things."

I assume she's thinking about Bita, and the compromises people make to keep from being alone.

"I'll call you Saturday morning. And I'll look into buying a ticket. Swear!"

The next day, walking down the hallway to my office, I am greeted by a sight that I can only liken to Mia Farrow waking up mid-drugged-encounter with the Devil in *Rosemary's Baby*. Paige

Prentiss is all but arm-in-arm with none other than Antonius
Block. He's not so much walking as he is sauntering, and I am
not making this up, whispering in her ear. Paige reddens slightly
and appears a bit embarrassed when she notices me looking at
them.

"Well, hello, Dr. Weatherall," Antonius says, nodding in my
direction with Southern-boy grandeur.

"Good morning, Dr. Block."

"Ms. Prentiss has been telling me all about your classroom.
Sounds *very* lively."

I look at Paige, who won't meet my gaze.

"Well, Ms. Prentiss helps keep it lively," I say. She blushes an
even deeper crimson.

"Ms. Prentiss is uniquely gifted." He's daring me to think what
he must know I'm thinking. That he's pervy and using power
and seduction to praise, but ultimately undermine Paige Prentiss's
competence and talent.

"That she is." I unlock my office door. "And I'll see her later
this afternoon."

"And we," he says, directing a bit of that pervy seductiveness
in my direction, "shall drink bourbon again in the very near
future. Dr. Weatherall and I had an afternoon of Byronic inten-
sity."

If he were not senior faculty, I would be going seriously bal-
listic. Instead, I smile politely and gently open then close the
door. Not two minutes later, I hear a soft knock. Asa. Asa
looking like last night was long and rough. Her eyes seem tired,
slightly swollen, with dark circles beneath that not even David

Blaine could make disappear. A half-filled coffee mug dangles precariously from her index and middle fingers. Yet her voice is high and measured when she says hello. It's friendly in that fake way that signals she might rip my lungs out if the conversation goes wrong. And if it weren't just plain awkward on the baseline human level, I must remind myself that this is also a woman who will someday have a say in my bid for tenure. While she is not technically my boss, she can still technically make my future extremely unpleasant. I mentally gear up to choose my words as only a Ph.D. in English can: very, very carefully.

"Sooooo," she says. "I hear that you're the latest on the Dean's hit list."

"Yeah. I got my demerits through the mail. No more political discussions, or I'm going to get a little talking to."

"Get used to it." Asa gestures widely with her mug. "You can never stop thinking about what you say. It all comes back to haunt you."

Thus begins the uncomfortable silence.

I shuffle my papers.

Asa puts the cup to her mouth, but seems to forget to drink.

"Look. This is a little weird for both of us, but I know that you met David before. He told me. That he saw you at a coffee shop, and that you might have gotten the wrong idea about something. He knows that it was probably partially his fault, since he doesn't always remember to make clear that he's in a committed relationship. That came out wrong. We had an open relationship for a while, but it wasn't working, so we're back

s letter, found moments before the bride was to walk
he aisle, allegedly reads: "Maggie Mae, I always loved
ut this isn't what I wanted. And I can't stand Scarlett
." The bride could not be reached for comment.

hear Toni opening and closing my cabinet doors,
oking for a mug. Below the rest of the article was a
etailed list of the expenses, most of which were of
lly nonrefundable variety. Whomever Maggie Mae's
r-Jones was, he had screwed her and her family over
assive-aggressive fashion.

tionary tale for bridezillas everywhere," I comment.
e decided it just wasn't worth the money?"

now," Toni hollers. "It definitely gives one pause.
ere was some Ashley Wilkes out there that no one
out. Maybe she should have read the whole book
lanned the wedding. She could have seen this

es from the kitchen and sits on the sofa with her
op-Tart.

to be even more grossed out?" she asks. "I just
e literary agents have already contacted her for
tory—how she's going to 'carry on' in the face

ng? Tell her to try working for a living to pay off
erself. Now that's a story I'd like to see. Did
now that there were moments that even Scarlett
for a living?"

to nonopen, but then sometimes he blurs that line. Committed seems to be among the many liminal spaces David is interested in exploring."

And that, my friends, is academic for "my relationship sucks and my boyfriend is probably cheating on me, so I'm going to half blame you, even though I am totally feminist in my non-dating incarnation."

"Great. I probably did get a mixed signal, but no real harm done. I don't want things to be strange with us. I value you too much."

This is academic for "please, lady, don't go psycho bitch on me. I don't want your sad, lying excuse for a partner—not for coffee, not for dating, not for nothing. Nor, however, do I want to get in any form of discussion with you that might lead you to believe that I am either looking down on, or patronizing you, so that you can hate me later." This is academic for "please, lady, I've got problems of my own."

"You know the stress of writing your dissertation," she says. "I think that if we can just get through this…"

But it doesn't even feel like she's talking to me now. And this is past academic speak to plain old person speak. Trying to rationalize a relationship you know is going down the tubes, but you can't seem to let go.

"I still have nightmares about the dissertation. No need to explain that to me."

"Uh-huh," she says, and I know exactly what she's going to ask, I just know that I won't have a good answer. "I have one more question. David said that you told him that you were a stewardess. Is that supposed to be some kind of a joke? Or was he trying to get a rise out of me? I really can't tell anymore."

The only thing I have going for me in this conversation is Asa's clear disorientation. If I say yes, then she'll think I lead some kind of *Looking for Mr. Goodbar* double life where I tell unsuspecting men that I am, in no particular order, a stewardess, a hot librarian, the night nurse and a Catholic schoolgirl. If I say no, I'm deeper in the middle of whatever home drama is taking place.

"I was trying to say scholar," I lie, yet again, "but I had a mouth full of oatmeal raisin cookie, and he misheard me, and you know us creative writers. I just thought it would be funny to go with it. I really didn't think I'd ever see him again."

A good lie! Not only does it faux (and might I add, poorly) explain the "misunderstanding," it emphasizes my complete and total lack of interest in Andrew (or David, or whatever he's calling himself these days).

And I know that it's worked because Asa's face changes, almost like someone who's been hypnotized, and she snaps back to reality, taking a swig of her coffee as if it's laced with something stronger. She leaves, but not before popping her head back in.

"Paige Prentiss is the devil. Just don't ever forget that. And don't hesitate to call for backup if you need it."

"Check," I say, and then, because I'm already known as the wacky, girly one, and I can almost get away with it, "We girls have to stick together."

And, although Asa probably finds the word *girl* for *women*

even more loathsome than I do, s in my direction.

"Check," she says.

The next morning, Toni knoc and dejected than she has in th she's changed out of her ter slippers. She hands me the which reads: "GROOM IN WITH THE WIND." The p Maggie Mae Mischner prep portions.

"Nooooooooooo," I say, p

"Just read. I'm out of co Toni asks.

"There's a pot I made a my kitchen. "Knock your

Toni forages for caffei horrible karma delightir that was the Mischner- Maggie Mae smaller le day for jilted bride." P is still a jilted bride, ar however vapid. Altho empathy I feel.

Atlanta's A-list, in
lennium, were i

groom
down
you. B
O'Hard

I could
probably l
long and d
the decided
Rhett Butle
in grand, p
"It's a cau
"You think
"I don't k
Or maybe th
yet knows ab
before she
coming."
Toni emer
coffee and a
"You want
heard that thr
rights to the s
of it."
"You're joki
the wedding h
anyone let her k
O'Hara worked

Toni shakes her head. "You mind?" she asks, lifting the Pop-Tart. "I couldn't resist. You have strawberry frosted."

"I know. Some people talk to their inner child—I just buy mine sugar food products."

Toni takes a bite of the Pop-Tart and closes her eyes in a state of bliss.

"God, I love sugar and hydrogenated fats in the morning. Best thing about being broken up. My ass can go temporarily to hell."

"So you want to talk about this crackhead," I say, pointing at the paper. "Or you want to tell me what happened with Tino?"

Toni leans her head against the back of the sofa and rolls over on her side.

"It was gothic. It's still gothic. I decided the best thing to do would be to rip it off, like a Band-Aid. So we went out to the Atlanta Fish Market because we're always cracking each other up about the big fish in front, and dinner is so good, and I'm sitting there thinking about how much I like him and how much I hate him at the same time for being such a bigot underneath it all, and I..."

She closes her eyes and takes a deep breath.

"This is so nuts," she says. "It's embarrassing even to say. I start crying, not blubbering, but start sniffling there in the middle of the restaurant. Then, I swear, it devolved into some of the highest melodrama ever, where sometime between the valet and my apartment, I was like, *I'm black, and you don't even know who I am, and you won't even date black women, and who do you think you are, and the hell with you,* and door slam, pounding on door,

Lotto in the background yelling, 'nice can, beeatch.' It was five-star shitty."

She puts the coffee mug down and heads back to the kitchen.

"You mind if I have another Pop-Tart?"

"Please. I only ever eat them in pairs."

"I tried going on another date, but I just hate everyone right now. And he's left, like, ten messages, but I don't want to talk about it."

"Did he have anything remotely sensible to say for himself? Not that there's anything that would make it better. I'm just curious."

"Doris. I don't know what's wrong with me. I barely even gave him the chance to speak. I mean, who isn't fucked up about race in this crazy city, in this crazy country? The last black guy I went out with in Atlanta, he was always going on about how 'Asians can't drive' and I know he just liked that I was light skinned, even though I didn't call him out on it. Why do I pick this guy to eviscerate? The one guy I like."

She breaks the Pop-Tart in half and picks at the filling.

"Well, if that's your concern, you can at least let him say his piece. Just for the sake of really knowing."

She finishes hollowing out the Pop-Tart, and wraps the edges in her napkin.

"You're probably right," she says. "I'd better get changed and head to work. Thanks for hearing me out."

"I thank you for the newspaper. And don't hesitate to knock when you need to talk. Let me know what happens."

The best part of being an academic is having the occasional weekday afternoon entirely at your disposal. And since the park trails are now safe, I decide to take that as an opportunity to try jogging. I lace up my New Balance running shoes and stretch as if I can go more than half a mile without wheezing. I think that I make it about seven city blocks before I have to downgrade to power-walk, which thankfully, is embarrassing only to me. More embarrassing only to me, my iPod is blasting some scary old Duran Duran, and I am cheeseball enough to wish that I'd down-loaded the entire album. Strapped to my other hip is my cell phone, which vibrates gently against my leg just as I'm about to pick up the pace. I look at the display. Zach.

"Hold on," I say. "I have to turn this down."

"What? I don't hear anything."

"'Girls on Film.' It's my favorite part about not dating you anymore. I don't have some music snob rolling his eyes every time I break out Journey's *Greatest Hits,* or crank up the badass Duran Duran."

"Then that would be both of our favorite part about not dating anymore."

I seriously think about throwing the cell phone on the ground.

"You know you're interrupting my exercise regimen. Got a good reason?"

"Just saw on the news they found that Altanta bride. I told you that marriage does stupid things to people."

I now have a little unironic Air Supply kicking in on my right ear, and the god of cynicism echoing in my left.

"I'm sorry," I say. "I can't hear you over 'Lost in Love.'"

"Doris," he says, "do yourself a favor and destroy that CD. Do everyone a favor and destroy it."

"Why? Because your shriveled little heart has no room for marriage or Air Supply? I know you think marriage is a bankrupt institution of state control and blah, blah, blah. Do you know how unoriginal that is? From an academic? It's so predictable it's like guessing country music lyrics when you've got the first half of the rhyme. And I think we had this argument about a million times already."

"Fine," he says. "I just wanted to tell you that I'd been thinking about you."

"Were you thinking that you'd like to come down to Atlanta and tell me that in person? Or that you'd changed your mind and wanted to work things out?"

Long pause from the other end.

"Zach," I say, "I have so much on my mind right now. I don't even know if they like how I'm doing my job. I can't do this other thing right now. I just can't."

"I have to go," he says.

"You called me. *I* have to go. *I* have laps to jog."

I click the phone off and, motored by sheer annoyance, make it a mile around the park without stopping.

Much as the story of Maggie Mae Mischner annoys me, on a gross-conspicuous-consumption level, I think it bothers me even more after talking to Zach. I tend to err on the Meg Ryan in *When Harry Met Sally* side vis-à-vis men and marriage. In other words, if a man tells you that he "just doesn't want to get married" or "can't move to be near you right now" it generally means "I sure as hell don't want to marry you" and "living closer to you is my idea of hell." Ronnie disagrees with me on this, as she has no desire to be married, to Earl or anyone else. That, and she accuses me of being overly dramatic. I told her that I think she has a latent Y chromosome somewhere in there affecting her thinking, and she told me to stop reading so many women's magazines. But I can't help it. I loved the idea of Zach and I having some (nicely furnished) half-hippie homestead where we wrote, and had some kooky bratty kid, and he knit booties for the kid, and I mail-ordered inappropriate clothing from Bluefly to wear around our hippie home. When I got my job, however, the dream shifted. It became more practical. Would Zach be willing to take a step out of his comfort zone for me? Could he be the person who followed me to a new town, and let my career take the lead for a year or two?

I was actually the only one of us who ever mentioned marriage.

I believe I said something like, "Why don't we just get hitched and move to Atlanta?" Very, very romantic.

Zach let me know, in no uncertain terms, that he respected my views on marriage almost as much as my taste in music. "It's as though you've never seen an actual marriage," he said back. "Marriage isn't a bandage. It's not going to make us get along better, and it's not going to make me want to move to Atlanta."

To hear him tell it, marriage was nothing if not work. A long extended battle for solidarity punctuated by huge losses, small victories, and an ongoing march forward. He made it sound less like raising the flag at Iwo Jima, and more like trench warfare. And I know that Zach is half-right. When Ronnie talks about Bita and Charlie, I think, "Yes, that is what marriage does to two perfectly happy people. It makes them strangers. It reduces them to sneaking around a house they share." Yet, I still have to think that some people make it work, some people can love and support each other, some people feel joy for making the plunge.

Maggie Mae Mischner is a cautionary tale about romance writ large. I don't really think that Maggie Mae Mischner deserves a book contract because I can't imagine she has anything much different to say than any other woman spoon-fed decades of wedding stories and celebrity nuptials. This is where Zach never understood my point of view—he would have put me in the Mischner camp, but I was advocating something different. Not romance, but love. Not weddings, but a life together. Not white dresses and picket fences, but a person who knows you totally and has your back. And that, on occasion, requires sacrifice, from the man, as well as the woman.

None of the romantic comedies end with the couple loving each other but wanting different things. I don't recall seeing Meg Ryan end a movie with, "I'm sorry, but I've worked too hard to get where I am, and I'm just not ready to give that up yet. Maybe I'm just not sure." Conversely, what is the Tom Hanks of the real-not-romantic world supposed to do? It seems that when couples hit a crossroads, there's this whole check-and-balance system of whose dream matters more. I know that in my real-life scenario, I've been slightly fascist about this—my dream matters more because I stayed in school, because it makes more money, because I stuck with it, because it was harder to come by. But really, is that a fair way to look at things? Is Zach supposed to change who he is because it doesn't suit my lifestyle? Just because I don't understand what he wants, and honestly, I do not, does that necessarily make it wrong?

By the end of most films, the characters have reached a paradise that looks nothing like compromise, and chucked whatever veneer of individuality they had for that most elusive of romantic ideals: love. Their two become one so, so seamlessly.

But normal men and women? For normal men and women, hard choices with unsatisfying ends are what we deal in all the time. And it starts to feel like a lot of half-baked choices that aren't so much choices as forced hands that have you checkerboarding across the country, possibly losing the people that you truly care about. The people who made your life what it once was: special. And am I expected to go on like this for the sake of an academic career, coasting from place to place, from person to person, feeling slightly more detached at each juncture? Or worse yet, getting good at it?"

Given my general level of grouchiness, it's probably best that the end of the week is the actual day of my date with Maxwell, which brings me back to the one place where romance still thrives. The poetry classroom. Paige Prentiss and I are engaging in an uneasy standoff. I try to pretend that I don't know or care that she's possibly sleeping with a man old enough to be her grandfather and also, perhaps, studying my liberal tendencies and reporting me to the university higher-ups in a so-called attempt to protect her right to an apolitical education. She tries to pretend that she never saw me in the hall with Antonius Block that day, let alone reported me to her conservative coalition.

This week we're discussing sonnets, and I don't even pretend that all this nonsense hasn't gotten to me. I could have brought in biting social commentary by Claude McKay or Gwendolyn Brooks. The sonnet transformed into political statement, divorced from its romantic roots and rejuvenated for the twentieth century. That, of course, runs the risk of discussing actual issues, so I settle on Edna St. Vincent Millay, also on occasion political, but politics aside, one of the definitive writers of the anti-love sonnet.

As I'm collating today's packet of material to hand out to the class, a tall, tanorexic woman who looks close to my age, but of an entirely different genus of female, enters the room. She'd probably be pretty were she not wearing a full pound of makeup, salmon-colored skirt-suit in a size four or six, gold dripping from her neck, wrists, and fingers like she bleeds the stuff and started to hemorrhage before class. Her hair is dark and professionally blown out. The supershiny lip gloss is a trampy nude. It's one of those outfits that is supposed to signal money, but mostly signals a complete lack of taste or judgment.

"Ms. Weatherall," she starts.

And then Paige Prentiss corrects her, "It's Dr. Weatherall, Mom. Don't be an idiot."

Paige Prentiss has a mother. An actual uterus from which she was no doubt ripped. A tacky, clinging to her twenties, clearly overchurched (this judging from the hubcap-size cross hanging prominently between her pushed up breasts), probably twice-divorced mom. Ms. Prentiss looks slightly stung, but immediately overcorrects with a hyperwide smile and officious shrug of the shoulders.

"You don't look like you could be more than twenty-five," Ms. Prentiss says. "I do apologize. I spoke to the dean, and your department chair, and they said it would be fine for me to sit in on your class today. Just to write up my own little report, part of the parental front line in the classrooms. Showing concern for the students, my little girl."

Ms. Prentiss removes her suit jacket, revealing a white tank top with red piping, and inexplicably, a red bra that all but glows through the material. Paige, for the first time since I've met her, looks potentially suicidal. She refuses to make eye contact with me or anyone else in the room.

"Jesus, Mother," she finally says, adjusting the bright red bra strap peeking out from Ms. Prentiss's tank top.

"Praise the lord, Paige."

Paige cringes.

"Ms. Prentiss, I assume. No one, but no one, told me that my class would be observed today, although you're welcome to sit in."

"Actually, I'm Ms. Cartwright. I never even was a Ms. Prentiss, but thought that Paige shouldn't suffer for my mistakes."

She's polite, but examining me from head to toe like Rocky sizing up the opponent before stepping into the ring.

Paige tugs at her mother's arm. "Class is starting."

"Now you be quiet, Paige," she says without a hint of authority. And then to me, as though we were suddenly co-conspirators, "I know that you received a letter about my coming some time ago, and I apologize for being so late with my visit. I've been planning a wedding, and it takes so much time. I always try to be sure to say something positive in my write-ups."

Ms. Cartwright puts her arm around her daughter, who pushes it off like someone attempted to drape her in last year's Banana Republic irregulars. Ms. Cartwright looks embarrassed, but then starts doing what she clearly does best. Smiling like a monkey who hit the banana motherload.

I make a mental note that if I survive the afternoon, I deserve not only a ticket to Los Angeles, but the luxury of investigating first-class airfares.

Ms. Cartwright is quiet the first twenty minutes of class, while I give a thumbnail sketch of the sonnet's history, form, rhyme and meter, and the value of using something as antiquated as form in the twenty-first century. I read some Shakespeare that we've all heard before, and we discuss ideas of romantic love, the love object, etc. Ms. Cartwright even sits still while I read the first of Millay's poems, fiddling with her bracelets instead of looking at the page like the rest of the class. Paige is understandably quieter than usual, answering only the most innocuous of questions. Then we move to the first of the "love" sonnets, Millay's "I shall forget you presently, my dear."

I start by asking an obvious question or two.

"How is this different from, say, what we saw going on in Shakespeare's poems? Look at the first line, does it seem tonally similar?"

Two hands go up, but before I can call on either, an unsolicited, "So what exactly is the woman saying?" comes from the mouth of Ms. Cartwright. "Is she saying that love just doesn't last? I think that's a rather hateful thing to have young people reading."

"Mother," Paige hisses. "It's ironic. Millay is using irony."

"Good," I jump in, "in what way is she using irony, Paige?"

Paige gives me a drowning look. She's caught between the good mommy and the bad mommy, and even she has no idea which is which anymore.

"In the difference between feelings, the fact that they are impermanent, and a drive for sex, which is underneath the feelings, and how the two confuse each other."

"Good." I ask, "Can anyone else elaborate on that or clarify what Paige just said?"

Ms. Cartwright's lips tighten, no doubt erasing thousands of dollars of good face work. She crosses her hands in her lap and interrupts.

"I don't know anything about irony," she says. "But I do know that these children should be reading something with a better moral lesson. How are they supposed to take anything of value away from a poem like this?"

Between "children," "morals," and "take-home lessons," I am truly, truly, truly at the end of my deeply frayed rope. This is more like Romper Room than college. I take one deep breath and do my best to respond.

"This is some serious bullshit," Jack Moynihan mutters audibly from the right side of the room. I've been letting Jack audit the class since his born-again liberal arts experience, and for the most part he's been quiet and listened. But even a frat boy has his limits. The obscenity is followed by more murmurs of aquiesence.

"God, Mother," Paige says, the fury in her voice now totally unmitigated. "I told you not to act this way when you came to class. You don't understand. Dr. Weatherall isn't like you, and this isn't like high school. It's poetry. It's about language. But you wouldn't understand that. You don't understand anything. You can't even wear the right *bra,* how can you even talk about Millay!"

Jack Moynihan laughs, and Paige seems to suddenly to remember that he's in the room.

Ms. Cartwright gives Paige a death look. "Of course," she says, with guarded Southern politeness, "you would be able to tell me what to do, since you know everything. Since I gave up my youth to send you to some fancy school, so you can tell me how you know better."

And suddenly, my classroom has become the Jerry Springer show. I wouldn't have believed it possible, except that Paige had to have learned a total lack of boundaries somewhere, and now it was crystal clear where the lessons have been taking place. No wonder she hates women in any kind of authority. I felt sorry for both of them, and dismiss class early before the shame spiral tightens further.

"I'd be happy to answer any questions you have at a later time," I offer to Ms. Cartwright on the way out the door. "But as I didn't know you were coming, I have other appointments this afternoon. Paige has my e-mail if you need to contact me."

If she writes me up as Satan herself and mails it to the actual president of the United States, not just Atlanta State, I am overjoyed to realize that I no longer care.

I confess. In the scant three hours between returning home from my afternoon at school and my date with Maxwell, I probably down a good five ounces of vodka. Alcohol in mod-eration has generally been my post-grad-school motto, and alcohol in moderation on first dates is one of the ten command-ments of dating. As are: thou shalt not boss thy date around, and thou shalt not complain about thine own life, thou shalt not talk about thyself all the time and thou shalt not express too many strong opinions. If there were such a thing as a dating heretic, I was gearing up to be burned at the stake.

When Maxwell knocked on the door looking finer than fine in a cream-colored silk shirt and an only slightly creamier pair of pants, I had already decided that he was driving.

"I'm sorry," I say. "Normally I would be coy and charming, but this has been a day for the record books. Welcome to the longest week of my life. As a result, you are the lucky man who gets to squire me to dinner, your choice of venue, as driver, of course."

Fortunately, I could apply makeup well from beneath the door frame of a collapsing house in a 6.0 earthquake, so I look positively glowing, not to mention smiley from the liquor. For all he knows, I console myself, this is my actual personality.

"Longest week of my liiiiiiife," I sing. "How was yours? Less brutal?"

"I was looking forward to telling you this," he responds. "Since you've been following the papers, I presume. My company just landed Maggie Mae Mischner. It's going to be an-nounced tomorrow. Evidently, she decided that she wanted to return the dress."

"And that calls for legal representation?" I interrupt.

"She feels that the store mislead her not only about the return policy of the dress, but also about the nature of the dress itself. She thinks that all of her problems with her ex-fiancé began when she brought the dress home, and as a point of pride, she wants the money back. The boutique owner, who'd been nothing but understanding up until then, told her that the dress had been altered, and had a 'tawdry past.'"

"Please," I beg. "Please, please, please tell me that 'tawdry past' is a direct quote."

"Indeed it is. Maggie Mae considered the comment a sort of verbal assault, and allegedly pushed the boutique owner, who is alleging that Maggie Mae caused her to spill a pitcher of their complimentary champagne punch on a rack of new dresses. Maggie Mae is pleading 'mental distress' and the owner wants the cost of the dresses covered."

"It's like, if Chekov wrote chick lit," I say. "Only the 'gun in the first act' is a fifteen-thousand-dollar wedding dress. It has to go off by the end. Flaw-less."

Maxwell isn't smiling exactly, in fact, something in Maxwell's demeanor leads me to believe that he *feels sorry* for Maggie Mae Mischner. I'm not sure that I approve.

"Just promise me that *you're* not defending her."

"She's genuinely distressed." He folds his arms like he's about to start some grand closing argument.

"She's an embarrassment to women everywhere."

"But you're not bitter," he says.

"Not in the slightest."

"For the record, ma'am."

eye to eye

"Do NOT ma'am me today, mister."

"For the record, Ms.," he corrects. "She's got some mental problems of her own."

"Please," I say. "Tell her to JOIN THE CLUB. Next excuse."

"Not here," Maxwell remarks. "Over food."

Maxwell and I drive to a hole-in-the-wall vegetarian joint near Virginia Highland, run by vegan Indians and populated largely by a crowd that I recognize well from my days at Langsdale: socially-conscious white folks in hempware and smelly thrift-store jeans. Silent Bollywood films play on the two television sets at either end if the restaurant, and Maxwell and I are beyond overdressed. I like that we are sitting at some ratty diner-style tables, ordering delicious ginger carrot juice and debating the future of a one-time bride to be.

"If you do meet Maggie Mae Mischner," I warn, "tell her that I deeply resent her representing women who want to get married, in a crackheaded crazy-bitch fashion. Tell her it makes us all look like crazy bitches."

And I was violating dating commandment number six left and right: thou shalt not curse like a sailor.

"You're gonna eat with that mouth?" Maxwell asks.

And at that exact moment, our food arrives. Macaroni and cheese made with neither milk nor cheese, a concoction called kalebone, which was some form of grain shaped to look like a rack of ribs, along with some greens cooked without pork of any form. It *looked* delicious, but from the moment that first piece of kalebone entered my mouth, I knew we were in trouble.

"You like?" Maxwell asks, excited. "It's amazing what you can do without meat."

All I could think, as I attempted politely to masticate the eco-grease in my mouth, was that I should have ordered all vegetables. Grains pretending to be meat is like Ian pretending to be black, or David pretending to be Andrew, or Asa pretending to be normal or me pretending not to be all but gagging on this overfried piece of greasy bulgur, the consistency of cartilage, doused past recovery in barbeque sauce. There is no way I can get through more than three bites. And the next course I attempt, macaroni and "cheese"? It's like eating that food I got when I was super little to feed to Baby Alive. The whole experience reminds me of when I finally talked my parents into buying me freeze-dried ice cream at the National Air and Space museum, which in my seven-year-old brain was going to taste like ice cream, but actually tasted like sugared fiberglass. All I can think in the face of my rack of kalebone is that somewhere, across town, at the OK Café, there are diners eating actual macaroni and cheese that came from cows and not from whatever bastardized plant they'd pulverized into grainy yellow sauce.

"I love it," I lie.

Maxwell seems pleased, but I wish I was having dinner here with Ronnie, who would have elevated the whole meal past disgusting and into heresy. It was no fun eating ass-y food with someone who clearly had so deprived himself of delicious meat products over such a long period of time, that he found said

ass-y food delicious. Then I notice the cook peering out at me,
clearly not fooled by my faux-pleasure. Clearly annoyed. Eating
with Maxwell was definitely better than eating alone, but I
made a mental note that the moment the evening was over, I
was buying my ticket out to L.A. With each bite of kalebone I
promised myself a rack of real BBQ, cooked specially by Earl,
followed with another side of meat and Ronnie's own macaroni
and cheese.

"You seriously eat this on a regular basis?" I ask him.

"How do you *think* I keep this body?"

Even my poorly socialized, just-back-in-the-wild dating self
can smell the promise of nudity thick in the air. Hurrah! Which
leads me, unfortunately, to violate *many* other dating command-
ments. Ronnie would be hitting me over the head, as she
believes in no more than a single kiss on the first date. Eroto-
mania later, but just a teaser on date one. Exhaustion, booze,
and the thought of Maxwell's earth-friendly body all create one
big rationalization in my head about why it's okay to go home
with him. But once we reach his house, however, the dream dies
a bit. I was expecting übermetrosexual digs. Instead, he has a
large denim sectional sofa plopped across the room from the
largest television set I have ever seen in home use. The floors
are covered in dingy white wall-to-wall carpeting, and a lone
picture of a tiger in a jungle is mounted slightly crooked over
the sofa.

"Sorry," Maxwell says. "I just moved out from my ex's last
month. She took most of the furniture."

It's one of those moments where that little inner voice chants, RED FLAG RED FLAG RED FLAG RED FLAG RUN DORIS RUN RUN.

But no, just like the girl who heads up the stairs instead of out the door in the face of danger, I say, "That must be hard. I broke up with my ex not too long ago. Although he didn't have any furniture, unless you count some ten-year-old futon worn down to a frayed nub. Which I didn't."

Maxwell tries to laugh, but the chortlelike grunt that comes from his mouth is deeply and decidedly bitter. And just then, in ever-dying embers of my Atlanta fantasy dating world, with more perfect than perfect Maxwell sitting across from me, I miss Zach.

"Let's not talk exes," he says, the bitterness now gone from his voice. "I don't want to focus on anything but you."

A line! A dirty, well-delivered line! God, how I've missed those.

"Okay, but nothing too crazy. After all, we've only just met."

And then, in spite of exes and kalebone, and the unromantic reality of life in the city, I let Maxwell help me break at least two other dating rules, and one that I hadn't even thought of.

ronnie

Kalebone. I don't understand. Where Earl comes from, kale is a green, and where I come from, bone is not rubbery. So, Doris's work may be cut out for her with this Maxwell dude. First of all, I never heard of no brother (who wasn't Muslim) who preferred fake ribs to actual ribs from an animal that doesn't deserve to die, blah, blah, blah and all that vegan stuff. I know I must sound like Ian, talking about what "black people do," but what can I say? Grad school didn't completely indoctrinate me with its hippie politics.

Maxwell, if he were normal, meat wise, would be a catch of sorts. But it's funny, if there's one thing I've learned with going back and forth on trying things out with Earl is that you can't fit round holes into square pegs. And even if it seems to be a fit, like for example, Maxwell and I presumably going together better because we're both black, educated, single, and share the same politcs, etc., etc., those are all superficial things, on one level. La Varian Laborteux back in grad school was the exact same package as me and he was a square peg to my round hole, and I'm not trying to be sexual here, because he was actually *way* small-minded when it came to basic rules about how you should treat women—with generosity, respect and kindness, as you would anyone else. And by that I mean telling the woman you're dating (me) that you're *married* to someone else (your, uh, WIFE!) The black man plus black woman equation in that particular instance equaled not so hot together.

I've been thinking a lot about this lately since Doris will inevitably keep trying out Maxwell even though she still loves Zach. After that, one of two things will happen. She'll either get over Zach and fall madly in love with Maxwell, or she will discover that she and good old Maxwell aren't quite the right fit, which will have nothing to do with race. Although that will be the first thing that people will suspect, and sometimes it can be. But it will have everything to do with his man-made material shoes. And kalebone.

I have always thought about this stuff since I, like Doris, am a Rainbow Coalition kind of gal. I've dated representatives from all over the globe. Earl, though, he's always been a different proposition, admittedly because of my own prejudices, mostly because of his cultural markings, as we used to say in grad school. There's the white guy who's dating a black woman, and then there's the *white* guy who's dating a *black* woman. Earl and I, we're in the second category, in the "Oh, like those two people would really go out with each other. Puhleeze. That's fiction, right?"

Uh, no. Fortunately.

I don't mean to bring the man-woman relationship chatter to a screeching halt to talk about identity politics. I only mean to say that, if I'm going to be generous and kind and respectful and all live and let live to my fellow humans, I should give Katie, the All-American Beach Blonde Pain In the Ass some slack for trying to wedge herself in front of my Badass Sexy Biker Man. I should. And I should be more generous and kind (I'll get back to you about respectful) to Ian, The Devil's Spawn, whenever he's mouthing off about my "cowboy biker dude." Poor kid can't see his own blind spots about *his* cultural markings, though I'd bet money that he's about to find out.

My nephew's one of these kids trying to make it in hip-hop. He's got a group and all that, and they write their own lyrics and he's pretty good at freestyling or spiting or flowing, as the kids say. I'm not as up-to-date on the lingo as I could be, because I'm officially too old school or bookworm-y to keep up. But I do know that the kid, my nephew, is good, actually. Just as a listener of hip-hop I can tell shit from Shineola and my nephew Blake has the goods. So I have this idea that Blake and Ian should meet up somehow. Ian's got drive and ambition (and a fuckload of dough) *and* connections. Blake has the talent (and a fuckload of attitude) and *no* connections, so who knows?

I've driven out to Riverside so I can broach the subject with Blake who, like Ian, is too cool for school. Literally. He's dropped out and is working temp jobs so he can do the music thing at night, which my brother, Joe, can't stand. "That boy needs discipline, is what he needs! Needs someone to put a foot up his ass so he'll quit all this hip-hop bullshit!" He actually kicked Blake out of the house until my sister-in-law, Tina, said she'd kick Joe out if he didn't let her baby back in the house. Joe cussed and carried on for an hour until he agreed. He's like Mike Brady, my brother. A genuine Ward Cleaver. It's a Wednesday, on of my days off from Ian, and even though I've not told Ian my grand idea, I want to invite myself (and Ian) to Blake's next gig. It's a showcase somewhere out in Corona, California. Not very Hollywood, but according to my nephew, showcases like this are where "all the good shit be happening."

Blake has just made it home and is poking his head in the fridge, looking for something to eat, which, my brother always says, "He should damn well pay for since he's got a job." My brother and sister-in-law are in the living room watching a fight on pay-per-view while I try my best to play Cool Aunt. You know, be casual and nonchalant and bored, *like I care*. Blake finally pulls his head out of the fridge and when he stands up tall, he's a good six-two to my five-seven. Hard to believe, but years ago I used to change this kid's diapers.

"Hey," I say, when he turns around with a plate full of leftover meat loaf. "You don't give your aunt a hug?"

He smiles a lazy smile. He's happy to see me, but, you know, gotta play it cool. Classic teen and newly post-teen maneuver. "What up, Auntie Ronnie," he says. He puts his plate down on the counter and bends down to give me a hug. "What you doing here?"

I sit down on one of the bar stools and watch him cut up his meat loaf to microwave it. "I thought I mentioned it? That showcase you told me about? I wanted to talk to you about it?"

"For real?" He squints at me. "You never have asked me to go to a show."

"I know." I'm a little too fast and apologetic. "But that's just because I've been gone so long, in Indian-ner. If I were here, I would have gone."

He nods, grabs his plate and puts it in the microwave. I continue my spiel over the loud hum. "You know how much I like your music, right?"

"Yeah, and what about that last demo thing we did, were you feeling that?"

"Yeah." I nod gravely. "Felt it *strongly.*"

The microwave dings. "Corny, Auntie Ron," he says, digging into his meat loaf.

"Soooo. Do you mind? If I come, I mean."

"*Hell,* no," he says. "I don't mind. That'd be cool. You could see me do my thang." He takes the last bite of his meat loaf.

"There was, like, a pound of meat loaf on that plate. When did you eat all that?"

He shrugs. "I'ma go back in the fridge to see what *else* is in there."

"Better leave a twenty-dollar bill on the counter, boy." My brother is suddenly behind me and slaps me on the shoulder. He's almost as tall as his son and is sporting a black track suit. He runs a hand over his cleanly shaved head. "See what happens when you don't finish high school and get a crap job? You end up being a broke-ass, mooching off your parents." Or you go to grad school and become a broke-ass...

Blake rolls his eyes. "I ain't mooching. One of these days when I'm sipping Cristal and living in my mansion, you gonna be asking me for a loan." Blake winks at my brother. "And I might even give you a couple bucks if you're cool to me now."

"I haven't killed you or kicked your ass out on the street," Joe reminds him. "I'm cool to you now. Trust me."

"Anyway." I clasp my hands together and put them on the countertop. "I'm here on business. You're messing up Blake's and my negotiations."

"Please," Joe says. "I'm going back to watch the fight. You owe me twenty," he says, pointing at his son with a long, no-bullshit finger. "I'm not playing with you." And then he leaves the kitchen.

This warm show of family support reminds me of Ian and how easy he has it, with tutors, any clothes and the latest technological crap his black heart desires. I couldn't even imagine the Bernsteins threatening to kick Ian to the curb, let alone actually doing it, like my brother did. I had an insane image of dragging Ian here so that my brother could give him a little physical therapy and a gentle talking to, then...Ian dissolving into a pool of tears and quickly coming up with something way more creative than *whatever* whenever Joe asked him a question. Alas, such a thing would never be so. I'd have to settle for Ian and Blake meeting, if Blake is okay with it.

"I want to bring someone," I say. "This kid I tutor. He knows a lot about music, about hip-hop, and he'd really dig your show."

Blake leans into the counter and raises an eyebrow. "A kid? That you tutor?"

"He's all right." A bit of a lie, but so what?

"What are you, bringing him just to be cool to him, or something?" Blake crosses his arms. He's getting suspicious.

"Trust me. Really. It'll be really cool if he can come. His parents are *loaded* and he has access to folks you could maybe hook up with."

"For real?"

I nod, waiting for the green light.

"Sure. Whatever," Blake says, running his hands over his cornrows. "Whatever whatever."

Blake's show is two weeks from now, and Doris is going to be in L.A. just in time for it. "Let's scam on the kids," she said. "I can go zygote as good as the next guy."

"Or Ian. You can scam on Ian," I'd said over the phone while I watched Earl make fried chicken. Damn, that man can cook. And *real* food like fried chicken and catfish and collard greens and meat loaf, as a matter of fact. He can cook a mean meat loaf, not a kalebone in sight.

"Scam on him? I'm going to kick his little pip-squeak ass."

"Get in line. First Earl, and then you. But I'm warming up to him lately. He secretly likes subversive, corny, obsolete stuff like original thought and ideas. And books. I think he was just bored in school before."

"He's faking," Doris said, "being interested, I mean. Very sneaky and Internet date-y of him. You're getting sooooft. Sucker."

"I'm not." Though I do have a guarded hopefulness. I'm starting to like Ian. Craziness, I know, but I think he's changing a teeny bit, or at least letting his guard down so that I can see that he isn't *all* satanic, just partially so.

"Just because your wolf put on sheep's clothing, expensive, designer sheep's clothing from Lucky Brand or Abercrombie or wherever the chillens shop these days, doesn't mean that he's changed. You sound like one of the broads that's always saying that 'He's going to change, I know it. He's sorry he smacked me.'"

"Let's not get crazy," I said, as Earl delicately placed the final juicy piece of fried chicken on a plate. "A shred of credit, please."

"You watch," Doris said. "Just you watch. But in the meantime, you better be planning truckloads of fun for me in Hellay. I *need* a really good time."

"We'll see what we can do, won't we, Earl?" I winked at him.

"Tell Doris I'ma take her to the Baseline for some proper drinks so she can stir up some trouble like the good old days at the Saloon back home." He wiped his hand on a towel and shook his head. "Trouble's headed our way," he said and grinned at me.

Trouble, I'm looking forward to, actually. The glamorous life that I'd imagined in L.A., after shaking off the dust of Langsdale, Indiana, had turned into a very weird job tutoring some kid and getting by on every form of chicken and egg I could conjure. I had an advanced degree with no advancement. I was just hanging out, really. Floating on a life raft, scared of getting knocked off. *Not* what I imagined as I marched to "Pomp and Circumstance", trying to keep that ugly mortar board thing pinned to my head.

I think of Doris calling me soft now that I'm sitting outside, trying to connect with Ian. We've just sat down at the table. Each time I come, I never know what I'm going to get. I look at Ian, sixteen years old and not a care in the world, only the fear that something will suck unless it goes exactly the way he wants it. I try not to have the attitude of the kid in the sandbox who wants to snatch the other kid's toys from him. A lesson I thought I learned was never to envy what other people had because you never know what else is in those seemingly comfortable shoes you're dying to walk in. Death and all kinds of equally fucked up stuff could be there. Plus, I'm being generous and all that now, giving Ian more credit and hopefully doing something good for my nephew.

Even though Ian is wearing sunglasses that he refused to take off for fear he'll actually have to look at me, the Venus and *David* statues are not looking as sorry for me as they did earlier in the game.

"You look like you got this," *David* seems to be saying.

"Thank God you're not letting him run all over you like you used to," Venus chimes in.

I don't know. Ian seems to be in a mood. The sky's a clear blue, there's a slight breeze. The pool water is making little ripples and Ian keeps staring off in the distance, at the water, at the sky, at anything but me. It's not a pissy mood, but just an unusually contemplative mood for Ian.

He's just given me a paper he wrote discussing *White Boy Shuffle* and *Catcher in the Rye,* books I'd asked him to compare and contrast. He'd also been asked to watch some hip-hop videos and analyze them. The books are wildly different, but both have narrators that don't quite fit into the cultural expectations others have of them. Both narrators are smart-ass, smarty-pants, too, which I thought Ian would appreciate. I skim the opening paragraph, which seems pretty strong. "This looks good, Ian. You liked them?"

"Holden was cool. All that stuff about phonies and being stuck having to be with all those people he couldn't stand." Ian slumped in his Frank Lloyd Wright patio chair. "All those rich guys he hated, even though he had serious bank, too."

"What about Beatty?"

Ian shrugs. "I don't know...a lot of it was weird. A lot of that stuff I didn't get. Like, the title? *White Boy Shuffle?* What's that?"

I know that Ian is going to get annoyed, but I can't help but go into teacher mode. "Even after reading it, you don't quite see how the title fits?" He considers my question and pulls on his hair, which used to be blue-black, but now has some sort of red streaks in it. I knew that when I assigned the book that it wasn't exactly teenager-reading material because there are all kinds of historical winks and references he likely hadn't known, but still, I thought it a worthwhile book. This skateboarding black kid ends up leaving the beach for the inner city and keeps trying to avoid or fit into whatever it is that people, white and black, expect him to be. Sharp satire and all that.

"I'll have to think about that title some more," he says, "but one thing that bugged me was this one scene where he's making fun of rap videos." Suddenly he sits up, straight in his chair. "I think those videos are sick."

"You mean sick in the good way, right?"

Ian bit off a hangnail and spit it out. "Yeah, Grandma. Sick

like cool, sick like, those dudes are saying 'fuck you' to people
telling them they have to act like white people want them to."

Hmm. But his paper totally ripped apart *Laguna Beach,* so he
can't just be swallowing all of that clichéd imagery. Guns. Money.
Women hanging on dudes like jewelry. Still, Ian had a point. That
was how it was, at first, back in the day when NWA first came
out with "Fuck the Police" and everyone was all, "That's crazy,
they can't say that about the police," and then the police were all,
"Hold that thought for a minute while we beat Rodney King's ass,"
and then at least some folks were all, "Oh, okay, I can kind of see
their point." But now? The whole turning society on its head,
bitch, ho, AK-47, drive-by-shooting thing is a wee bit played out,
in my opinion. Except now, the only hip-hop guys who seem to
be making major "bank," as Ian says, are the ones who still glorify
that shit. And the ones who can't make serious money are the
more intelligent artists without a jiggling booty in sight.

"Ian." I pick up *White Boy Shuffle.* "That scene is satire, and so
it's an exaggeration of a true thing and since you watch MTV
every single day of your life—you don't have to tell me—but
just think about it. What do you see all the time? You don't even
have to say anything. Just think it." I flipped through the pages.
"That's all Beatty is saying. Also, if you can only do the one thing
that makes money, that all the people in charge demand of you,
isn't that a form of acting the way people want you to?"

"Ugh," Ian says. He stands up and stretches. "I need a sandwich
or something. Don't you ever quit with that preachy shit? Next
week you're going to be all, "Hi, Ian, I just discovered the secret
to world peace."

"Maybe I will." I sneer at him. "And then you'll be all, 'Please tell me, I want some world peace, man, come on.' And I'll be all, 'Too damn bad. You were mean to me last week.'"

"You are one crazy chick. Totally tweaked."

"Whatever that means."

Ian sighs dramatically. "You hungry? Want a sandwich or something?"

A sandwich? With actual meat that's not poultry? Fancy cheese and gourmet mustard? On real bread that's crunchy on the outside and soft and tender in the middle? Thank you, lawd!

I shrug. "Sure. Whatever."

Later that day, while we ate our sandwiches, I casually asked Ian if he wanted to go to my nephew's show with me. I waited until he took a big bite of his sandwich so he'd have to keep his ginormous mouth shut. He stopped chewing and held his half-chewed sandwich in his mouth as if he were barfing it up. I smiled amiably and chewed my roast beef as if I had just mentioned the most normal thing in the world. It went like this:

"A *show*? With *you*? Why are you fucking with me?"

"I'm not fucking with you. I'm serious."

"*Why?*"

"Because he's good, and you might like him, and it's a way for you to see some new raw talent. You're connected right?"

And then Ian said he'd rather spend all day with his parents at the synagogue than hang out with me. "Fun like cleaning toilets," is how he described hanging out with me. I *almost* said, "How in the hell would you know *anything* about cleaning toilets," but I let it slide. Long story short, I *happened* to have my nephew's CD and Ian liked it, although he pretended to think it was just okay. So he's going. I asked the Bernsteins and everything. "Totally random," as Ian would say.

Today, Doris is finally arriving after weeks of talking about all the fun, nonteaching, nonacademic stuff we're supposed to do while she's visiting L.A. All the cheap, between-us-we-can-scare-up-about-a hundred-and-fifty-dollars things to do. Bita is driving because my car is still acting up, and Charlie is working late. And we all know what that means. So it's going to be a girl's night out—if we can find Doris. This is the third time we've circled LAX and I've tried her on Bita's cell twice. No answer. Bita has been cussing out the various people who have almost run into her or vice versa as we weave in and out of traffic.

I've been gripping the handle above the window and trying not to scream every time I think Bita and I both are going to see Jesus and I occasionally ask questions that I think will get Bita talking about her situation with Charlie. Since Charlie has moved out, I've not heard much. As her best friend, I should be the first to know, and I suppose I will be—when Bita feels like letting me in on things. I try one more time, though. As we approach Doris's airline, I ask Bita, "So, B., do you think you and Charlie are going to do the counseling thing, or is he gone for good?"

Bita leans into her steering wheel and peers off into the distance. "Is that her? Is that Doris?"

Curbside, I see Doris wearing a long, drape-y dress the color of the rainbow, lots of yellow, red and orange. And a big, chunky red necklace that looks like something Betty Rubble from the *Flintstones* would wear. I lean out the window and wave like a crazy person. "Mrs. Roper! Welcome to L.A."

Doris gives me a big smile and the middle finger as we stop in front of her. I step out of the car quickly enough so that I don't get hollered at by the airport security fascists and give her a big hug. We throw her luggage in the backseat and then she climbs in.

"Bita! Thank you sooooo much for picking me up. I was trying to get you guys but my shit phone wasn't getting reception." Doris pauses long enough to take in the car. "And look at this. Wow."

I twist my body around so that I can see Doris. "I know."

"What is this car, exactly?"

"It's a Mercedes SUV." I raise my eyebrows at Doris. *Get a load of this thing.*

"I know," Bita says. "I don't want to hear it from you two, the cultural police."

"I think this car is great," Doris enthuses. "Would that I could afford something like this. Sorta like this…maybe a little bit smaller, something that uses less gas."

I flip down my visor to block out the sun—and to look at Doris and give her the SHUT IT signal with my eyes. "I ain't saying nothing, Bita."

Bita rolls her eyes. "Rare." We're finally out of airport traffic and merging on the 405. "Besides," Bita says, running her fingers through her thick, black hair, "I'm thinking of trading it in for something less fancy. You know, simplifying my life and all that."

I want her to keep going because I know this must have

everything to do with the Charlie Situation, but Bita changes the subject, as usual.

"Tonight, though, I don't want to simplify. Let's go someplace to eat that's nice, someplace fancy."

Doris is quiet in the backseat because she can't say what I can most definitely say. "Bita, Doris and I are broke asses. That's Latin for teachers. Wherever you're thinking of taking us, we cain't afford it."

"No worries. It's on me. My treat."

"No. . . ." Doris and I both say. Weakly.

"Don't even try it. Unless you're going to jump out onto the freeway and die, I'm in charge and we're driving to wherever the hell I want to."

"Wow," Doris says. "You're hard core."

"We're going to Morton's," Bita announces. "We're eating big, juicy steaks and drinking a couple bottles of wine."

Steak. Yay!

"Yay!" shouts Doris. "I loooove this car. I loooove fancy restaurants. I looooove cow. The cultural police are keeping their big mouths shut."

"Bullshit," Bita says, laughing. "It's in you guys' *blood*."

As Doris and I get ready to go to the show out in Corona, I have to shake my head. Earl had said trouble was coming to town, and I certainly feel something like trouble percolating. I try not to be so fatalistic about things. And how bad can a little show be, really?

I'm dressed already, as dressed as I'm going to be with square-toed Frye boots and a turquoise flowered shirt with pearl snap buttons. I pull on my jean skirt, which keeps twisting to the side, for some reason. When Doris comes out of the bathroom we both freeze and stare at each other.

"What are those *shoes?*" I say.

"*Me?* Is Earl dressing you? You're going to a hip-hop show in *that?*"

True, my ensemble is a little on the cowboy side, but I *like* it. I'm going to be comfortable in it, unlike Doris, who is wearing metallic green platforms with pink glitter lightening bolts on the side. And a star, a giant pink glitter star on the toe of each shoe. "You're blinding me with those things. You're like Bootsy Collins exploded into Ziggy Stardust."

Doris clomps toward me with a big grin on her face. "We'll just see who the hip-hop zygotes go for. Me, who actually has something cool on and, dare I say, very, very unique, or you, in your hayride, hoe-down outfit. I'm scared to think about what you'd be wearing if we stayed in Langsdale, Indiana, a day longer."

I look down at my skirt and boots, and I consider changing. "Yeah, well, I'm scared to think of a lot of things if I'd stayed in Langsdale a day longer."

"Amen, sister." Doris checks her makeup in a compact. "The lighting in this kitchen is god-awful. Or I look like somebody's mom."

"Bad lighting," I say. "Definitely." I grab my keys. "Let's hit it."

"What, we're not waiting for Earl?"

"No." I feel a bit guilty. To my surprise, Earl had been excited about the show, had wanted to come, but I talked him out of it.

"Oh, Earl," I'd said. "It's not a big deal. It's just a small thing."

"I don't care," he said. He had laid two T-shirts out on the bed. "Which one looks better to you? I like the black one."

"You always wear black." I pointed to the grey one. "It doesn't matter, though. Really. There's no need for you to go." I stood in front of our bedroom mirror and checked my lipstick. I could see Earl's image in the mirror and he stared back at my eyes until I looked away.

"You sounding like you don't want me to go. I told you I don't need to go out with Jake. We go out all the time. It'd be fun to hang out with you and Doris. Scare that boy some."

I didn't answer, because I didn't know what to say. My silence answered his question, and he put on his grey T-shirt and left while Doris was in the bathroom getting ready.

So now, I decided to joke about it to Doris. Something was happening between Earl and I, but I didn't know what. "You're kidding, right? It's bad enough that you and I are going to this thing—with Ian. Adding Earl would tip the situation over to surreal. We have you, who has time traveled from the seventies, who seems to be going through a glam rock phase, Ian, who seems to not even *like* me, but who I nevertheless feel very responsible for, and Earl, who, I swear, thought I was talking about a children's book about bunnies when I first said the phrase hip-hop. Besides, he's got something going on tonight. He bartends late and then he's off to some weird party with Jake. I wish I could see that, Earl at a Hollywood party."

"Speaking of surreal," Doris says. "I'm ready. I can't wait to meet Mr. Sixteen-Year-Old Badass. Get my hands on that little piss ant."

I hear tell that there is always a moment when a person recognizes that they're no longer a child, that they're no longer able to get by on the charm of youth. It's taken me a while, this epiphany. Not even when I was teaching undergrads, who first heard Madonna on their Fisher Price cassette players, while I first heard her my last year of high school, did I feel that I was no longer a child. You're in your teens, and then you're twentysomething, and then suddenly you're thirtysomething, but you still feel like you're a kid trying to figure stuff out. But then it hits you, rudely and squarely on the mouth.

When Doris and I pull up in a Honda that is so not bling-bling, get out of the car to see what in the hell we've gotten ourselves into, we see it's a parking lot full of people. All young, all black.

"Whoa," Doris says, "one of these things is not like the other."

"What'd you expect?" I lock the car and stand by the driver's door while Doris makes her way to me. "This is a hip-hop showcase. Besides, black Doris would be down, would blend."

"Yeah, but white Doris was thinking hip-hop in a suburban, white boy, we wish we could be from the streets, too, kind of hip-hop. Like Ian. Damn, I got a rock in my shoe."

We stand by the car like outcasts who are afraid to walk into the big high school dance. Almost all the guys look like some version of my nephew, Blake. Sagging jeans and a white T-shirt. Cornrows. And all the girls had *their girls* out. Most people ignore us but some stare at us like the freaks we are when they pass by. I keep looking for Blake and Ian.

Doris hands me a foil package full of little cubes of gum. "We look insane," she says. She surveys my outfit again. "The hip-hop hick, you look like."

"Shut up, Ziggy Stardust." I pop out two pieces of gum and chew frantically.

"Well, we can't stand here like idiots all day." She sighs. "Let's at least walk around like idiots."

"Blake!" I see my nephew walking toward us in his usual lazy swagger. Tonight he's not wearing cornrows, but is sporting a medium-size afro with an afro pick stuck on the top of it. "Your dad would give you so much stuff if he saw you with that hair," I tease when he reaches us. "'Cut your damn hair boy!'" He pats his hair on the sides and top, clearly proud of it. "I know," he says, grinning.

"This is Doris. Doris, my nephew, Blake."

"Hey, Doris," Blake says, giving her a hug.

"Did you just say 'stuff' instead of 'shit'?" Doris asks. "Puhleeze."

Blake laughs. "Aunt Ronnie think I don't know she cusses."

"Yeah, well, somebody has to be the grown-up, the good example and all that. Space Girl doesn't count." I turn around, full circle checking all the cars in the lot. "I don't see Ian, the kid I told you about."

"Yeah," Doris comments, shifting her weight on her tall shoes. "I'm dying to meet the little angel. Your aunt has been a true grown-up, since she hasn't knocked this kid on his ass for giving her so much shit."

I give Doris the shut-up eyes. I don't want Blake to know about Ian's and my rocky relationship because I know that if he knows, he won't be nice to him. I just want everybody to play nice this evening.

"Damn, that's a nice car," Blake says, "that must be somebody with real bank coming to check out the show, give a brother a contract." And the BMW I know to be Ian's pulls into the parking lot.

"That's Ian." My nephew raises his eyebrows and I shrug. "I told you he was loaded." Ian parks off in the distance and we wait a while for him, looking for his head to pop up between the cars. It never does. "Let's go over there. I don't know what's taking him so long."

"Great, more walking in these stilts." Doris takes off her shoe and puts it back on, as if that will help.

"I'm not a nice enough person *not* to say I told you so." I let her lean on me while she adjusts her foot. Blake walks a bit ahead of us, no doubt going to check out Ian's ride. He reaches Ian's car before we do. When we get there, he's knocking on the door, but Ian doesn't open it until he sees me. He looks as though he's seeing his best friend in the world and it actually makes me feel sorry for him.

He gets out of the car and locks it with a series of beeps and clicks that tells everyone within earshot that it's locked and alarmed up the ass, impossible to steal.

"What were you doing, sitting in the car? This is my nephew Blake," I say, before he has time to answer.

"Oh. Hey, man," Ian says, holding his hand out. Blake hesitates before he shakes it.

"I was knocking on your door, man." Blake gives Ian a hard stare.

"I know." Ian looks at me and then looks down at his torn black Converse.

"Ian, this is Doris. She's visiting from Atlanta."

"Hey." He gives Doris a half-hearted tilt of his chin and shoves his hands in his pockets. He's trying hard not to look miserable and she looks at me as if to say, I can't believe *this* pitiful kid is the one who's been giving you so much shit.

"So Ian knows music," I say, trying to loosen everybody up. "Knows some folks."

"Yeah," Ian agrees. "That's what I was doing when you knocked, listening to music."

"I didn't hear nothing," Blake says. "I saw you looking around like you were scared to get out the car."

Okay. Maybe the playing nice wasn't going to happen just yet. I see something in Ian's eyes. That stubborn look he gets when he's had enough of my shit. A pretty girl walks by, dark, smooth skin, her hair in long braids and a miniskirt showing off her long flawless legs. When she passes the back bumper of Ian's car, Ian glances at Blake and then says, "Damn, baby, you look good. Come here and let me holla at you for a minute, mami. You looking finer than a motherfucker."

"Fuck you," the girl says and keeps walking. Doris nearly chokes on her gum and Blake looks at *me* like I'm the crazy one.

I turn my palms up and shake my head as if to say I have nothing to do with this dumb-ass white boy.

"Ian!" I frown. "What the hell was that?"

"What? She was pretty." Ian looks absolutely clueless.

Much like Ian, Blake has an excellent bullshit detector and he has had enough. My crafty little ebony and ivory hip-hop plan is a bust. "You know what?" Blake says, "I'ma be late for my show. I'm out. See you in there, Aunt Ron? Doris?" Blake completely ignores Ian and leaves us.

"So let's go in now," Doris suggests. "Get this party started. We don't want to interrupt the good times we're all having here. And by the way? This *so* doesn't count as us going out in L.A. What next? A teen disco-seminar on race relations? You really know how to have a good time."

"Ian?" I pull on his black T-shirt, the image of Tupac large and plain on the front. "Let's go."

"No," he says quietly. "I'm going home."

"What do you mean?" Doris and I exchange glances. "You drove all this way. To *Corona,* for God's sake. You love this music. It's going to be a good time."

Ian shakes his head. "I don't feel like it anymore," he says. He points his key ring at his car and unlocks it with the same series of beeps and clicks. "Nice to meet you, Doris," he says, and then gets in his car and drives away.

"Man," Doris huffs as we walk to the show. "I actually feel sorry for the kid. He is only sixteen. It's practically *illegal* to have a lick of sense at that age."

And Doris is right. Part of me was trying to do something

cool for both Blake and Ian. Blake would have gotten some exposure, and Ian would have gotten some exposure, too, in a way. But part of me also knew that the night might turn out exactly as it has, Ian being put in his place some kind of way. And that makes me a bit of a playground bully, luring the unsuspecting to the bathroom stall to get his ass kicked. Okay, not that dramatic, but still. And part of this is Ian's fault, pretending, putting on the verbal blackface. But knowing him, I should have seen he'd do that, too. And I should have asked Earl to come. I didn't because I was afraid of all the different negotiations that all of us would have to do: Me, Earl, Ian, Blake, Doris. So different, individually, and yet *together*. That's how it should be, no matter how uncomfortable. I should have known a lot, and now I do. Like a grown-up.

doris

The Surrealists: A group of poets writing in and throughout the twentieth century, trying to cope with the absurdities of modern life by representing them through disjunctive images and language. Holocaust survivors like Paul Celan, who depicted the concentration camps of World War II through images of black milk and graves in the sky, or ironists like Russell Edson who point to the holes in domestic life by likening the tedium of family to a child pretending to be a tree for his disinterested parents. The literary equivalent of Salvador Dali with his melting clocks, and...clearly postromantic. And their corollary in lived experience (aside from, most recently, kalebone): those of us who can't seem to put the different pieces of our lives together.

Surreal, I think, as Ronnie drives me around on the tourist's tour of L.A. Not just the landscape. Though it is surreal with its gigantic billboards, the bilingual signs and colorful murals of the Virgin of Guadalupe next to the free clinics, and the beautiful rise of the Hollywood Hills and the promise of beaches not far away. Surreal, too, that a mere two days ago I was on the couch alone listening to the wail of Lotto, pet to my half friend, Toni, leaving behind Maxwell, Paige, Asa, and the whole mess of folks I barely know, yet constitute my fledgling attempt at a new life, so that here I can sit next to my real friend Ronnie, dislocated but seemingly happy. More surreal, not two months ago I had a boyfriend whom I loved, whom I still love on any given bad afternoon in spite of my fledgling attraction to Maxwell, who unfortunately, has yet to call or otherwise contact me. Zach, at this very minute is probably lounging on his futon, plotting the grand opening of his movie palace, watching his half girlfriend put on her Bonnie Bell lip gloss and text message the other nymphets about an end-of-season sale at Forever 21 on her Hello Kitty cell phone. And alas, that final image, while surreal, is probably true.

"I'm having Zach thoughts," I tell Ronnie, who expertly navigates the narrow streets that snake up and down the hills, past precariously perched mansions that put the fanciest Buckhead, Tara rip-off in Atlanta to shame. "Remind me again why we decided it was a bad idea to say run-of-the-mill girl things like 'men suck'? What if they actually suck? God, it feels good to say 'suck' without the word-police looking at me like my brain is rotting out of my head."

Ronnie makes a last-minute left turn on red, something I've learned that's part of L.A. driver's etiquette.

"What would be the worst thing?" she asks. "What if you did go back to Langsdale to help Zach out with opening the theater? For the summer, at least. Teaching's clearly making you mental, and you can make a dollar go further there than in Atlanta. You'll have to do better than me and Earl. I've had more eggs than Cool Hand Luke. And if I never see another peanut butter and jelly sandwich, it'll be too soon."

"Which is why I'm buying you lunch. That and to help us both recover from the disaster that was last night. I know I'm supposed to hate Ian, but you gotta admit, even with the Beemer he looked kind of pathetic. Like the sad kid in gym class just waiting to get his ass bombarded with dodgeballs."

Ronnie looks sympathetic for a moment, then her face changes.

"I know, Doris. But remember this. That might literally be the one day out of his entire life where he's stuck outside his comfort zone. And let's not forget that young Ian can still have the last laugh. He can fire my cow-ho ass any day of the week, so just be glad your space-ho self has a job."

"How could you have let me wear that out of the house, Ronnie? How?"

"The better question is how you could have purchased those shoes with actual American dollars. I think some of the brothers thought they were being punk'd, not too many thirtysomething Judy Jetson types around."

I try not to bore Ronnie with all the minutia of my neurotic brain, but I seem to be having some kind of clothing identity crisis. I have no idea what to wear in Atlanta half the time, and given the chance to cut loose in L.A., it seems the only thing that I lost was my last iota of judgment. Then I start laughing because I think about what Zach would have said if he'd seen me.

"It's walking that fine line between novelty and circus freak. And for lunch, pick someplace decadent where we can gawk at celebrities and decide whether they're really as short and less-pretty-in-real-life as I hear. And where we can overhear their conversations if they start talking about their favorite Scientology centers or diet pills. But to answer your question, I am *not* going back to Langsdale. I spent the better part of a decade trying to get out of that place. Clearly you've forgotten what it's like there."

Ronnie changes lanes in front of an actual Rolls Royce, barely glancing in the rearview mirror.

"I know you'll hate to hear it, Doris, but you might have done the right thing getting that Ph.D. I mean, I'm happy that my book's being published, but it hasn't been smooth sailing on that front. And I don't think any school's going to be knocking down doors to have a Burning Spear author, or author-ette, or author-ina, or however they're marketing women these days, who're working at their institution. Don't let your head explode or anything, but I've even been debating going back to school."

Now, don't get me wrong. There's nothing that I'd like more than to see Ronnie live her dreams, but I view my Ph.D. the way some women probably view abusive spouses, or sadistic, soul-destroying employers. I appreciate that it made me the person I now am, but otherwise, what a horrific way to waste one's youth. In fact, I still feel as if every day away from Langsdale is one of active recovery, in which everything I say or do is not being picked apart like some fetal pig on a dissection table.

"Ronnie. Are you totally high from California exhaust fumes? Do you even remember what it was like back there? I want you to close your eyes and conjure the stale, pungent smell of the microwave in the workroom. Listen for the sound of some whiny, tight-ass telling you why they threw away their television ages ago. See the cold fluorescent lighting of the Langsdale library, built totally without windows so as to aid in the pasty-fication of all that doughy, white flesh. Is it coming back to you?"

Ronnie parallel parks the car near Mann's Chinese Theater, essential pit stop on any L.A. excursion.

"I do," she admits. "But Earl seems, shall we say, distracted these days. He barely talks about law school anymore, and I don't think it's because he doesn't want to go." She pauses and gives me a side glance. "I think it's because he's working so hard and still we can scarcely afford that proverbial pot to piss in. The Burning Spear money will help, but it's not like they've offered me a second book. I get no writing done, and I don't foresee a real break anytime soon. Don't get me wrong, I'm not moving back to no crazy-ass Langsdale, especially not after my book comes out, but I wouldn't mind finding some other smallish town or cheap city, cheaper than here, where Earl and I can get back on track. Because this, paradise that it is, is beginning to

feel like a detour. And just look around you, Doris." She gestures
to sunbaked homeless faces crouched against the walls. "Second
easiest thing to coming with a dream to L.A. is becoming L.A.
roadkill."

We've gotten out of the car and begun to walk the star-
cluttered, if pee scented, sidewalk.

"You'll never be homeless. You and Earl can always come
live with me in Atlanta. But I get what you're saying. What
does Earl think?"

"I don't know," she says, almost to herself. "I haven't really
talked about it yet."

I looked down at my feet, at the star on which I'd been
standing, having one of those faux-philosophical moments where
Hollywood is starting to make a lot of sense. Heck, Burning Spear
Press is even making sense, with their nutsy escapist storylines
and heroines who can afford to shop the nonsale rack. Who
wanted to be stuck in their own life all the time, worrying about
real problems like money, and frustrated ambitions and whether
one was making the right choices in love? I was wrong to revise
my Meg Ryan and Tom Hanks drama. It's not just verisimilitude
we need, but outright fantasy. Isn't that what these stars were
supposed to deliver? Cary Grant, the original metrosexual, ban-
tering urbanely and charming the socks off deserving women.
Humphrey Bogart and Robert Mitchum delivering rapid-fire
dialogue and seducing the ladies with tough-guy exteriors and
bedroom eyes. Heck, I'll even give Brad Pitt credit on a good day
for raw sex appeal when he's not doing a valley-Roman accent
on the beaches of Troy.

"Um, Ronnie, don't take this the wrong way. But I think you loooooove Ian. I saw that glimmer in your eyes last night, as he rode off into the Bavarian Motor Works sunset."

Ronnie gives me her patented eyebrow raise.

"Seriously. Desert island. Ryan Seacrest and Ian. With whose nubile young body would you rather wile away the afternoons. And no booze. Just ass. Whose do you pick?"

"I don't know, Doris. Let's make it challenging. You're on a desert island—Maxwell or Zach? The ass you know, or grab-bag ass?"

"Silly woman," I say, looking for a star of which I can be proud. Finally, I stumble on Mary Tyler Moore. "Who's to say that it's grab-bag ass. It might well be ass that has been both grabbed and bagged."

"Nothing like an informed shopper."

We're close to the actual theater by now. A theater I know well from Academy Awards shows on television and old footage of Marilyn Monroe and Jane Russell vamping it up goddess-style even with hands coated in cement. Now that is the glamour for which I came to Hollywood.

"You know how you feel about talking about Earl and Ph.D.'s and the future and teaching Ian and all that? You know how I felt wearing my space shoes on the soul train last night? Take that level of discomfort, and that's the pit I have in my stomach when I think about choosing wrong. And it's like I'm para-lyzed. Like there's a right choice to make, and I'll only figure out what it is when I don't make it."

Ronnie and I push our way through a crowd of tourists who

look straight from Langsdale. They're all ooohing and aaahh-hing over Mel Gibson's tiny little paw prints.

"Remember that Lucy episode where Lucy's hands fit in all the different imprints, and Ethel's only come close to fitting Trigger's?" Ronnie bends over Ava Gardner's square, her hands expanding well outside their slender outline. "I think I'm more of an Ethel than a Lucy."

I move from square to square, imagining what it was like to be Marilyn, or standing next to Gary Cooper when he signed off. "Look, I say. I think I fit Sylvester Stallone. How totally tragic."

"Man hands," Ronnie says. "Better put that in your Internet profile."

"Rocky's hands," I say. "It could have some homoerotic fas-cination for a slightly repressed yet still-straight jock. Don't kid yourself, m'dear. There is something for evvveryone on ye olde Internet."

One of the old fellows from the Langsdale-esque group, whose mother clearly never taught him that it was rude to eaves-drop, gives me a knowing nod. For all I know, he might actually have *seen* my profile on the Internet. Deeply, deeply terrifying.

"Earl wants us to do karaoke tonight. You game?" Ronnie asks. "Barragans, this Mexican joint down the street, is Earl's new favorite L.A. stomping ground. He wants to show it off. Don't break his heart."

"It's not his heart I'm worried about," I say. "You ever heard me sing?"

"Noooooo."

"With good reason. But it's not like I *know* anyone in L.A. And if it makes your fellah happy, who am I to rain on his parade."

"Indeed," Ronnie says.

Before returning to the apartment, Ronnie and I pit stop at a purely functional Internet café. Ronnie's computer is on the fritz again, and I am far too paranoid to be toting mine around, residual fear from hearing urban legends of disappearing laptops with non-backed-up dissertations. I weigh my desire to check e-mail against my irrational paranoia of someone taking my password, and sign on to a computer that looks like Fred Flintstone hocked it when the new models hit Bedrock.

"Classy," I say to Ronnie.

"Welcome to poverty. Enjoy your stay."

I'm actually nervous as I check my e-mail, mostly because having violated so very many of the dating commandments early in the evening, I violated the remaining few about playing hard to get, not putting out on the first date, and waiting for him to contact you. I dropped a "had a groovy time, am now going out of town" note as a last-minute gesture of self-sabotage before heading to the airport. So I'm curious, of course, as to whether the dating laws are right, or if one can, in fact, defy the universe and reap an occasional reward.

And as the universe so cruelly and frequently answers: maybe, maybe not.

Maxwell has, indeed, written back, but it's beyond cursory and doesn't really allude to a definitive future date. The requisite, "I enjoyed meeting you, too. Travel safely. Peace." I resist the urge to send a long e-mail asking how Maggie Mae is holding up, and whether he's binging on kalebone to make it through the night without me. One cannot be one's version of funny with someone who might not even think that you are funny. Once upon a time, I might have moped slightly about the e-mail, but today I actually feel detached in that surreal way that makes Maxwell more like a character in some sitcom version of my life, not a man I actually considered a potential short- or long-term partner.

"Lame," I say to Ronnie. "That desert island question is looking easier by the minute."

The e-mail that I most dread opening has the subject line as, "CLASS YESTERDAY" and is sent from none other than HRH Paige Prentiss, who probably wants to pass down another order or two from on high. I debate letting her ruin my day, but curiosity gets the better of me.

Dear Dr. Weatherall—
I would like to talk to you about class the other week. Your office hours say that you are out of town on business. Is there a time that I can reach you when you return? Thanks.

Typically cryptic little princess. One of the downsides of teaching is that it quintuples your volume of "I need to talk to you about something, but I'm not going to say what," conversations, which are up there on my list of things I love with black jelly beans, parsnips and root canals. For a solid week after her mother's visit, Paige refused to speak in class. And because I am a masochist, I even noted that her posts on the "Dr. Weather-all is a Liberal Bitchess" Web site had subsided. However, I have watched enough horror in my life to know that just when you think the Freddie, Jason or Hannibal of your life is down for the count, there's always the chance that they might jump out of a closet, or show up at the door when you very least suspect it. The devil, in my life, does in fact wear Prada.

"Almost finished?" Ronnie asks.

"You know when you were talking crazy about that whole back for the Ph.D. thing? Well, you should think long and hard about it. It doesn't remove the Ians from your life, it simply triples their number and gives them institutional channels by which to torture you. Just some food for thought."

"So long as it provides food proper of the nonegg variety, tell the little monsters to have at it."

On the way home, traffic has slowed from "jogger" to "glacial." I'm starting to get my bearings, and wondering what every visitor to L.A. must wonder: how any sane human being ever survives this traffic. Atlanta is no walk in the park, not by a long shot, but this is positively masochistic. My cell phone keeps cutting out, but I leave Toni a message asking if she's talked to Tino. For just a moment, having seen how hard Ronnie and Earl are struggling, I admit how lucky I am at this juncture in my life. I may not have long-term friends, but I do have kind acquaintances. And if the Paiges of my life, or the smug Asas, or the indifferent Maxwells occasionally get me down, Ronnie is right to point out that at least I go home to a sweet apartment with a fixed computer and yuppie snack food in the refrigerator.

"This is insane," Ronnie says. "We've moved approximately two city blocks in the past ten minutes."

"But there's Mexican food at the end of the rainbow. And Earl behind a microphone. I miss the way he used to sing at the Saloon."

Earl used to serenade Ronnie back at the bar in Langsdale, changing the words to whatever song was on the radio to some rhyme-free bluegrass yodel like, "When you gonna ride my hoooooog, city gaaaaaaal," or "L.A. woman, ride away with meeeeeeee." Ronnie always put her hands over her ears, but deep down she liked it. And Zach would shake his head when I asked why he never sang to me like that.

"You on a bike?" he'd say. "That's a laugh. Pardon me if I don't know any diddies about you riding off into the sunset *after* you've finished the latest eBay auction for your twelve thousandth pair of shoes. But seriously, I'll be thinking about it."

I looked out the window at a pair of half-naked blondes teetering down the street in too-high slingback heels, and I knew exactly why Ronnie was thinking about leaving.

"You know any car games?" I ask. "This is worse than traveling cross-country."

"Tell me about it. On a normal road we could have been in Vegas by now."

Ronnie fiddles with the radio, and my cell phone rings.

"You mind if I take this?" I ask. "It might be Toni."

"No problem," Ronnie says, turning the volume down slightly.

"Doris?" I hear a man's faraway voice through the static, "Doris? Where are you?"

"L.A.," I say. "Who is this?"

"Zach. What are you doing in L.A.? Are you with Ronnie?"

"I am," I say, mouthing the word "Zach," to Ronnie when she looks over. "She says hello."

"Did you tell me you were going to L.A.? Must have slipped my mind."

I think of saying something snippy about teenager girls causing brain-rot, but bite my wicked tongue.

"I won't keep you," he says, "but I wanted to put this thing in the mail to you about the opening of the theater. We're shooting for December, but I don't have your address."

It's a good thing I'm biting my tongue because the following thoughts are vying for first place in racing from my mouth: Why, why, why would anyone EVER open a theater in DE-CEMBER, when you can't even walk to your driveway because of the snow in Langsdale, when all the little ticket-buying children of the corn are heading home for the holidays? And THEN I'm thinking YOU DIDN'T EVEN KEEP MY AD-DRESS, YOU ASSHOLE! But since I am in some form of Zen, pre-decision-making mode, and I know Zach well enough to know that this is, in fact, his anemic version of effort, I do what my mother and kindergarten teachers once taught me: I say nothing at all.

"Doris?"

"Bad reception. I sent you my address, ages ago. Twice, even."

"Well, I can't find it. And I'd really like for you to come. I checked your school calendar online, and the opening is after you're done with exams, before the holidays, so if you want to, I'm hoping you can squeeze it in. I'm even screening *What Ever Happened to Baby Jane?* in your honor."

And I know I'm just being pissy because I say, "Thanks a lot. Why? Because you think I'm some kind of hag so you're starting with a hagfest in my honor? I'll be sure to block out the dates." About halfway through I stop saying it bitchy and start laughing. Zach laughs, too, because he's the kind of guy to whom you can say "hag" without his thinking "breakup."

"That's exactly right, Doris, and you can tell your cohag that I'd love to see her and Earl there, as well. I'll save you seats front and center and you can recite every word."

"Which, of course, we know from our years in hag school."

"Naturally." He sounds like he's smoking, and I feel a little worried for him. Zach may date a youngster, but he's not the sort made happy by just anyone. No, it takes a special breed of faux hag to keep him on his toes. "It's not the same without you two here, but have fun tearing up the town, and say hi to Earl."

"Okay. Can do. I'm down to a bar, but I'll call you when I'm back in Atlanta."

"Miss you," he says. "Really."

And then the phone cuts out.

There must be some mystical force at work in California that turns people healthy before it turns them homeless and or overcoiffed and or skeletal. Like in vampire movies when the victim is first bit and looks eroto-ravenous, rather than simply corpselike. Whichever force it is, and however tired he may be at the end of the day, Earl looks fabulous. He and Ronnie have both dropped a bit of weight from the I'll-be-rich-in-my-next-lifetime diet, but underneath Earl's teddy-bear exterior is a clearly defined set of muscles and abs that, while not washboard, are hardly the doughy mass I've come to expect on myself, or even Zach. His hair has lightened a bit, and Ronnie is still bitching about the fact that Katie, the nymphet with whom he works, convinced him to wear tighter T-shirts for bigger tips from women *and* men. And while I completely understand Ronnie's territoriality, I have to say that Earl looks hot.

But if his exterior has morphed, the Earl I remember is still the one who greets us at the door, spatula in one hand and the other giving me a half hug, then squeezing Ronnie on the arse.

"You ladies have a good afternoon?" He stares at Ronnie a little longer, searching her face. She walks over to him and kisses him softly, holding his hand. It looks like a makeup kiss to me, but for what, I don't know.

"Mellow," I reply. "We're conserving our energy for karaoke. And fictional shopping with our fictional money tomorrow. I have a whole pretend L.A. life now, with imaginary Chanel sunglasses, an imaginary fake tan and an imaginary tight little ass. If only I could move out here and live the dream."

Earl gestures us into the kitchen, where he's been slaving over a hot stove, grilling shrimp in the pan. Huge, elegant, expensive shrimp. It's one of those "Gift of the Magi" moments where I wish that I could make the meal disappear and give Ronnie and

Earl back whatever portion of their income went into making my evening special.

"I figured you'd had enough of the steak with Bita," he said. "We'll load up on dinner here so we can stick to drinking at karaoke. Get yourself ready, Doris, because they make one mean margarita."

"Mmm," I say, my eyes glazing over only slightly. "I can't wait to get good and toasted. That's the thing about Atlanta, it's destroyed my tolerance. I have to drive myself everywhere, and one does not drink and drive on the freeways. It's not like Langsdale where you could sort of fake it down the back roads. I'm practically a teetotaler these days."

Ronnie frowns. "So that would explain your evening with Maxwell?"

"Maxwell?" Earl asks, the "tsk tsk" in his voice barely masked. "What happened to Zach?"

I give my best vacant Hollywood answer. "He says 'hi.'" Earl leaves it and I go back to Ronnie's question.

"Okay, so there was that little glitch. Let's not talk about Atlanta. I go back soon enough, and I'm so enjoying being around you both. Even if you are morphing into scary 'beautiful people,' and I may be reduced to eating pork products and ice cream all alone by my next visit."

"Not likely," Ronnie says. "As soon as I get that check from Burning Spear, I am never, ever touching an egg again. Not even on Easter."

We eat dinner on the small patio behind the apartment, and even if Ronnie and Earl are living on the cheap, the view from outside is both free and beautiful. I wonder how it is that L.A. gets such a bad rap, when as much as I love New York, there aren't any vistas quite like this, not available to the under-employed, at any rate.

"Look," Earl says, as if reading my mind, "smog finally lifted."

After dinner, we head over to the Mexican dive bar. In some ways, it's an L.A. equivalent of the Saloon: unpretentious sur-roundings, cheap liquor, sauced clientele. However, you can't miss that this is L.A. Every other song is some heartfelt Mexican ballad, sung in Spanish, blending seamlessly into the tragic renderings of Patsy Cline and Johnny Cash. Tragic largely in that they're sung by hipsters who no doubt discovered Johnny from his *American Recordings* and own *At Folsom Prison* in a strictly ironic manner.

"I love this place," I say to Ronnie. "We don't even have to sing. It's great just watching."

"Nice try, Doris," Earl winks at me. "But I've already signed you and Ronnie up."

Earl changed into a fitted black T-shirt and equally fitted jeans. When he saunters up the bar to get the songbook, I notice that Ronnie isn't the only one checking him out. In fact, as he was standing at the bar, a slight, blond woman sidled up beside him and gave his left butt-cheek a firm squeeze. And much to my surprise, instead of telling her to mind her own person, Earl hugs the girl.

"Are you seeing what I'm seeing?" I ask.

"Every day of my life," Ronnie replies. "That's Katie. If you look her up in the dictionary, the second definition is 'obvious' and the third is 'really, really obvious.' She once had the nerve to tell me that she and Earl had some inside joke that involved her hands on his ass. I can only guess it involves Earl showing her what one looks like, since she clearly doesn't eat enough to have one herself. Earl says he doesn't want to hurt her feelings, so I said that as long as the punch line doesn't involve his pants below his knees, to suit himself." She shoves a chip in her mouth and chews it like a robot.

I can't believe that Ronnie is being so calm. It's either a manifestation of extreme security or defeat. I, however, am racked with sympathetic paranoia.

"Okay. Don't take this the wrong way, but if that was Zach, I would like seriously be thinking of murdering both of them. What is the *matter* with that girl? And not to be the stunningly huge bitch that we both know I can be, but she's not even that cute, especially in this town. She's clearly a C-list kind of blonde."

"Which is why I pay her no mind."

Earl returns to the table with drinks for us and Katie trailing behind him.

"Doris," he says. "This is Katie."

She barely looks in my direction.

"Hey, Doris," she says, then gesturing in a cutesy half-wave, "Hey, Rhonda."

Ronnie takes a loooooooong sip from her glass. I detect the faintest smell of blood diffusing through the proverbial waters, but Katie continues, "I'm begging Earl to sing one of those sweet country songs. He's so funny. I tell him he's like that Uncle Jesse guy in the *Dukes of Hazzard* movie. The singer."

Now she's starting to piss me off.

"You mean Willie Nelson?" I ask.

"Yeah. The one Jessica Simpson's character is always saying she's in love with. That old dude."

Katie tilts her head flirtatiously in Earl's direction and starts to braid her strawlike hair.

"Katie," Earl says. "What you don't know about music is a lot."

Ronnie puts her hand on Earl's knee and squeezes.

"I always think of Earl more like Tommy Lee Jones in *Coal Miner's Daughter*. Might not be the best singer, but all man."

Katie looks disinterested.

"Must be an old movie," she says. "He's, like, what, a thousand now?"

"And hot," I add. No-one knocks Tommy Lee Jones on my watch, especially not someone who would clearly prefer Tommy Lee. "A flawless movie. They don't make 'em like Loretta anymore."

Katie smiles politely, like she's humoring her grandmother in order to stay in the will.

"I don't know Loretta Lynn," she says. "I mean, I know she's the old lady that Jack White did that CD with, right?"

True. I had to give her that one.

"Sing some country," Katie pleads, now just ignoring Ronnie and myself. "Please," Katie says. "I wore my cowgirl boots just for tonight."

I now add definition C to the growing list of synonyms for

"Katie": really, really REALLY obvious and just a liiiittle tacky. In a deeply strip-aerobics move, she reaches down and rubs her leg, tracing a line to the top of her red leather cowgirl wear. Her boots are no doubt expensive, acquired from some boutique on Melrose with eight hundred percent markup, but country they are not. No more country than the faux-twang she puts on when talking to Earl.

Ronnie inhales the last half of her margarita.

"Listen," Earl pipes up. "Speak of the devil. It's miss Loretta herself, Ronnie. I asked them to put this one on special for you, and there's some Dolly Parton cuing up in your near future, Doris, so get ready."

"Thanks, Earl." In the background, I can hear the karaoke machine wailing the first chords of *You Ain't Woman Enough to Take My Man,* and I can't tell whether or not Ronnie is amused, pissed or some frightening hybrid of the two. Regardless, she pours herself another margarita from the pitcher and heads to the front of the bar, patrons hollering at the surreal sight of Ronnie getting ready to belt out a country standard. A vision right up there with hip-hop Ian and Ziggy Doris. Surreal, and then some. Ronnie has a decent voice, and starts into the song with no small degree of conviction. Earl leans back in his seat. Katie looks bored and annoyed. She puts a hand on Earl's shoulder, but he shrugs her off.

By the second verse, I can tell that Ronnie's had it. She's still mouthing the words, but something inside has changed. Having read multiple Internet articles on how to spot liars, I can see that she's faking any form of joy. Her mouth is smiling, but her eyes are hard as the pavement outside Mann's Chinese Theater. And maybe I'm projecting, but I think that she's having a similar moment about Earl to the one I had earlier with my clothing. That the sort of out-of-control mismatch of Earl, Katie, Loretta, Ronnie, Melrose boots, margaritas, bad karaoke and Mexican ballads is no longer wacky and zany, it's just taxing. If I could read Ronnie's thoughts at this exact moment, I'm pretty sure they'd be *I am officially too old for this here brand of shit.*

ronnie

It's been three weeks since the hip-hop showcase, and now I'm on a plane, sitting in the aisle seat, getting my knees obliterated every time someone passes by with their luggage. After she'd gotten back to Atlanta, safe and sound from "Hellay," Doris convinced me that I'd be sorry if I never met my very first editor and never visited my very first publisher. So I decided to go to Atlanta. Plus, it was an opportunity to see Doris, which is the real reason for her cheerleading.

I stare out the window of the plane, glad I'm not at the window seat. I just don't want to know how bizarrely high in the sky I am, in a hundred-ton plane that, still, impossibly, glides through the air. But here I am, flying, which I hate to do. Doris said that I really had no choice in the matter, since I was in major travel debt with her. The hip-hop showcase was not her fantasy. So, I got into more debt by charging my flight on my supposedly emergency-only credit card.

The hip-hop showcase, while amusing on some tangential level, and with really good music on another level, really wasn't our style. We've aged out of that scene, sadly. It was a hard night for Ian, too, but an important night. Something about him had changed. I could hear it in his voice on the machine. I'd tried to call him on his cell a few days after the show, but he didn't pick up. I called all day. I even called his mother, who said he was fine, but kept saying he wasn't feeling well and that he'd call me. And the next day there was a message.

"It was short," Earl said, taking chicken out of the fridge. "Something about being sorry and talking to you when he saw you."

Ian said sorry? That was about as rare as me being at a loss for words. But I was. "So that's it?"

"It's on the machine. You can listen to it still." Earl's already distracted by the chicken and poking around in the cabinets for flour and seasonings.

I listen to the message and it hardly sounds like Ian. It's a soft voice. I can't detect a sneer anywhere in the tone.

Hi, Ronnie. Um, Veronica. I'm sorry I left the show the other night. Stupid. I was stupid, I mean. So I'll see you, like, next week or something. When you come to my house.

Earl watches me listen to the message as he sprinkles flour on a cutting board. He stares at me long and steady until I hang up the phone. "You gone keep tutoring that boy or you had enough?"

"No," I reply, still staring at the phone, thinking and thinking. "I mean, no, I've not had enough." And it's true. I haven't. I know what enough is because Earl and I gave each other ultimatums the night of the hip-hop show. I'm not going to give up on anything else that easy, not anymore. It was the biggest fight we've had, and it was the best thing for us.

From the outside, to Doris and Bita, Earl and I are the perfect odd couple. But if I'm telling the truth here, from the very first time I saw Katie giving Earl hugs at the bar, I worried. Earl and I are always good to each other, but we also have, no matter how hard we've tried not to, somehow gotten into the habit of not making waves, of letting sleeping dogs lie, even after we promised each other we'd talk it through. I don't know, exactly, how many sleeping dogs Earl has tucked away, but Earl and I never mentioned that makeup smudge to each other. I had decided that sometimes stuff is small junk that doesn't have to be talked to death. And I'm always hearing Doris yelling at me like she did, telling me not to be such a girl.

But sleeping dogs have to wake up sometime.

After the show, Doris said that she had to take an Advil to stop the throbbing in her legs, go to bed and get some sleep so that she could dream away the evening, or she'd kill herself. But the night was still young by bartending standards and I knew that Earl sometimes hung out at the bar even after he got off work or went out with friends. He was home there, liked it there, and whenever I wasn't home, he'd kill a little time there. So I went looking for him after Doris crashed out on our couch.

When I pulled up, it was already two in the morning so

things were winding down and the Baseline was thinning out. I didn't see Earl, but saw Jake the hottie sitting at the bar. The jukebox was playing "Space Oddity", which made me laugh, thinking of Doris in her space shoes that night. I pulled up a stool and gave Jake a sideways hug. "Where's your running buddy?" I turned to face him and looked around the bar, noticing all the strips of black-and-white pictures they had tacked up from the backroom photo booth. There was a new picture of Earl, Katie and Jake mugging for the camera like the Three Musketeers. And Katie was kissing Earl's cheek, had her arm around his neck. That could explain some things, and yet, I wasn't letting it.

Jake sipped his light beer. He was forever working out and trying to keep his thirtysomething body looking good so he'd get work as an actor. Earl wouldn't be caught dead drinking a light beer. Jake looked me up and down, stared at my breast for a moment. "Nice shirt. I like those pearl buttons."

Even though his eyes said "Nice rack," I thanked him anyway. "So where's my baby?"

"Oh, he left with Katie. She needed a ride. Car trouble or something."

"Really. Car trouble." I felt that fear again, but tried to look as though it didn't bother me. Jake shook his head. He and Earl had gotten pretty tight and he knew how much Katie got on my nerves, although I thought I had kept my desire to break her tiny little neck on the down low.

"That's what she said." He shrugged and stared at his beer bottle.

"So why didn't *you* give her a lift?" It was late, but I suddenly wanted a screwdriver. I motioned for the bartender, a twenty-something guy with the stick-thin body of Sid Vicious.

"She seemed to want Earl's company more than mine," he said. "Earl was headed out, headed home, so it made more sense that he'd take her home."

"Oh." My heart started to beat fast. I got my drink and swished the straw around in it. Now that I had it I was too busy thinking to be drinking. "So why are you here drinking alone? Why didn't you head out for the evening?"

Jake chuckled and rubbed his clean-shaven head with his hands. "It was a *night*."

"Party suck?" I pinched my straw between my fingers and took a tiny sip.

"For me, yes, but for Earl, it was a pretty good night."

"Oh? What happened?" I sat up straight in my stool not wanting to hear what he meant by a good night. I kept looking at the picture of Katie kissing Earl, and it hurt.

"Well, I'm sure he'll tell you, but he met some casting agent at the party who liked his look."

I didn't know what any of this had to do with Katie. "What do you mean? So what happened?" I was feeling sick and nervous and I didn't even know why. I should have been happy for Earl, but all of what Jake was saying was really weird.

"She offered him a bit part in this new thing that's coming out."

What? None of this seemed even remotely likely. "Stop fucking with me, Jake."

Jake took a long pull on his beer. "Nope. Swear to God. I'm serious. And that kook of yours told her he'd have to think about it. That he wasn't 'one to be acting.'"

Good for you, Earl. That's the spirit. You had to put your foot down somewhere or you'd turn into the good old boy who drank light beers and got facials so that you looked good on film. I'd forgotten about Katie for a minute.

"Jesus," I said.

"Exactly," Jake muttered over Mott the Hoople singing about all the young dudes. "I've been busting my ass trying to get my break, and Earl goes to this party practically kicking and screaming and gets a role in a film handed to him. Fuck."

Fuck made me think about Katie and Earl together. I was ready to go and hadn't even finished my drink. "I think I'm going to head out, Jake. Get back home."

"Really?" He put his hand over mine resting on the bar. "I'll buy you another."

I looked down at our hands together and I imagined, for a second, about what it would be like to be with Jake, not Earl. "No, thanks, Jake. I should go." I pulled my hand out from under his, put money down on the bar and walked out the door.

But when I went out to my car, the piece of shit wouldn't start. Again. I thought about walking up that long hill, up Echo Park Avenue, but I was tired and it was past two-thirty in the morning. Not a good time for women to be walking around by themselves at night. So I turned right around and went into the bar and asked Jake for a ride. He sucked down the last of his beer and grinned at me. "I would *love* to give you a ride," he said.

When Jake drove me home, I was feeling strange hugging the waist of a man who was not Earl. When we got to the apartment, he turned off his bike and waited for me to climb off before he hopped off. When I gave him a thank-you hug, he grabbed me and wouldn't let go. He kissed me right on the lips and I didn't pull away as quickly as I should have—or could have.

"I've been wondering for a long time what that would be like," he said, when I finally pulled away from him.

"It's not going to happen again, Jake."

Jake shrugged. "Earl, he seems to get all the women." He straddled his bike. "And all the jobs." He turned the key, revved the bike and saluted me as he drove off.

I didn't know what had happened, exactly. I knew I felt guilty, because I let it happen. I guess I was thinking about Katie kissing Earl when I let Jake kiss me just a little too long.

I turned the key very quietly because I didn't want to wake Doris, but Earl was sitting at the kitchen table with beer in his hand, looking dead serious. His look made me feel like a kid sneaking in after curfew.

"Hey, baby," I whispered and bent down to kiss him on the lips. He didn't kiss me back.

"Where you been? I didn't know what to think when I saw Doris on the couch and didn't find you in bed."

I put my fingers to my lips and signaled for Earl to follow me into the bedroom. I shut the door behind us. "I went looking for you."

"That was Jake's bike," Earl said, sitting up tall on the bed. "I looked out the window and saw him driving away. Why is he giving you rides home?"

I pulled my boots off and unsnapped the buttons of my hip-hop hick shirt, as Doris so respectfully called it. Earl had a *tone* in his voice. He was not happy. I was getting defensive and nervous as if I'd actually done made out with Jake when I remembered that *I* was the one who should have been pissed off.

"Why are you giving *Katie* rides home?"

Earl's face changed then. He turned bright red. "Her car broke down, Ron. She needed a ride home is all."

"Yeah, well, so did mine, so did I."

Earl stood up and leaned against the wall with his big arms crossed. It's a strange thing to be pissed at someone and to also notice at the same time how hot they are. "Goddammit, Katie was lying," he said. "She wanted more than a ride home and I gave her more credit than she had coming to her. I should know better than that by now."

"Yes, you should have. So that's what this caveman routine is all about? Katie tried to put the moves on you—again—and because she's an operator, you think Jake's trying to do the same thing?"

Earl got quiet.

"She only tried, right?"

Earl sighed and suddenly pulled his black T-shirt off. "She did a little more than try," he said quietly.

I don't want to know the bullshit she tried on Earl, but I decided on the spot that I would fuck her up if she tried one more thing. I kind of wanted to know what she tried to pull, but then I would have had to tell Earl about Jake. The Jake Situation, I decided, was the last sleeping dog I would let lie.

"Dang, it's hot in here," Earl said. "I been drinking." He rubbed his face and the back of his neck with his shirt.

"I can tell."

"Both me and Jake been drinking. We got to talking and he let slip what he thought about you, thought you were just the kind of smart, beautiful woman he'd like to take home to his mama. Said I should trade you for Katie, so he could take you home to that mama."

That bastard. "So what are you mad at me for?"

Earl walked over and pulled me to him. "I ain't mad. I'm just a little drunk. It was kind of a strange night."

"I heard." I wrapped my arms around Earl and he bent down to kiss me. This time he did it like he meant it.

"I'm just..." His voice trailed off. "More of the same stuff. Sometimes being together is harder than I thought. You never know when somebody says something to make you feel mad or hell, even sad."

Welcome to my world, I wanted to say, but we have to take everything one conversation at a time. "Well, then. Just tell me whenever you feel mad or sad." I sat on the bed and patted the space next to me, but Earl just stood there. He looked serious.

"Okay, then. Sometimes you make me mad, and sometimes you don't make me feel good about myself. Sad, I guess."

My mouth hung open. "What?"

He held his hands up. "Let me finish. I feel like I'm trying, Ron. Really trying. And I feel like you're always looking for a way out of this while I'm trying hard to stay in this thing with you. I feel like you're ashamed of me, sometimes. I feel like you, not other folks, think I'm not good enough. I know you like what you're looking at whenever you put your eyes on me, but that's something else from really wanting to be with me."

"Earl—"

"Still not done," Earl said, putting his hands up again. "I have come all the way here to this." Earl gestured around the room. "I don't know what all kind of place…I'm so far away from home. And I'd move again. But what makes me sad is that sometimes I don't believe you'd ask me again. I believe you'd just as soon have me be back in Langsdale where I started out."

I sat there. My heart was beating so hard. I had no idea that he had been thinking all of this. But I let what he said settle in and decided that he was right. I'd just never admitted it to anyone, not even myself. Another part of it, a part that Earl was still a long ways from understanding, was that on some level, I was feeling like I wasn't good enough for him. In grad school, for the first time I learned about structuralism, the ways in which a culture is ordered. We read Franz Fanon's *Black Skin, White Masks,* an exploration of how colonized blacks internalized the ideas of their colonizers, namely that the binary structure of black versus white is fraught with connotations having to do with the notion that blackness is inferior to whiteness. I'd read all the stuff in a book, but didn't have to, not really. When I looked at Katie, I'd let that voice get in my head that told me, *Pssst. You know that Earl would like her so much better.*

After all, who's canonically pretty, you or her? And anyway, you and Earl, you're binaries! You're binaries!

I patted the side of the bed again, and this time Earl sat down next to me. I thought of the Katies, looking me up and down whenever I kissed him, the Ians who smirked at Earl, at the way he dressed, the way he talked, and me, who didn't want him at the hip-hop show with us because he wouldn't fit. But in that moment, I realized I was more afraid of losing him, and that was worse than all the bullshit I was letting get to me. I grabbed his hand.

"I'm scared, Earl. And I don't ever want to make you sad. I don't want you in Langsdale. I want you here, with me. We have to work. I want to work at this." I squeezed him. "We've got to trust each other, Earl. I'm not going to run off with every black man who looks at me, and I have to trust that Katie and any other bitch like her is never, ever going to get into those Wranglers of yours, especially if you're going to be a big star."

"I don't know about that," Earl said, stroking my hand. "I don't even want to be in no movie."

"Not even if it pays a few bucks?"

"We'd have to see about what kind of bucks they're talkin'."

"Big bucks!" I yelled. I'd forgotten about Doris out there on the couch. Earl shushed me.

"Enough for you to get yourself a proper car, one that don't quit on you every time you turn around."

"Amen, brother."

Earl stood up and slid out of his jeans. "How was your night?"

"Ooohhh," I said, scrunching up my face, thinking of Jake, the show, Ian. "That's a conversation for tomorrow. Let Doris tell you about the show. She's guaranteed to give you colorful commentary."

Earl shook his head and grinned. "Hey," he said, stretching out on the bed, "Did we talk enough? Are we all right?"

"Yes…but we'll always have to keep checking in."

"Okay," Earl said. "Will do that. No question." Then he smiled at me. "Ain't you hot with all them clothes on?"

"Know something?" I raised an eyebrow. "I *am*. I am *hot*." I stood up in bed, took off my shirt, twirled it around my head, and threw it so that it landed on Earl's face. And then I got out of my skirt and kicked it to the floor.

"You sure are, darling." Earl whistled softly, a long, low whistle. "Come on over here."

In less than the two hours since I've landed in Atlanta, I've had biscuits, meat loaf, macaroni and cheese and key-lime pie. "You're trying to kill me with food," I say to Doris as we're handed the check.

"I've got this," blurts Doris, slapping her credit card on the table. "I've got an actual job, as crazy-making as it is. Not a bad way to go, by the way, death by food."

I look around the café. "Everybody here is so coiffed. Like really put together. Pearl necklaces and all that."

"And in L.A. they're not?" Doris is gathering her things. "I will never forget how folks dressed for the *supermarket,* for God's sake. Miniskirts and thigh-high boots to get your cereal and milk in the morning?"

"*I* don't dress that way, and I'm a native."

"Yeah, but that's just because you got brainwashed by Indiana—and that big, hot man you got living with you. You wore fishnets, you taught in fishnets when you first got to Langsdale. Classic L.A. fashion, apparently. And now look at you. Cowboy boots. Who'd a thunk it?"

"I love those boots. By the way, where are your space shoes?"

"Two words for you. Good Will."

"It's actually one word."

"Do you want a ride to Burning Spear or not?" Doris asks, getting up from the table.

"This is exciting," she singsongs as we drive to Burning Spear. "I don't care what you say. This book could be your big Terry McMillan moment."

I stare out the window at the scenery. Atlanta *is* a cool city. It feels citylike, but dignified in ways that L.A. won't ever be. I tell Doris this and she tells me not to get all romantic about the place.

"Here in Atlanta, a particular brand of woman reads too much Margaret Mitchell, spends all her daddy's money, and gets paid more money to tell the world her demented views on marriage and feminity, so don't talk to me about dignity."

I settle in my seat. "Well, I still think it's very nice."

I think about what Doris said about my McMillan moment and I don't know about that. The problem with Burning Spear Press is that they're trying to make us all Terry McMillans. That's cool, nothing against Ms. McMillan. It's impossible not to feel appreciation for her success and what it's meant to black women writers. But I'm a black woman writer who wants to do something a little different. I had made as many of the changes in *F: The Academy* that they wanted me to. I made Doris black, which, I have to say, was really, really hilarious. I made Dottie's and Wanda's circle of friends almost exclusively black, no other ethnicities, which seems, inexplicably, the norm in a lot of contemporary fiction. It's one or the other kind of folk, nothing in between. I even threw in a couple of "girlfriends" and "sho nuffs" to make it more "friendly toward their market," is what they told me.

I also added all this relationship bullshit because the first draft was seen as too much of a character study—what we used to call good writing in graduate school. But after all that, it's not the book I envisioned I'd write, not by a long shot. And yet there's no denying that a writer is lucky to get published these days, ever since everybody started relying on Harry Potter to save the literary day.

"I'm going to be in that café across the street," Doris says, pulling up to the curb. "I'm going to have a coffee and read *People* magazine and pretend that I have a glamorous life."

"Make sure you have condoms."

"Ew." Doris gives me the thumbs-up. "Good luck. I hope you hit it off with everybody." And then she pulls away.

Just like all the publishing houses on TV, the building is one of those slick, modern types, but inside, it's still going for the velvety, antique, curly-furniture thing. Very schizophrenic, and very *Gone With the Wind,* in fact. I'm on time for my appointment, on the dot, so I wait outside Arianna Covington's office until I hear her secretary announce that I'm waiting. When the door opens, a tiny woman in sleek charcoal slacks and a white silk shirt pokes her head out and turns first to the left and then to the right looking for me. This is something that I'd get on Ian about, making assumptions about people and all of that, but for some reason I had assumed that Arianna Covington was black. I mean, since she was running a black imprint and everything. Instead, she was a pixie-ish redhead, with blue catlike eyes and freckles across her face. Young, too, of course.

"Veronica Williams?" She extends her hand and gives me a big smile. "Please. Step inside my office."

Her office is well-appointed, as they say. Elegant fixtures and silver-framed photographs of what must be her family. There's a picture of Arianna with a handsome, grey-haired man and a red-headed toddler on a bookshelf to the right of where I'm sitting.

"Cute," I say, pointing to the picture. "How old is he or she?"

Arianna laughs. "You can never tell what they are at that age. She. But she's much older now. Three years old. Little Jocelyn."

"Your husband, he's handsome." I stare at the picture. Really, they look like the perfect family.

"Ah, well," Arianna says. "Ex. We've been divorced for about three years."

"Oh." Damn. Somebody must have really acted up for one or both of them to jump ship *immediately* after the baby was born. I think about Bita and the choices she's making, and all of it seems hard.

"So," Arianna says, clasping her delicate hands and getting down to business. "I do have to say how happy I am to meet you, since we rarely meet the authors we edit. We are very excited about the book and think it's going to do very well."

"I'm excited, too…" I pick at a hangnail on my not-so-delicate hands. "I'm worried, though, about all the changes I've made."

"Oh?" Arianna frowns and tips back in her seat. "What are your concerns?"

How long did she have? "Well, I've made an awful lot of changes to make it more reader friendly, or whatever, and, well, I'm afraid it might be too bland or something." And will totally suck. "Too much like everything else that is already out there. Not brave enough. Not interesting enough. Not smart enough. And there's already so many of those types of books out there. The McMillan clones."

"Yes," she says, smiling amiably. "But your book is different. It's set in academia, and that's something we've never quite seen so far with this press. That's a good thing."

"Really?" I cock my head just a tiny bit in that do-not-bullshit me tilt.

"Really. Don't forget. You cover many topics in this book, the ivory tower, how women are treated in the academic setting. And it's funny, too. It's a good combination. A winner."

I'd read some sections to Doris over the phone, a section with Dottie, and we laughed, mainly because it was too funny imagining Doris black, but also because I had fun with the dialogue. My character, Wanda, was supposed to be the nerdy, bourgeois black girl from Washington, D.C., and Dottie was supposed to be "from the streets," at the university on scholarship. The whole thing was absurd, so I just decided to go with it. Dottie had lines like, *"Mothafucka, I will cut you."* And *"hell, naw."* And *"Bitch, do you think I'm playin' with yo silly ass?"* Doris and I almost hurt ourselves, we were laughing so hard.

Still, Arianna makes me feel better. She may be young, but she knows what she's doing it seems. She even shows me reviews from some of the press's more successful titles. We talk some and laugh some and I leave the office promising her the final manuscript within the next month. And after that, nothing to do but wait.

When I leave the building, I can see Doris sitting in the window of the café across the street. When I get closer, I see that she's talking to someone, someone handsome.

"Ronnie," Doris says, putting her coffee down. "This is Maxwell."

"Hello." I grin at him like an idiot. "I've heard a lot about you. Good stuff," I add, a little too late, guessing from Doris's *what in the hell is the matter with you?*

"And," she says, narrowing her eyes at me. "This is Ronnie, Maxwell. The soon-to-be-published author. Her very first book."

"Wow. Congrats," Maxwell says, shaking my hand, strong and sturdy. He has nice ones.

"Did Doris tell you she's black?"

Doris and Maxwell stare at me openmouthed. *"What?"* they say.

Maxwell gives Doris a good long look. "You're black? You never said anything about being black."

"That's because I'm *not,*" Doris says, smacking me hard on the arm. "Are you insane? Did you do a line of coke in old Arianna's office? What my crackhead friend *means* is that she turned the character based on me, in her book, black."

"Oh," Maxwell says, in a long breathy sigh that seems almost like relief.

"Yeah, 'Oh,'" Doris says. "Anyway, we were just headed out." She stands and grabs her bag.

Rude. What's going on here? "Nice to have met you, Maxwell," I say, before Doris damn near rips my arm out of my socket, dragging me out of the joint.

"Jeez." I gently rub my arm. "You got a fire in your panties? What's going on?"

"Pick up the pace," Doris orders, hustling down the street. "Okay, even though you were completely nutty, turning me into a tragic mulatto back there, I was glad to see you because I have blown off Maxwell for a long time now, told him I was traveling, sick, the whole repertoire. I was feeling quite busted."

"I didn't know you two were seeing each other. I thought he vanished."

"He did. Then reappeared. Then another bad date, after which I felt more lukewarm, which of course made him heat up. Now we're just sort of halfhearting it on the phone. I don't know. Maybe I'm crazy."

"Maybe?"

I'm out of breath from the spontaneous track meet by the time we get to the car. I collapse in Doris's car and we lurch onto the street. "Easy, Charlie's Angel or Starsky or Hutch, whichever one you're trying to be. Remember, we were going to die by eating ourselves to death, not in a fiery car crash."

"I don't know what's wrong with me. Maxwell's nice. He's a nice guy."

"And handsome. I wouldn't kick him out of bed for eating crackers."

"What about, like, curds and whey? Would you kick him out of bed for eating curds and whey?"

"I know about Little Miss Muffet, but is that some *actual* vegan thing? Curds and whey? You've seen him eat that?"

"Well," Doris says, flipping her sun visor up and down, "not the curds, but the whey."

"I can't believe we're having this conversation."

"So I'm a horrible, rotten person because I don't like Maxwell."

"Oh, no. Don't even go *there*. It's not the skin color that's bothering you, it's the whey—and the faux-leather sandals. Damn, those are some ugly shoes."

"With khakis, he was wearing those. Why, God, why?"

"So maybe you get him into some kind of other shoes."

We're pulling into Doris complex and it's my last night with her. Who knows how long it will be before we see each other again? I miss her already.

"Wahhh." Doris watches the garage door close behind us. "I'm holding you captive in here. You have to live in my garage and not go back to L.A."

"It'd be cheaper. Could I bring Earl?"

"Like there's any choice about that. You guys? You guys are stuck like glue."

I let Doris have the breezy view of our relationship because I really hope it's true. If we're lucky, Earl and I will always be talking. Race relations is a bitch, but some things are worth the hard work. And some things are not, as in the case of Bita and Charlie. "Unless Hollywood sucks him up and he becomes a jackass." Or I go to jail for killing Katie.

"Never happen. Not to Earl. Not in a million years. He's jackass-proof."

Probably. Most likely so. But if you're not an idiot, then you know that life is always and forever transitory, shifting into one shape or another. I should have told Doris all about everything that happened after the hip-hop show, but I don't. I just let her good faith wash right over me.

Bita's picking me up, as always. There's a special place in heaven, I'm sure, for people who pick their friends up from the airport. I keep looking out for her ginormous car among all the crawling alongside the curb and ignore the little hybrid honking and honking right in front of me. I ignore it as long as I can until I'm about ready to cuss the driver out, but it's Bita.

"*What?* Oh, *man*. Now you've really gone and done it." She grins at me as I struggle to get in the car. "I'm so happy to see you. Give me a hug, dammit." I squeeze her as hard as I can and stare at her. I can't believe she's gone and gotten this itty-bitty car. An LAX parking security guy blows his whistle at us and motions for us to get going.

"What in the world is going on? I'm only away for a few days and already with the new car? I thought you were joking."

"I'm doing what is called getting my shit together." Bita runs her fingers through her thick, dark hair. "New car, new life."

"Good for you," I say. "Good for you."

I hold on to the side of the door because as I've said Bita drives like a wasted rock star sometimes. And in the big car, that was cool, but in the itty-bitty, environmentally safe car, I'm scared shitless. I know, I know. Hypocrisy. But maybe a medium-size car would be better for Bita—and her passengers. "Why the sea change?"

"The what?" She glances at me and frowns. "Don't sound so teacherly and corny."

"Why the complete turnaround?"

"Better," she says smiling, and slaps my thigh. "No more golden handcuffs."

"Bita. I really don't want to know."

"You dummy. Not sex handcuffs, metaphorical handcuffs."

"Oh."

"Anyway, I went for the golden handcuffs, marrying Charlie, living that lifestyle, and at first, I didn't think it was that bad a choice. Now, ten years later, and probably a lot of affairs later, I see it was a real shitty choice. I'm tired of it, tired of turning the other cheek, ignoring God knows how many vaginas Charlie's been into."

"Bita! Watch out for that asshole. He didn't use his signal." She calmly slows down and lets the person cut her off.

"Don't sweat these fools," Bita says, all Zen. She *is* changing. She's the person who I was always sure would get into some bizarre road-rage episode, be on the news with a telephone number asking viewers to please call if they've seen this woman, who is considered armed and dangerous. "It's that simple. You decide what you want, what you can take, and then you go from there. You change."

Somehow, after returning to L.A. from Atlanta, a million years passed, and Earl became, well, not a jackass, never a jackass, but he got a lot more excited about this film stuff. When I called him from Doris's place, he told me that he'd called back home to Indiana and his family and buds had put some stars in his eyes. Now, as I peer through our screen door, I can see and hear him in the bathroom *practicing*. His *delivery*. "Jack on the rocks? Jack. On the rocks. John Daniel, coming right up. Johnny Daniel suit you?"

"Okay, De Niro," I call out as I come in and drop my bags on the floor. "What's this?"

"Hey, baby!" Earl's face is lit up, happy to see me. "Come here, girl. I missed you something terrible. Better put your arms around me."

"It was only four days." I grab his behind and pull him to me.

"Them was long days, baby. Looong days."

"And now you're a method actor."

Earl blushes. "Sit down. You want a beer? I want to sit at the table and have a beer with my woman."

"Pretty please. A beer would be nice. It's around happy hour."

Earl twists the beer caps off and pulls up the one other kitchen chair we have so that he's facing me, our knees touching. He leans toward me and I stick a finger in one of his dimples. "I missed these."

"I ain't going Hollywood, you know. I'm just meeting with the woman on Friday. Said she wanted me to read something. I didn't want to mess up." Earl scratches at his beer bottle with his thumb, looks down at the floor and then looks at me, sheepish, through those long, sandy eyelashes of his.

"I'm not worried. Not yet." I kiss him and take a sip of beer. "But you shouldn't try to get too slick. Bet you ten bucks they like you just the way you are, especially the way you are."

"I know it," Earl says, staring at the street through the screen door. Neither one of us speaks until Earl clears his throat. "I didn't come out here to bartend, Veronica. Not saying I hate it, but I remember telling you back in Langsdale that I wanted to go to law school because I couldn't bartend for all the rest of my days, and now look."

Something about the way Earl says this makes me sad and out of nowhere my eyes well up. Moving back to L.A. has mostly been about me. "I'm sorry, Earl. I know you wouldn't even be here if it weren't for me. And what are we *doing?*"

"Hey, hey." Earl tips up my chin so he can look me in the eyes. "Where's this coming from? Are you going to cry on me? We're fine, baby, we're having a good time here together. That's something."

Yes, but what is the something? Coasting isn't really "something." Even Bita had figured that out.

"Hey," Earl says again. "Look at me. We only got here not too long ago. It hasn't been but, what, five months? Give it some time. Let's you and me just decide to do what it is we really want to do. For now. You told me once: that life is transitory. That's what we're doing now, being transitory."

Check him out. I was creating monsters everywhere, poisoning Ian and now Earl with the lingo of grad school.

I nod. "So you really want to act? Are you *serious?* Actors are the worst. *Almost* as bad as academics," I add, sniffling. "I hate actors."

"Wellll." Earl chuckles. "I ain't no actor, but I can sing. I know that. Let me just see what's what about all this. They might send me packing before I'm in the door good. Now smile for me."

I give Earl a weak smile and hold his face in my hands. "You're a damn good guy, you know that? They don't make 'em like you anymore."

"For that, I'll whip you up some fried chicken for supper," Earl says, and gets up to get himself another beer.

doris

Modernism: A literary movement directly tied to life as it is now, distinguished as it is by fragmentation, a mix of high and low forms, and a latent nostalgia for the days when things were whole. Some lovely high-end writing, and the great heyday of the dead white man. Well, that's a stretch, but it is the movement of William Faulker, Ernest Hemingway, Ezra Pound, T. S. Eliot…all the writers my students think of as "real." But it's also a time when writers like Virginia Woolf, Millay and Marianne Moore entered the playing field as not only equals, but challengers: who lived life on their own terms, asking for that proverbial room of one's own, trying to figure out a way for women to have it all, or at least have what they ask for. A problem still not solved.

A sure indication of modernity is the rapid dislocation of the subject, the separation the subject feels when confronted with their own tenuous construction based largely on surroundings rather than some innate sense of self. In other words, is a person still herself if she gains thirty pounds, dyes her hair brown, and gets air lifted to some deserted island where skinny blondes are one step shy of hagdom? Doubt it. Dislocation, however gentle, is hard on the self. When one moves from place to place, it's natural that one's new surroundings feel alien for quite some time. I imagine that even Cinderella took a few months to adjust to castle living, probably scrubbed a toilet or two and hemmed a couple curtains just to feel like herself again. Two sure benchmarks on the road to adjustment involve travel from the place and the arrival of houseguests. As wonderful as L.A. was, there was something comforting about returning home to Lotto's newest catch-phrase, "you're in or your auf," in his most diva-licious Heidi Klum.

It was also nice to be greeted by Toni the second evening after Ronnie's departure. Toni was back to her usual glam-boho self, hair teased out wildly with a think headband holding it off her forehead, wildly patterned free-flowing minidress and cool go-go boots that only a truly daring soul could wear.

"Look at you," I say. "You taking an author photo for the new book?"

"No," she replies, handing over a magazine story folded neatly into quarters. "I thought you'd get a huge kick out of this. It's the revisitation of that story from years back, you know, the one that said a single woman was more likely to get trampled by a

herd of angry buffalo than get hitched after age forty. They
changed it to buffalo because of the whole terrorist situation
making the odds a little different."

"That was big of them." Toni makes a beeline for my couch
and flops back, crossing her legs defiantly. "Well," she says. "Not
only have they revised the odds, but they proved what we've
always suspected. That single women in their forties are some
badass broads. I think this is a paraphrase of a direct quote,
'Single women in their forties are cream of the crop, men in
their forties, who have never been, are bottom of the barrel.'
So ha. For once we're not the crew being dumped on."

"But, Toni. We're not in our forties."

"But we could be single fortysomethings, and I'm just glad
that I can put in my book that we are not hallucinating. That it's
confirmed that women who stay single are not necessarily
pariahs, but potential demigoddesses."

"So you're now single and proud."

She gives me a little smile as if she's been sneaking in while
I was in L.A. and hording the Pop-Tarts.

"Actually, Tino and I are back together. And I think it's
really serious."

"You're kidding! Details, details."

"Well, as it turns out, when he was in college he was practically engaged to a woman who was black, and his family was
just awful about it. Called him up, told him he was bringing
down generations of race purity, that people would think he
was trash, what would the neighbors say, and all that shit that
folks who claim not to be racist start spewing when interracial
dating is the issue."

"Yikes. That's harsh."

She gets up and paces a little as she continues.

"So he does the right thing, tells his family to screw them-selves, and then the almost fiancée cheats on him. Totally dumps him for some hippie joker she met on a job interview. So he's totally screwed, blew the family off, then she blows him off. So he figures, once he feels like dating again, that it's just easier to date a white girl than go through that same hell with his family."

"I guess that makes sense."

"I'm not sure it makes sense, but it's the best explanation I could possibly have received. And he's totally down with dating a black girl, and he says he'll go nuts if he loses me. I swear, he sounded like some cheap-ass romance novel, but instead of wanting to throw up, I just wanted to thank God and the heavens and everything else that this one thing was not going to total shit."

"See. Thank goodness you heard him out!"

"I know," she says. "So I have an idea. Let's go get loaded. I'm all dressed up, and Tino's out of town for the weekend, and we haven't had an official girl's night in millennia."

"Godfather, that is an offer I can't refuse."

Hungover, the next morning, one of those laws of thermo-dynamics came to bite me in the face. The one about how for every action, there is an equal and opposite reaction, or put in dating terms, for every reconciled couple, some poor beeatch (to quote Lotto) is getting dumped on her arse. This morning, said arse was mine, and said dumping took place over the inglorious medium of voice mail. Specifically, Maxwell saying somewhat sheepishly, *I was hoping to talk to you before you saw the paper this morning, but I guess you're still sleeping. It probably wouldn't have worked anyhow.* Not words to warm one's heart before the first cup of coffee. And, of course, I'm thinking *which* paper, and I don't even *get* the paper, and would Toni notice or care if I stole hers first thing?

Fortunately, Toni was up and running ahead of me, and I answered the gentle knock at my door to find her looking sad and sympathetic. She held out her newspaper like some tract on how Jesus was going to save your soul.

"Don't shoot the messenger," she said, handing me the Life & Style section. "Open to the gossip page."

And there, on page three, was a picture of Maxwell with Maggie Mae Mischner, canoodling over something that was decidedly not beet juice and bean sprouts. Beneath the photo was the caption: "CELEBUTANTE MOVES ON WITH DEBO-NAIR LAWYER."

"Oh, for God's sake," I say. "Must every man alive have some form of savior complex?"

As far as I was concerned, Maggie Mae Mischner might as well have had actual pinwheels spinning at the center of her eyeballs, and a veritably bunny farm in the backyard ready for easy harvest, when the next poor bastard crossed her. And Maxwell was dating her? In a way, it could make a perverse kind of sense. Anyone sensitive enough to care about the fate of cowhide could probably get sucked in by a slow dose of nut bride.

Toni looked at the picture again and laughed.

"Guess he never heard that old saying that when you see crazy coming, better cross the street."

"He heard it," I say. "He's just confused about which direction you cross to. He is officially doing the emotional equivalent of walking into oncoming traffic."

"In pleather," Toni adds.

"I wash my hands of it," I say, gesturing dramatically.

The next day my invitation arrives for the opening of Zach's movie theater. The layout looks like an old pulp fiction cover, heralding the arrival of the "Langsdale Lounge." Evidently, it's going to be a place where one can order a coffee, a small meal and watch art films or re-releases. And as promised, the back announces the inaugural series on "Femme Fatales and Fallen Females." I question the use of "female," but give Zach credit for attempting consonance. First film is, indeed, *What Ever Happened to Baby Jane?* followed by *Mildred Pierce, Out of the Past* and *The Last Seduction.* An absolutely fantasy lineup, to my way of thinking, and I wonder if Zach isn't doing a little bit of covert seducing himself. And while I know that calling on one's ex is standard just-dumped protocol, that's not the only reason I pick up the phone to see how Zach is doing.

The real reason is that I miss him.

"Got the invite," I say when he answers. "You're really in touch with your inner gay man these days. Are you sure there's not something you want to tell me?"

"Just to buy a ticket now because airfare's going to go up."

I twist my hair unconsciously, flirting with Zach visually even in his absence.

"So it's all good to go?" I ask. "Do people seem interested?"

Note to self: do not be maternal. You are not dating. Any failure is his alone.

"Great response from the community. We're going to do a series on Italian cinema, from neorealism on, and then one on vintage comedies. And I think they're going to let us use the park to set up a screen next summer, not that it will make any real money, but it will generate even more interest."

I try to stop myself from asking, but can't. "What about your dissertation?"

Zach pauses for a minute, and I fear that I've blown it again.

"I wrote nearly two chapters since you left. Every down minute, I'm working on the book. I'm practically a hermit."

Again, I try to stop myself from asking the obvious, but cannot. "What about your girlfriend."

Zach laughs. "She wasn't *exactly* my girlfriend, Doris. Those are more your words than mine. Just trying to see how easy it would be to get over you."

"How could you not get over me?" I ask. "I'm such a pain in your ass, it's probably a relief."

"Maybe at first," he says. "But you were a lot more than a pain in my ass. My thought is that you should come here for the summer, see how things are, and then we'll figure something out for the fall."

Now he's pissing me off. I stop twirling my hair and gesture at the invisible Zach in front of me.

"Problem one—I *know* how Langsdale is in the summer. It's a festering hellhole of mosquitos, hundred percent humidity, tornadoes and bad English department parties. Remember? I *fled* Langsdale, and while I might miss you, I don't miss that place one minute of my life. Not one lonely, shitty, crappy, I-am-alone-in-Atlanta minute. I hate small towns. I hate running into my students at the three normal venues in the entire place. I hate everything about living there except for you."

"Can't that be enough? Just for one summer. I'm not asking forever, just a summer that we can not fight, and try to get ourselves back on track. Because I know you love your job, Doris, and I know you've worked hard for it, but don't you want someone in your life to share it with?"

I look at my empty but fabulous apartment, and close my eyes to keep him from tricking me with his codependent babble.

"Like we wouldn't fight," I say. "I'll have to think about it. Can we talk about something else?"

"How was Ronnie's visit?"

"Fun. We ate enough macaroni and cheese that even I'm sick of it now, and Ronnie got most of the work finished on her novel. They made her revise it so the thinly veiled version of me is black. It's slightly hilarious."

"Another black valley-child. Just what the world needs."

"But black Doris is very sassy. She grew up in the hood, and being in Langsdale tapped into her inner militant. She and Wanda are cotokens, but in true novel fashion, they handle things very differently."

Zach laughs. "Does black Doris dress like you? That'd be funny."

"I didn't check. But I hear in the book she dates some real jackass from her English program named Mack."

"That black Doris," Zach says. "Whatever does she do with him?"

"You'll have to read the book to see."

Zach laughs again. "Ronnie must be going crazy with that. What'd they do with Earl, make him a Black Panther?"

"You'llllll seeeeee."

"I gotta run," Zach says. "But I have it under good authority that black Doris would spend the summer in Langsdale to see how things turn out with Mack. I heard she's just that kind of madcap, risk-lovin' gal."

"You could come here," I say. "Does that thought just flee your mind every time you think of our possible future together?"

"I never said I wouldn't come there. I just asked that you make this one step toward me for the summer. Then we'll see."

We'll see is what high school boys say to their girlfriends whom they want to sleep with but not necessarily date. It's what producers say to fat models and ugly actresses when they go on auditions. *We'll see,* is most often, *Leave me alone until I have the balls to say "no."*

"Are you going Buddhist or something? I hate 'we'll see.' It smacks of self-righteous detachment. And what am I supposed to do for money?"

"I thought you'd just write. If this all works out, I'll have enough money for both of us, for summer at any rate. Just keep it in mind. And buy your ticket for December. I'm working on

Earl to get him and Ronnie out here, too. A regular reunion, you know, between you two sistahs."

"Shut up, Zach." I'm smiling even though he can't see it.

"Word."

"Don't be an idiot," I say.

And then I hang up the phone.

If Zach had been lighting candles at the local parish for a change of heart on my behalf, he couldn't have lined up a better first customer of the day than Paige Prentiss. I thought that I'd dodged a bullet when I first got back from L.A. Two weeks of office hours passed without her mystic tan and Gucci bag materializing in my office. If she'd once wanted to talk to me, the desire seemed to have passed. In fact, it was almost as if her desire to talk, period, had passed. She wasn't even sullen proper, just withdrawn during class. And while a good teacher-mommy, since mommy and teacher are often cross-referenced in the average student's mind, would have called her into the office to find out what was really going on, I had clearly crossed over to bad teacher-mommy, and was just relieved to have some time without the thought police hot on my trail.

So I almost wondered if Zach hadn't paid her off when I see her outside my office first thing on Tuesday morning. As usual, I am juggling two tote bags full of papers, books and unread memos about department meetings and the like. At least Paige has the good, Southern manners to take an armload of books while I opened the door. Paige looks a little tired, a little less made-up than I'd come to expect, and her hair, while still close to camera ready, is looped in a decidedly unfashionable pink and blue scrunchie straight from the back page of *Glamour* magazine don'ts.

"I'm sorry it's early, Dr. Weatherall," she starts. "But your office hours do start at nine, correct?"

She's right, although it's already just past nine fifteen. This might have been a barb, but it sounded strangely like a plea. We enter my office and Paige sits straight backed in the chair across from me. She folds her hands in her lap and then closes her eyes as she says, "My mother is getting married. Again."

I have no idea what this has to do with anything English related, but decide to quiet my inner voice, which is all but screaming, "GO PAY A THERAPIST FOR THIS," and ask, "Is that a good thing?"

"Her third marriage, *since* my father. And every time she changes completely. Phil, the guy, runs a construction company that's building a new skyscraper for Ted Turner. He's rich, but so, so tacky. You cannot buy taste. Did you see that bra my mother wore to your class? That's not my mother. Even I don't have a red bra, too hooker-y. That's Phil. And Phil has enrolled her in good wife classes at his church. I want to get married. I know that. But my mother…"

I am thinking, in this order, "I have two red bras," and "is *hooker-y* an adjective?" Paige is clearly frustrated, but I'm still not sure what any of this has to do with me. I slip out of my tennis shoes, working-girl style, and slide into my less comfortable but much cuter work shoes, a pair of gold-tone ballet flats that I didn't want to get wet in the morning rain. The third thing that crosses my mind is that I'd really like to find out is what they're teaching in good wife classes, but I don't want to seem like a total smart-ass.

"Then there's you," Paige says. She says it like she's pointing to my chalk outline sketched across the carpet. "You have this job where people listen to you—" (dubious, but I'll let it slide) "—and you have your independence, and you say what you think no matter what other people think. I can't see you going to church class for some guy named Phil, but at the same time, you're not married. None of you all are married. Not you, not any of the other women professors. Is that because you have so many opinions? Do you even want to get married?"

This is rapidly becoming worse than talking to my own mother. I can see what's happening. It's no longer good mommy-bad mommy time with the mama Prentiss as my foil, but a Goldilocks situation, where one is too hot, the other too cold, and the younger Ms. Prentiss cannot seem to fathom where one finds the life equivalent of just right. She, and everyone else I know.

"That's a personal question. For one thing, there are a lot of married or partnered professors, they probably just don't wear rings or announce it. And it's not that marriage or having children are things that I never think about, but I'm happy with most of the choices that I've made. I'm happy to have this job, and the chance to put my education to something that at least approximates good use. It's not that I don't date or think about having a family, but that doesn't automatically solve the problem of who you are, or who you want to be in the world. There are lots of unhappily married people in the world. It's not a cure-all for loneliness. And believe it or not, there are lots of smart, independent women with boyfriends."

I'm thinking *at least I hope there are,* but now is not the time to show weakness. Paige sighs.

"My mother thinks being married proves something."

"Well, the beauty of life is that we don't have to model our lives on our mothers'. We can model them on whomever we choose, or pick some course that's totally different from anything they might have imagined. But I'll tell you, just because you pick a certain kind of life, doesn't mean that everything will go as planned. You need to get to a place where you are not only happy with your own choices, but you can let your mother make her own choices and mistakes, as well. Or me, God knows I make some mistakes." And at that exact moment I'm thinking about Zach, wondering if I'm not being a bit too cold, too uncompromising. I continue, "But the nice part about life is that if you live long enough, you can at least work to correct some of those. You're young. And you're going to make some good choices and some bad choices—it's just a given. Though you'll be a lot happier if you cut everyone some slack, including yourself."

She sighs. "I'm sorry about my mother coming to class. And the other things…"

Either she's been possessed by a good demon or shelling out mucho dinero for therapy. It's actually a little frightening, like one of those gangster dramas when things are going really, really well and you just know the massacre is a moment from your door. But the massacre never comes. Instead, Paige picks up her bag just as Asa ducks her head in my office.

"Doris, can I talk to you when you're finished?"

"Sure," I tell her, trying to conceal my utter lack of enthusiasm. "Just a minute."

Paige notices my tone and smiles. When Asa leaves, Paige lowers her voice a bit. "I wanted to talk to you about something else."

She holds her bag a bit closer to her and whispers, "Dr. Block. I didn't want you thinking that... I know there are things people say about him. And I didn't really believe them. But I think he might have tried to kiss me. I just..."

So the silences in class aren't only about me.

"Paige, it's not your fault."

She sniffles and looks toward the ceiling. "I just thought that he believed I was this amazing writer. And he's such an incredible writer. I just..."

"Don't worry," I say. "Was it just the one incident?"

"Yes."

"Do you have to have any contact with him?"

"No."

"Then don't."

"But I need his recommendation to help get me into law school."

"Oh, well, don't you worry about that. He's going to write you the *glowing* recommendation that you *deserve* for your *writing*."

Paige looks relieved.

"You don't think less of me."

I shake my head. "I hope you go back to talking in class. The last thing I want you to feel is silenced. Even if your opinions are different from my own, I do want you to have opinions."

"I know. It's not that. It's just been a bad few weeks. But I'll be back to normal soon."

"Threat or promise?" I ask, wondering immediately if sarcasm is the right approach. But Paige comes back quickly.

"Promise."

Asa walks by again, looking quickly in my office. Scary that at this exact moment I like Paige better than I do Asa.

After Paige leaves, I spend a few minutes prepping for my morning class, then I go to check on Asa. She's a bit more chipper than usual, surrounded by stacks of papers and opened books. Either she's working her ass off, or just far better than I at creating that illusion. On close inspection, though, her eyes look watery, and her hair, while brushed, is at least two days' worth of dirty.

"I just thought you should know that David and I broke up." She folds her hands together. Her nails look professionally manicured. So Asa is at least part regular girl underneath it all, heading for the salon in times of crisis. "And I wanted to tell you because I wanted you to know that I know what went on between the two of you."

She says this with zero affect. Like she's cross-referencing a witness to see if she can trick her into talking.

"Nothing went on between the two of us," I say as clearly and unemotionally as possible. If there's one thing I know about a liar—that is to say, David and/or Andrew—it's that he never lies about just one thing. If he lied about his name and lied about their relationship, it's highly likely that he lied about whatever allegedly happened between the two of us.

"I know. I should probably thank you in a way. He was so nervous that you might have told me something, that he came clean, from out of nowhere. I guess he feels threatened by the fact that I have this job, and he's still in school. He said that he needed to feel important, like the 'alpha.' Can you believe it? He actually said that. 'Alpha.' Like he's some mutt and I'm, what, his bitch? A Ph.D."

"And not even like some saucy music video kind of bitch, he's talking actual dog. God, that burns me up. Like you can't win for trying if you do well in this world."

Asa sniffs and wipes her hand against the corners of her eyes. "I thought he was better than that. I really did, that's the thing. He never acted this way when we were both in school."

I sit down, and push the candy dish filled with mini-Snickers across the desk.

"People change, Asa. You really don't want someone who speed dates behind your back. For all you know he'll start dating Paige. That's all you need."

Asa smiles, and even though her eyes are red, they crinkle genuinely.

"Thanks. For not telling me. I wouldn't have wanted to hear it."

She has, of course, proven what I feared. That she's half-crazy. But right now she is half-crazy and contrite, and I'm still in the position of trying not to alienate anyone.

"I honestly wasn't sure what to do. But at the end of the day nothing had transpired, and I didn't feel it was my place."

She nodded. "I was angry at you at first. I thought you should have told me, but then I could see why you wouldn't want to get involved, and that maybe you thought in some way that I was better off not knowing."

Which is academic for "we all have situations in which the course of action is grey, where you're not sure if it's best to involve yourself or stay out of the way, where you can't say for sure if what you've been seeing is something or nothing, and you don't want people to hurt unnecessarily." It's academic for "thank you for behaving like a friend."

The rest of the afternoon, I stew over what I'd like to say to Antonius Block the next time that I see him. Unfortunately, I am in the unenviable position of David to his Goliath. Untenured junior faculty taking on the one departmental institution. Yet, if I'm the archetypal David figure, what does that make Paige? Who's going to stand up for her, and what message does it send if the Antonius Blocks of the world are not merely tolerated, but tacitly encouraged when people like me turn the other cheek?

It's not so much that Block hit on Paige, as that by hitting on her he undermined her security in her own accomplishments and intelligence. And the whole thing is so clichéd that my inner writer cringes. Antonius Block, of all people, should know better than to fall into such a bastardized narrative. Antonius Block, whose sonnets I shall not again be able to read with any degree of pleasure, and damn him for that, as well!

I decide that the best thing to do is confront him directly. If there's one thing I've learned from the paper trail of class complaints, it's the courtesy of direct address. Block's office door is half-open, the inside lit with the last natural light of the day. He has on reading glasses, and is reclining in an oversize leather chair with a book by Robert Pinsky held arm's distance from his face.

"Why, Dr. Weatherall," he says. "To what do I owe this pleasure?"

I take a deep breath.

"One of my students came by this afternoon. Paige Prentiss. It seems she had a rather troubling encounter with you recently."

Block waves his book at me as though he's swatting a fly. "You know how imaginative girls that age can be."

I wait two more seconds before committing possible career suicide.

"No, I don't. I don't think she was being imaginative at all. I think she was upset, and felt betrayed, and you're responsible for that whether you like it or not. You. Are. Responsible."

Block raises an eyebrow and lays the book down.

"Well, you seem to know everything having heard only half the facts. Did Ms. Prentiss mention what she was wearing into my office that afternoon? Did she stress her own half-clothed state?"

I measure my response.

"You're the adult. She admires you. And you know better."

He hesitates a half second before squint-smirking at me as though everything I've just said is beneath his consideration.

Then he sighs, picks up his book, and says, "Well, if that's all, Dr. Weatherall, I have some reading to attend to."

And I know better than to argue any further, to quit while I'm not completely in over my head. I look him straight in the eye, hold the gaze so he knows that I mean it, and then leave. Career suicide, possibly, but there still have to be a few causes worth dying for.

The next day, I decide against leaving my bed. Part of me is still angry at Antonius Block, angry that regardless of how badly he behaved, he will never, ever, ever acknowledge it—not even to himself. I fantasize about writing a rebuttal book of poems to his sexist-but-brilliant sonnets, a Phair-esque "Exile in Guyville" to his Stones-canonical "Exile on Main Street." Delusional, yes, but nice that I'm finally fantasizing about writing again.

By midafternoon, I still have not received an e-mail letting me go, so I finally change out of my sweats and decide to face the day. It's been autumn for a while now, but this is one of the first afternoons that really feels like fall. Sweater weather. People are outside enjoying the sun, the crisp air and the cool breeze. There's something wonderful about being alone, about walking in silence among the pairs of people, the groups of people, even the solitary readers nestled under the trees, carefully chosen books in hand. The little dogs are out en masse, and I have canine envy, trying to decide whether a Boston terrier or an Italian greyhound would be a better companion-savior from this life of thwarted intentions. Atlanta isn't yet my city, but it's a great city, and I love being here. Funny how you can suddenly become attached to a place just when it seems like the option to stay might evaporate.

I consider whether I haven't been engaging in a bit of Paige Prentissing myself, drawing an unnecessary line in the sand between Zach and my life here. Sure, long distance isn't anyone's first choice or fantasy, but I've been working so hard not to give an inch of ground, to prove that I'm not the kind of woman who tosses everything away for some guy, that I've forgotten that everyone who has a healthy relationship cedes an inch or two of turf in the interest of peace and parity. And that taking two steps toward Zach doesn't necessarily mean that I'm taking three back in my life. Even I know that summer in Langsdale wouldn't be that different from summer in Atlanta: hot and sweltering. I just wouldn't have to spend it alone. *Not,* I might add, that there's anything wrong with that. It just seems that my life lessons lean toward the other direction—toward understanding that it's okay to learn to need a person, faults and film series and all.

If Zach has been lighting candles, he must be on God's good side, because the phone is ringing and it's Ronnie. I park myself beneath a tree, and the light filters through the leaves and freckles across my legs.

"I got blown off over voice mail," I tell her. "For the nut-bride."

"Noooooo," Ronnie says. "I saw that picture online here, and I thought it was just a coincidence. You know, two hot black men in Atlanta, both named Maxwell, who like dating crazy white women."

"Har-har. No, that's my very own fetishist. Maybe she's willing to give up burgers for him."

"Maybe she sees another good publicity opportunity."

"Yeah. I guess. I hate being dumped."

"Why? Because you were so deeply in love with him and your soul mate is gone? Every time I talk to you you're finding reasons not to like him. He just beat you to the punch. And didn't you go on three dates? I'm not sure you can even be dumped after three dates."

A beautiful-past-heterosexual man with a miniature pinscher walks by and gives me a sympathetic smile.

"Random strangers in the park feel more sorry for me than you do."

"I don't know, Doris. This seems to me to make your life easier. You've had one door closed for you, so you can concentrate on the one that's been half-open this whole time. I think you need to decide where you are with Zach once and for all before you take on another Maxwell or anyone else. Besides, I simply cannot think that it's a bad thing to lose a man who won't eat meat. Think of all the other things he might abstain from on moral grounds."

"I do like them a little depraved." I wish that Ronnie were here, and that we could have this discussion over two martinis and a bowl of hot wings. "So Zach wants me to come stay with him for the summer."

"In Langsdale?" Ronnie asks, barely disguising her horror.

"Thank you, yes, in Langsdale. I feel like if I go, I'm like one of those women in a horror movie who's escaped from a dungeon, but goes back into the haunted house to look for her cat, or some shit like that. I worked so hard to leave that hellhole behind."

I get a raised eyebrow from a passerby.

"Depends on how important Zach is to you."

"Why can't I be so important to Zach that he comes here? Why!"

"Deep breath, Doris. Maybe it's because you have the summers off. Did you talk about the possibility of his moving?"

"How can he, with that stupid movie theater? See, I end up back in the same place. And I can't give up my job for him. I worked too, too, too hard. Even if I am one of those miserable career women that Toni clips articles about in the newspaper. I simply don't think it's fair that I move on right now. Not when I just got here."

"You haven't even seen the stupid movie theater."

"I know. And I'm only getting mad because I miss him. I really, really, really miss him. He would never, ever, ever in ten million years date a Maggie Mae Mischner."

"Unless she were a lesbian."

"Or a twelve-year-old," I say, laughing. "And this is the person I so romanticize."

"He's a good man, and he loves you. I'd say see the theater with an open mind. I really think the two of you need some face time before you make any more decisions about the rest of your life."

Maybe I am giving in to nostalgia for the past, or the desire to be the person I was when I was with Zach, but upon arrival home I book a ticket for Langsdale. I leave December tenth with an open-ended return date. Obviously I won't stay there any time past when school starts here, but I'm going to try to leave judgment at the door and see what happens in freezing-ass Langsdale with my pseudohippie un-ex-boyfriend. The minute I buy the ticket I feel relieved. I remember what it was like the first night I spent with Zach, the way his hair smelled, the way his voice sounded lower in the dark. I remember the time he made me dinner with anemic farmer's market vegetables that had wilted in his refrigerator, and the hat he knit me, shaped vaguely like a beret, even after all the times I'd barbed him about knitting. I remember driving around in the middle of the night when neither of us could sleep, and parking near the lake to listen to the frogs.

And although the odds might be against us, at least now I'll know that I gave it every shot I could. That Zach and I tried to be one for the decade if not one for the ages. It's also nostalgia that makes me forward the e-mail of my itinerary immediately to Ronnie, even though I know she's doing final edits on her novel and I should probably be leaving her alone. Because as much as I love my new life, I still clearly have one foot firmly planted in the old. And maybe it's disjointed, and maybe it's dislocated, and maybe there's not much else for a modern girl to be but a little fragmented and unsure, but this evening, I am ninety-nine percent positive that I'm making the right decisions.

ronnie

The great irony of being an academic, or professor, or teacher of any kind is that you're likely the biggest idiot on the planet when it comes to real life. The last to know what any B-list actor would know. Perhaps it is unfair to say likely, but damn, it's been a coincidence that in my life I have observed this to be true any number of times.

Like, I actually thought I was in some epic power struggle with Ian, but he's just a kid. He's still just a kid who's a colossal pain in the ass, although I'd forgotten what it was like to be sixteen, for one, and I'd also mistaken his insecurity for some sort of threat against me and who I was. When really, in spite of all of his dough and privilege, and big-mouth bravado, he has a huge deficit in the Figuring Out Who He Is Department, whereas I—even if I have been stumbling around a bit since coming home to L.A.—pretty much know what I am. It's just a matter of applying who I am to the world at large. You can read a ton of books, teach a ton of classes, and still take a while to come to what Oprah calls "The Aha Moment." I call it the "Duh! Moment."

Ian and I put the hip-hop showcase fiasco behind us. We revisited the hip-hop video paper he had written, and now after going to that show, Ian said he understood some things. He looked miserable, having to tell me I was right, but he told me anyway. He was scribbling on his paper, doodling stars and daggers.

"So, like, does your nephew think I'm a dick or something?"

I watched him doodle and started scribbling on my legal pad. I did happy faces. "You didn't make a good first impression, no. Not your strength, first impressions."

Ian kept scribbling and then threw his pencil down on the table. He turned up his lip like Billy Idol used to, back in the day. "At least I admit I'm an ass."

"*Now* you do."

And Ian rolled his eyes for, like, the hundreth time since I've known him.

Today is my last session with Ian, but I've got a lot of other students set up thanks to Mr. and Mrs. Bernstein. They think I've worked a small miracle by tutoring Ian into a B+ in his English class. Turns out there are all kinds of lazy, overprivileged kids in Hollywood, Bel Air, the Palisades and Malibu, with parents who are desperate for somebody to bully their children into shape. This is what Ian is telling his "friend" and my new tutee, Shonna, built like a brick house, dressed "down" like she's still got money to burn, chew up and spit out. Punker chic is how I'd describe her. She twirls her bone-straight, blue-black hair and stares at me with heavily lined brown eyes. She's got three blue stars tattooed up her forearm, and is wearing a black T-shirt that says YOU SUCK. The old lady in me wants to say, "Honey, why, oh, why would you wear a mean shirt like that?" But after almost half a year with Ian, the not-so-old lady in me thinks her shirt is practically charming.

"So you guys aren't dating?" I have to ask. I'm packing up all my books except the one I gave Ian as a We Survived Each Other Gift. It's Aldous Huxley's *Brave New World*. When Ian asked if it was fun or a bummer, I said it was a sneaky-fun book. It snuck up on you and you ended up liking it for all the lessons it taught you about the way you didn't want to live your life. He said that sounded like a fucking bummer, all right.

Shonna grinned at Ian, who's as red as the polish on Shonna's nails. "Nah, we're not dating," she replies. "We just hooked up a couple times."

I know that "a hookup" can be anything from kisses to marathon intercourse, so I quit while I'm ahead. "That's cool," I say. "Ian's a good guy."

Ian gives me a look like, I *am?*

Shonna grabs Ian's hand from across the table. "Ian says he thought you were a total bitch and a complete idiot when you first started tutoring him, but that's just because you didn't take any of his shit." Leaning in, she gives him a kiss on the cheek.

"Well, Ronnie couldn't stand me, either," Ian adds defensively, chewing his metallic green fingernails. "She totally hated my guts."

"Not your guts," I clarify, standing with my book bag slung over my arm. "Just your completely fucked-up attitude."

Ian grins when I say that. "See?" Ian turns to Shonna. "I told you she's no bullshit."

"Are you sure you want me to tutor you?" I ask, checking my watch. I have to meet Earl and Bita in a little bit.

"Yeah," Shonna says, nodding slow and easy as if she's listening to music on headphones. "I'm totally cool with you."

"Good." I move to leave the study. "Because I'm cool with you, too."

"I'll be right back," Ian tells Shonna, and follows behind me.

"What?" I adjust my book bag as we make our way down the hallway and toward the door. "Don't tell me you're walking me out. What a gentleman."

"Fucking with me to the end," Ian says, shaking his head.

"Old habits die hard." I open the door and step out. "Thanks for the word of mouth. I may actually make a living."

"And get a cell phone, I hope."

"The very next thing on my list."

"Later." Ian leans on the door. "I hope your car starts."

"Fucking with me to the end," I say before I get in my car. Ian juts his chin out, the cool person's goodbye, and it's a small miracle, but my car starts—loudly—and I watch Ian close the door in my rearview mirror.

As I drive away, I remember when I returned Ian's phone call after the hip-hop show. He said he'd learned something about himself, something he thought was really shitty. And I told him I'd learned something about myself, too, since I knew, on some level, that things were going to happen exactly the way they did. And maybe there was something shitty about that. Very know-it-all and obnoxious, since Ian was too easy a target. He was no match for me, not ever, really. I'm a "grown-ass woman" as my mother says. I had to leave academics and teaching in Langsdale, Indiana, for my home-grown academics and teaching in Los Angeles, California, to figure that out.

Earl's still bartending—and going on auditions. I can barely say that without gagging, but since he was the supportive boyfriend all these months, I have to be nice about this, surreal as it is. When I think how concerned I was about Earl, concerned about how the good old boy would blend in L.A. I have to laugh. It's amusing as hell. He's still the same old Earl, thank God. Sincere. Charming. Hot. But he's also figured out that he doesn't really want to do anything but give this whole singing, acting thing a shot. There's something in the water, I swear, that makes perfectly normal people want to take their shot at show business once they get to Hollywood. So now that I'm pulling in reasonable dough with the six kids I tutor, it's time for him to see what he can do. He did get that bit part in a film. One line: *Jack on the rocks, bud. Coming at you.* He says that might get cut. But he doesn't care. He's happy, and if he's happy, so am I.

Tonight, we're celebrating four things. For one, I've finished tutoring Ian, and everybody I know is happy about that, glad that it all turned out okay. Doris called and left a message on our phone, asking if I was dancing up and down the street naked with joy. She also said that I'd be all right, even if I didn't see Ian every day. "You were secretly in love with a sixteen-year-old!" she yelled into the answering machine. The second thing we're celebrating is Earl getting that teeny part in the movie, the third thing is a bit premature, but I'm about to see the cover of *F: The Academy* in a day or two, and the fourth thing we're celebrating is the fact that Bita's divorce is final, which is a happy and a sad thing. We're eating in the neighborhood at Farfalla, a place where a man like Earl can get an actual piece of meat if he wants it, but a place that's medium-scale Italian that actually feels fancy. And I can pay for my and Earl's meals—for a very shocking change.

"Let's toast," Bita says above the jazz softly playing in the background. She raises her glass. I was busy swirling my bread in olive oil and shove the bread in my mouth, so that I can hold up my glass. Earl holds up his glass of beer and puts the other hand on my leg underneath the table.

"I see that, Earl." Bita grins, but then stares off into the distance. Her hair is in a loose bun and she's wearing huge gold hoops. I think she's the most gorgeous woman I know.

"You okay, Bita?" I lean into the table, peering into her face and Earl and I exchange glances.

"Hey, buddy." It's been Earl's nickname for Bita and it always makes her smile. "You all right?" he asks.

"Ah, hell," Bita says. "You guys look so happy. I guess I miss that asshole sometimes."

"Sure you do," I say softly. I reach across the table and grab her hand. She let's me hold it for a while and then she pulls away, brushing her bread crumbs off the white tablecloth.

"I'm better off without him," she says, shaking her head, making up her mind.

"He didn't treat you right, buddy," Earl points out.

"You knew it the whole time," I remind her. "You just didn't listen to yourself."

"I was so scared." Bita pushes around the asparagus on her plate. "I was scared to leave and scared to stay. And I kept thinking how had this happened to *me?* The hard-ass, the woman who was always so together."

"You were a *baby* when you met him. We were just kids in college, barely older than Ian."

"I believe you are in love with Ian, just like Doris said," Earl says, pinching me on my side. "That's going on, what, the third time you've mentioned him tonight."

Bita agrees. "If you leave Earl for Ian, I got dibs on Earl," she says, winking at him.

Earl blushes. "You got yourself a deal, buddy."

"Sick." I put more salt and pepper in my olive oil and soak my bread in it. "You guys are sick."

All the talk of Ian reminds me of the last time I saw Charlie. He wasn't with Bita, he was at the Bernsteins' house for dinner—with the little chippie he was dating. He'd been long kicked out of the house and was staying at the fancy-ass W Hotel in Westwood. It was strictly a horrible accident that I'd run into him in the first place. Ian's tutoring session had gone

late. We were talking about James Baldwin and Dostoyevsky—
more bummer stuff that Ian still liked, even if he pretended not
to. I was walking down the hallway as usual, leaving the house,
when the Bernsteins came through the door, with Charlie and
the chippie in tow. The Bernsteins knew Bita, of course, knew
I was her close friend, so we all stood in the hallway looking
miserable until Charlie summoned up the balls to introduce me
to *Kiya,* who looked about as old as Shonna, which made Charlie
a big fat cliché. If I'm to be the mature woman that I'm claiming
to be, I should honestly say that the *child* was pretty (in a predictable kind of way) with manners (gave me a sincere hello)
and didn't seem to have a bitchy bone in her body (unlike myself
at that moment). And God bless her, Kiya seemed *into* Charlie,
who seemed alcoholically bloated.

"Kiya's our receptionist," Mr. Bernstein said, nervously
tugging at the cuffs of his Oxford shirt. He had a thick shock
of wavy, grey hair that he was fussing with the whole time. Mrs.
Bernstein appeared to give me a *look,* a look that said, *Can you
believe this motherfucker?* But I couldn't be sure.

"Liking your job?" Charlie asked, wasting no time in remind-
ing me that I had a check coming to me every week because of
him.

"I *do,*" I replied, my eyes darting between Charlie and Kiya.
"I love working with kids, just like you."

"Charlie," Mr. Bernstein said, "let's get you a drink." He
pulled Kiya and Charlie into the sitting room, and that was the
last time I saw Charlie.

"What was the 'kids' business?" Ian asked. "I'm not a fucking kid."

"Mouth, Charlie," Mrs. Bernstein said. "Goddammit." She turned to me. "It won't last," she blurted. "And I never liked Charlie, anyway. He's not that great a writer. Ira has some attachment to him, for some reason."

"Yeah," Ian said, snapping what seemed like two dozen black bands on his wrist. "That guy's a complete tool."

Mrs. Bernstein shrugged. "Whatever that means. Night, Veronica." She looked at Ian. "And if you sit down to dinner with us, you didn't hear any of this."

"Whatever," Ian said, and took the stairs up to his room two at a time.

I let myself out.

And I thought, Good for you, Bita, for letting yourself out. Kids grow up, kids in college who marry too soon. And she had the smarts to get out when it all went wrong.

Coming back to the conversation at hand, Bita and Earl are talking about Bita taking some head shots for Earl. Jesus. *Head shots.*

"I will capture your true essence, Erardo Lo Vecchio," Bita says, laughing. "The rugged you, the country boy, all that."

"Sounds good," Earl says, taking the final bite of his steak. He's chewing thoughtfully when we both hear someone calling his name, all squeaky and excited.

"Earl!"

Before I see her, I know it's Katie. What in the hell is she doing here?

"Hey, Earl-y," she says.

Earl-y?

She's with an older man who, I hope, is her father. His thinning black hair is combed back, sleek and greasy, and he's wearing a white silk shirt, khakis and sneakers. Very chic. Or something. She's hardly paying attention to him, she's slobbering over Earl so much.

"Hey, Katie," Earl says, tense. He grabs my hand under the table as if to say, do not go postal. "Who's this you got with you?"

"Oh. I almost forgot." Katie tugs on the man's arm. "This is Reginald. We met at the bar. He's recently divorced," she says, tugging on her pink belly shirt. "He lives in Bel Air and I'm just showing him the neighborhood." Her hair is in two ponytails, which at twenty-six she can barely get away with.

Reginald gives her a look that says, *Bitch, tell everybody my business, why don't you,* but then he composes himself and puts his arm around Katie's waist. "Hello, everyone," he says.

Katie still hasn't thrown in the towel. She's looking at Earl as if he's her last supper, meanwhile, she and Reginald are blocking all the waitstaff's way, standing around like they are.

"Reginald, this is Earl, Vanessa, and..." She raises an eyebrow at Bita.

"Bita," Bita supplies, picking at her bread. She shoots me a look that says, don't get crazy.

Hard not to. "It's Veronica, Katie. You have to know that by now, as many months as you've been chasing Earl and pretending to ignore me."

"Veronica Williams," Earl warns, part amazed, part keeper of the peace. "Easy now."

Bita drinks, long and silent from her water glass, and I know she's thinking that this little catfight is *so* not good for the sisterhood, but I don't care.

"I'm sure!" Katie says, looking at me like I'm crazy.

"Honey." Reginald turns to her. "We should sit down now."

"Yeah," I say. "Go eat something. You look hungry."

"Ron," Earl warns again. But Katie and Reginald are already walking away. "See you later, Earl-y," she singsongs, as Reginald leads her no doubt toward her life of trophy wife-dom. I share this theory with Bita and Earl.

"Naw," Earl says, "I don't believe I see that lasting for the long haul."

"And you." I scoot away from Earl. "I've never seen you tell her to really and truly knock it off. You just let her get away with murder." Maybe it was my two glasses of wine, but I was suddenly pissed at Earl and his humoring Katie all this time.

"I have to go to the bathroom," Bita tells us, and carefully lays her napkin on her chair before hurrying off.

Earl lays his napkin on the table and shifts his body to face me. "We worked all this out, didn't we?"

"You've never, ever told her off, not really and truly, not that I've ever heard."

Earl strokes his face and blows out a puff of air. He rubs his palms on his jeans and shakes his head. "You're going to make this our third big fight? Over the same thing?"

"Tell me I'm wrong." I glare at Katie and Reginald across the room. She's laughing and tossing her hair all around, not eating her bread, even though the waiter had brought it to them right away. Typical.

"I got one word for you. Ian." Earl takes my hand.

"I have no idea what you're talking about."

"Remember when we were on about Ian the other day, and you said he was just a kid, trying to figure himself out, that he wasn't a threat to you, no how, no way?"

"Uh-huh." I'm coming down from my sudden, irrational anger. It was Katie and her True Religion jeans and her calling me Vanessa that upset me. I squeeze Earl's hand and slide closer to him on the bench.

"Well, that's Katie. A kid. Harmless. Never going to be a threat to me or you, so ain't no need of me paying her no mind, not anymore."

I *guess.* And just like that, I'm almost feeling bad for Katie, for the fact that she's got a whole mess of mistakes ahead of her, a whole lot of stumbling around. Earl is right. I fast-forwarded Katie's life and if she didn't wise up, she was going to be stuck with some guy who doubled as her dad. She was a kid, making kid mistakes. But me, I had the higher ground. Thank God I was a grown-up and picking drunken fights in a restaurant for no reason at all.

We have some Frangelico after our meal, which Earl doesn't drink, and some tiramisu, which Earl doesn't eat. He just has another beer. "If it ain't plain and simple chocolate cake like Mamaw makes, I don't want none." And he waits until Bita and I are good and drunk to ask me if I wouldn't like to take a trip to Langsdale with him, to see some family and be there with Doris for Zach's theater opening.

"You're kidding, right?" I ask Bita if she wants the last bite of tiramisu and she pats her stomach and says no way. "It took me nearly half a year to get Langsdale out of my blood, and now you want me to go *back?* And we're just barely getting back in the black. Can we afford it?"

"Emergency credit card," Earl says. "We'll manage."

"I dunno know, Earl." I scrape my fork on my plate, playing with leftover icing. "Seriously?"

"I ain't been home in a long, long time, Ronnie. It's time I go back and it's a good time to go, since Zach's doing his thing then." Earl gives me one of those soft looks with those blue eyes and long, sandy eyelashes, and "no" is out of the question.

Bita waves our waiter down for the check and I suddenly wonder if she's game.

"How about you? Want to go to Indiana?"

"For *what?*" Bita takes one last bite of tiramisu.

Good question. "I don't know, it'd be fun? Plus, you're a single woman now. You could leave L.A. for a few days. You have no one to answer to." I'm half kidding, but I *do* think it would be fun to have Bita there.

"Except myself," Bita says. "No offense, Earl, but I didn't fall in love with Langsdale the few times I was there."

"Well, you weren't shown the right way." Earl stretches and yawns. "I could show you all the good stuff about Indiana. And, I got a cousin." Earl winks at Bita. "Y'all ready to go?"

More irony: here in this restaurant is the first time I've felt as though my life were truly coming together, not in the way I expected, but in a way that I like very much and yet, here we are, talking about returning to Langsdale. I knew, of course, that

Earl would always do so from time to time, but not me, not after
F: The Academy.

Doris says that I will be strung up and burned at the stake for
the book, but I think that, if it's basically true, the folks at Langsdale University will appreciate it.

We shall see.

doris

Among the academic hair-splitting debates that drove me to near insanity while I was preparing for my Ph.D. oral exams is the difference between modernism and postmodernism. Suffice it to say that had my dissertation committee read my little explanation of modernism, I would still be underlining literary theory in the dark corners of the Langsdale University library with a dog-eared copy of "Ph.D.s for DUMMIES" close by my side. However, since I am no longer forced to be in Langsdale, I am at gleeful liberty to continue with my little definitions. For postmodernism, my favorite definition is that it's very much like modernism, only there's none of that sad longing for the past, for the fallen whole subject. Instead, the postmodern subject revels in her fragmentation.

That, I have decided, will be my theme for the week: reveling in fragmentation. Atlanta Doris will allow a space for her latent Langsdale Doris, much as she loathes her memories of that particular incarnation. Yesterday, December 15, marks the first day of my return to Langsdale since leaving for Atlanta. Zach was nouveau-boyfriendly enough to meet me at the airport, easing me more gently from the fifty-degree Atlanta winter, to the twenty-degrees-with-the-sun-shining butt-cold deep freeze of Langsdale.

Today, we're getting ready for Ronnie and Earl's arrival. They actually came into town three days earlier, but went to a family reunion at one of Earl's relative's farms just outside of Bean Blossom. I received one broken phone message from Ronnie, who said Earl's relatives were hilarious, all wanting to know if he'd met Steven Spielberg, and why he was getting so skinny, and if the women were really as pretty as all that. Not one had heard of the movie he'd been in. They were evidently far more excited about his upcoming commercial for Dr. Scholl's foot supports.

"Hope things are good with Zach," she concluded.

And thus far, they have been. Having not seen him for the past four months, it was a little like unwrapping a Christmas present that you'd picked out in July. Sort of like what I remembered, but not quite. In this case: better. In fact, I can't help but half wonder if Zach does better in my absence than my presence. Don't ask what I'd been expecting with the "Langsdale Lounge"—something scary, like a converted Subway restaurant with cheap tables and some crazy eggplant-colored paint job. But no. Zach was clearly possessed of redecorating genius. The place looked like a fifties cocktail lounge worthy of Sinatra or Sammy Davis Jr. Red curtains along the walls, dim lighting, beautifully intimate tables, and enough seating for at least a hundred.

"I'm working on the liquor license," he explains, unveiling the space to me for the first time. "Then I'll really be raking in the dough."

Looking around the space, I felt so proud of him that I could barely find words. It's a funny moment when the person you've been with reaches their potential, even if it conflicts with your vision of what the two of you might have been together. Zach the decade-plus student, Zach the knitter, Zach the career jumper, Zach the occasional dater of lesbians and adolescents, Zach the caring and engaged teacher, Zach of the unwashed hair and three-day shadow—all of these had been manifest intermittently throughout our time together, but never Zach the kick-ass businessman. I wanted him to know how much I admired what he'd done—even if I'd spent a solid four months pissed off about it. I wanted, also, to pull him behind one of those velvet curtains and have a cinematic fade-to-black scene of our own. Our time apart had made him a slight stranger again, and there was something vaguely erotic about the feeling.

And because I am such a champion at expressing my rich and complex inner life, I said, "A Jim Carrey retrospective plus a liquor license in Langsdale, you won't even have to bother buying lottery tickets."

Zach laughed. He looked older to me, but older in a good

way. Like his latent Tommy Lee Jones craggy-faced sexiness was starting to bloom. He was wearing the moss colored J. Crew sweater that I'd bought him last Christmas because it fulfilled all my latent lumberjack fantasies, and in loose-fitting Levi's with hiking boots, it was total hippie porn. I took his hand in mine and pulled him closer.

"Did I tell you how good you look?" he asked. "It's true. It's like you've really come into your own in Atlanta."

I put my arms underneath his sweater, beneath his T-shirt, and rubbed the warmth of his chest, the tangle of hair beneath.

"God," I said, "You sound like my freaking father or something."

Clever man he is, he had unhooked my bra without my even noticing.

"Don't get oedipal on me now, baby," he whispered.

As he kissed me I knew that what was going to happen next, had it been projected on the screen, would have made the "Langsdale Lounge" a theater of an entirely different kind.

For the next two days Ronnie, Earl and I helped Zach with last-minute preparations. We made sure that the tablecloths were clean and matched, that he'd hired enough help, that the copy of Baby Jane had arrived and was put in a safe yet easily remembered place. It was funny to see Zach so nervous, and it brought out the best in him. I even had a moment where, after he'd set out breakfast and headed for the library ("I know you won't be mad about this, Doris, but I have to stay on the dissertation or it just gets away from me."), when I wondered if he hadn't become out of my league in my absence. I ignored the fruit and yogurt that he'd left and met Ronnie for an artery-clogging fat-fest at Ralph's Country Boy.

They say you can't go home again, but whoever "they" are, "they" clearly weren't from Langsdale, Indiana. The conversation in the next booth is so stereotypically Langsdale that it almost feels like a setup. Two men in plaid shirts and John Deere hats discussing at length the nuances of which guns were best for hunting, and which for home protection.

Ronnie looks at me. "Can you believe we both *lived* here? And had the nerve to think we were normal?"

Ronnie was bundled up in about fifty layers of clothing, including a pair of fingerless gloves that she refused to take off, even indoors. She reminded me of the little match girl.

"I dare say we might have stood out. This is a crazy question, but do you think that Zach is now too good for me?"

Ronnie gazes at the ceiling with her "why, God, why?" expression. "I know we're back in Langsdale for sure because you're acting crazy again."

"It's not crazy," I say. "Maybe it's true. Maybe it seemed like I was doing well out of the gate, getting a job and getting out of here, but now look at where you and Zach and Earl are. You've got a veritable cottage industry tutoring in Los Angeles, Earl is poised to be the next Hollywood hottie, and Zach is this born-again entrepreneur. Only I am plodding along the charted course, reliving my exact life in Langsdale, but with no friends and a slightly bigger salary." I push a particularly greasy link of sausage to the side of my plate. "And better food."

Ronnie blows across the top of her coffee.

"Don't you think your exaggerating just a little? And aren't you happy for Zach?"

"No to your first question and yes to the second. I'm happy for all of you. I just feel like everyone has made some quantum leap forward, and I'm just coasting along my once-chosen path. Did I tell you that I haven't even written a poem since I've been in Atlanta? Four months and no poem."

I hate that Langsdale is doing what it always did to me, bringing out my anxieties and turning me into a quivering mass of insecurity and self-doubt. Ronnie is wisely choosing not to humor this line of thinking at all. Instead, she flagged the waitress for extra biscuits.

"Because, what," she asks, and not too friendly, might I add. "Wonder Woman would have written a poem? You remember how hard it was to get that job? And you just moved, you're still settling in."

I eat the final bite of my poached eggs. "I think, I can't say for sure, but I think that black Doris would have written at least a sonnet or two."

"I can tell you one thing—black Doris definitely wouldn't be bitching that her man got a job. Black Doris would have a lot more street sense than her crazy cracker cousin, white Doris."

"White Doris *can* be a little annoying. I think she's sorry."

"I think she better eat that last bit of bacon, or black Ronnie might have to take charge of the situation."

I push my plate in her direction, and Ronnie snags the last bit of meat.

"Sooooo," I say. "You've been quiet, but wasn't the cover of your book supposed to be FedExed this morning? If you've had it in your bag the entire time, I will literally kill you for letting me rant like a maniac."

Ronnie crosses her hands together and raises an eyebrow.

"Beeeatch," I say. "You do have it."

She reaches into her bag and passes a glossy mock-up of the cover across the table. There's a picture of what looks like a college campus in the background with a large brick wall in the foreground, and the words "F: THE ACADEMY" written on it in spray-paint lettering. To one side, a woman's outline is silhouetted, and beneath the silhouette, in funky but similar lettering is "a novel by Veronica Williams."

"I love it! They did a great job."

"It's a bit literal, but I don't hate it."

I gesture at the cover.

"Please. This is *fabulous*. Men and women alike would pick this up. And it looks fun and smart at the same time. What more could you possibly ask for?"

Ronnie looks at the cover again, and I can see that she's proud, that even she can't quite believe that the novel will be coming out, in hardback, in bookstores across America.

"You know it looks good. Don't even lie."

She nods her head slowly. "I guess."

"But enjoy your breakfast because you will *never* eat lunch in this town again."

The men at the table next to us stand up and toss one rumpled dollar on the table before leaving. They're hungry jack types, Earl in fifteen years if he hadn't been cleaned up in L.A.

"Doris," she says. Her eyes follow the men out. "You say that like it's a *bad* thing."

Probably because I was such a colossal snob about the town at breakfast, the rest of my afternoon in Langsdale is nothing but Mayberry moments. The campus is blanketed in a thin film of snow, everyone drives politely and with respect for the traffic laws, and the Langsdale students, dressed exclusively in non-designer wear, driving strictly functional cars, are a true relief from the Paige Prentisses of my new world. I half expect to see Jimmy Stewart running down the streets yelling "Merry Christmas, Merry Christmas."

That evening the Langsdale Lounge is scheduled to open, so in true Doris fashion I have brought a vintage black cocktail dress for the occasion. It's a piece that I inherited from a favorite great-aunt, worthy of Donna Reed's finest look-I-fixed-dinner-for-the-boss-so-that-my-husband-gets-his-promotion episode. The top is fitted with three-quarter-length sleeves and quarter-size fabric buttons running down the front until they meet the skirt part of the dress, which flares out from the waist in a halo of loose fabric. I pair it with pearls and some lovely black pumps that I found at Steve Madden, nouveau vintage for the nouveau vintage theater.

One thing to which I became accustomed during my time with Zach was dressing for an occasion only to have him by my side in a rumpled Oxford and jeans. Tonight, though, he's surprised me again. He comes out wearing a shirt, tie, and deliberately mussed blazer that definitely did *not* come from the local Old Navy. He has a Chet Baker–West Coast Jazz feel, with pressed pants and dress loafers, hair combed back and face clean shaven.

"If you've owned this getup the whole time I've known you and you've only seen fit to wear it now, I am seriously going to murder you."

Zach narrows his eyes and gives me his most wicked half smile. "I take it you approve."

I smooth the lapels of his jacket into place. "I more than approve."

He kisses me softly and says. "So you think it's going to be okay tonight?"

"I know it will, Zach. You did the best job ever. I'm so proud of you I don't even know what to do with myself."

He moves his attention to my neck, running his tongue around the edge of my pearls.

"I can think of a thing or two."

"Threat or promise?"

"A little of both. So you like the way the theater looks?"

"I love it."

"And you like the movie I picked out for tonight."

"I love it."

"And the music we're going to play before the movie starts?"

"Love it."

"Even if we can't yet serve alcohol?"

"That's why God invented flasks."

"And the light fixtures. They're authentic from the 1940s."

"Love them."

He puts his arms on my shoulders and looks me directly in the eyes.

"And me?"

It's so sweet and un-Zach-like, that even I am able to quell my inner intimacy-phobe.

"I love you, too. Most of all."

He gropes a little farther down my leg.

"More than that flask you're hiding underneath the dress?"

"Let's not get crazy."

Earl and Ronnie meet us at the packed theater. They're not quite as overdressed as Zach and myself, but they look very hip and very L.A. Ronnie has on an orange flowing tunic top with embroidery and an open V, with flared black pants and platform boots. She'd probably be freezing her ass off were it not for her appropriation of Earl's black leather biker jacket, which she has draped over her shoulders, warding off the cold. Earl is wearing a fitted black T-shirt, dressy jeans and cowboy boots. Very too cool for school.

"Look at you two," Ronnie exclaims. "Very Lucy and Ricky. You gonna put on a show, Doris?"

"No, ma'am," I say. "I'm going to be a good Lucy and watch my Ricky do his thing. But doesn't he look good? Who knew?"

"Who knew," Earl says, gesturing at Zach with arms open and palms forward like, "How'd we get with these two kooky broads?"

"That your Scorsese accent?" Zach asks. "Pretty good."

"*Not* the acting classes," Ronnie pleads. "Please, please not tonight."

Earl pulls her close and whispers something I can't quite make out in a Brandoesque mutter.

As the theater darkens, we all move to a table toward the center of the room with a Reserved plaque on top and an opened bottle of champagne hidden discreetly beneath. Zach welcomes the audience and concludes his short speech with, "Langsdale can be any place, really. I'd like to think that we can make this as culturally viable and enjoyable a venture as any this town has seen. We've got some great flicks lined up, and if you haven't seen tonight's you're in for a treat. And I'd especially like to thank Doris, and Ronnie and Earl for coming here, since it doesn't really mean much without people you love."

God, but Zach was getting corny in my absence! Corny, but *sweet*.

"So enjoy!" And on cue, the theater went dark, the curtains opened, and the fateful car crash that begins the film started to unfold. Zach sat down beside me, touching my knee. "How'd that sound?" he asks.

"Really, really good," I tell him. "And very sweet."

"Shh," Ronnie says. "You two have any home training?"

"It's him. He's a terrible influence."

I've seen *What Ever Happened to Baby Jane?* enough times that I could easily have my own Rocky Horror-esque banter with the screen, so instead of watching the film I look around the theater.

The house is full, and most of the locals have dressed nicely for the evening. A few undergraduates in black pants and white shirts serve light appetizers, and the mood is good, the vibe optimistic. People are even laughing at the correct parts, acknowledging the campy romp that the film is. There's no way to tell whether or not this place will have legs, just as I can't tell now whether or not Ronnie and Earl will still be laughing together in three years or whether Zach and I will figure things out by summer.

But watching their half-illuminated faces, I feel lucky. Lucky that at this moment everything feels perfect, as absolutely perfect as any evening could be. Bette Davis and Joan Crawford hag it up, arguing, fighting up and down the stairwell, cooking rats. And after all that drama, you find out they don't even have their stories right. I decide now there's a lesson to be learned. A warning not to believe in a story so much that you lose sight of the present. Maybe Zach and I don't have an easy ending in clear sight, or a story that sounds terribly smart or familiar, but that doesn't mean that a happy ending can't happen.

"Space Shoes," Ronnie whispers in my direction. "You're missing the best part."

I look at the screen and Bette Davis is letting roll with everything she's got.

"Best hag ever," I say.

Zach closes his hand over my own, and beside me I hear Earl murmur something soft and intimate in Ronnie's ear. For a second, I feel like Dorothy when she opens her eyes at the end of *The Wizard of Oz* to see all the familiar elements of two different lives blend in one instant of love and recognition. I click my black stiletto heels together, gently, in a gesture to myself, as Zach holds my hand tighter. It may not really be perfect, it may not even be forever, but it feels like home.

Lauren Baratz-Logsted

Delilah "Baby" Sampson got hooked on the Bard back in college. Then she got briefly hooked on Singapore Sling cocktails. And then she got tossed out of school. Yes, when Delilah discovers something she likes, she *really* sticks with it.

These days, her addictions include sudoku, lime diet cola and now… Jimmy Choo shoes. Oh, Baby's *gotta* have those shoes! But on her window-washer salary, $1,400 is a stretch. Which leads us to her latest obsession…gambling. Every win puts her closer to those beloved shoes. And as the "21s" keep dropping, so do the men…right at her feet. But for a girl who never knows when to fold 'em, gambling and casino guys are not healthy habits. She could end up losing her shirt, her head… and a whole lot more.

Baby Needs a New Pair of Shoes

"A whip-smart, funny voice."—Christopher Moore,
author of *Lamb* and *You Suck: A Love Story*

Available wherever
trade paperbacks
are sold.

RED DRESS INK ™